FOR JOSEPH

ENJOY !

GEOFF

Of Winter's Cost

GW00372479

by

Geoff Akers

Grosvenor House
Publishing Limited

Geoff Akers is hereby identified as author of this
work in accordance with Section 77 of the Copyright, Designs
and Patents Act 1988

The book cover picture is copyright to Inmagine Corp LLC

This book is published by
Grosvenor House Publishing Ltd
28-30 High Street, Guildford, Surrey, GU1 3EL.
www.grosvenorhousepublishing.co.uk

Although, Of Winter's Cost, is inspired by real events, it is primarily a
work of fiction. All characters and events are thus the product of the
author's imagination and any resemblance to actual persons,
living or dead, is purely coincidental.

A CIP record for this book
is available from the British Library

ISBN 978-1-78148-566-8

This book is dedicated to the memory of Israel Shahak, a tireless campaigner for justice and human rights in his adopted country.

My heart aches. I ask why are our memories so short? Have our Jewish sisters and brothers forgotten their humiliation? Have they forgotten the collective punishment, the home demolitions in their own history so soon?. Have they turned their backs on their profound and noble religious traditions? Have they forgotten that God cares deeply about the downtrodden?
Bishop Desmond Tutu

When do we Jews notice that Israel is insane?
Gideon Levy (Israeli peace activist)

...Like waifs their spirits grope
For the pools of Hebron again—
For Lebanon's summer slope...
Isaac Rosenberg

Prelude

Grandfather died two days after my fourteenth birthday. I remember being surprised that he was still asleep when I arrived with his breakfast that morning. Normally, he was propped up on his pillows waiting for me.

Preparing and transporting grandfather's breakfast was a solemn ritual performed at the same time each day. Watching him sip his orange juice and chew reflectively on a slice of toast, I looked forward to the moment when he would push the tray aside and begin one of his tales from the distant past. I would sit spellbound as images emerged from a time and a place so different from my own.

Occasionally, he spoke of his early life in Krasnow, the small Polish town of his birth and upbringing, but the main focus was always on the horror of the Nazi occupation. I found it hard to connect the frail old man with the hero of combat against a remorseless enemy. Only his eyes, alight with the memory of a particularly daring deed, or saddened by the recollection of a futile death, provided a palpable link with the past.

On the morning of his death, I called out to him but the blankets remained ominously still. Finally, gathering my courage, I pulled back the top cover and brushed his mottled neck with my fingertips. The skin was hard and cold to the touch. The realisation that death had stolen him away in the night, leaving this crusty shell behind, overwhelmed me. I rushed out of the room kicking over the tray and mashing the toast into the faded fibres of the carpet.

Over the next few days a host of strange and familiar faces floated in and out of my consciousness as old friends and comrades stopped by to pay their respects. I greeted them all courteously, but felt brittle and shrunken inside. Even now, it's hard to express my love for an old man who had been virtually bedridden for as long as I could remember. I suppose he was a refuge from my parents' endless squabbling.

Grandfather's death led to our relocation from Jerusalem to the West Bank settlement of Kiryat Arba, making it possible for my father to fulfil his long-standing religious ambitions. The rapid distillation of everything but fear and hatred, was the main outcome of my move to Israel's troubled frontier.

When I consider what I have done, my blood runs cold. How could I have been so blind, so impervious? I realise now that grandfather wished to preserve me from this fate – his stories an attempt to purge evil, not invest it. He desired above all else that I might live at peace with myself and others in a land liberated from violence. The state of Israel was to be a new beginning, free from enmity.

I shut my eyes and find myself seated once more at the foot of grandfather's bed, hearkening to his every word. His face tightens as painful memories are summoned up and appraised. His voice, rising and swooping like a bird in flight, carries me along in its slipstream.

CHAPTER ONE

The West Bank: Summer 1993.

Mr Dayane's pick-up roars out of Kiryat Arba. My father is up front with Mr Katz while Gad and me are sitting in the back trying to forget that the driver is our religious instruction teacher. In class he praises the courageous pioneers of Hebron, paying tribute to those brave souls who squatted in the town centre defying pressure from all quarters to move on. Almost fifteen years later, despite tough resistance from Arab terrorists and self-hating Jews, they're still here – stronger and more determined than ever.

We pile out of the truck and walk the short distance to the Cave of Machpelah. The truth is that no right-thinking Jew, living in Hebron, or Kiryat Arba, can stand the idea of sharing our shrine with Arabs, so we harass them at every opportunity. As usual, there's plenty of action at the foot of the steps leading up to the Cave. A gaggle of American tourists is being softened up by a *towel-head* guide. These twisters hang around offering their services for a few shekels. Mr Dayane speaks through clenched teeth.

"Why do we allow these creatures to ply their trade here of all places?"

"A good question, Yoel!" Mr Katz waggles his finger in our direction. "By the time these boys are running things, they'll all be gone. In the meantime, we can only show them how we feel."

Father smirks. He believes that expelling Arabs from Judea and Samaria will solve all our problems. Mother argues that we must share what we have with our "neighbours", as she calls them, and be more tolerant if things are ever to improve. She never lets him off with anything. She's so different from the other wives in Kiryat Arba who wouldn't dream of showing such disrespect to their husbands.

We move inside. The shrine is crowded with gawking tourists. Locals coming here to pray have a hard time of it, their anger often spilling over into violence. The Americans, we noticed earlier, are crowded round the Cenotaph of Abraham as their guide tries to hurry them along. Having been paid up front, he'll be anxious to get the tour over and done with. Mr Katz deliberately barges into him. He grimaces through a mouthful of yellow teeth and shakes his fist at us. He looks like an angry old goat. Gad laughs in his face as we follow our elders into the Tomb of Joseph. Here, we mingle with a dozen Hebron men holding Bibles and mumbling prayers. There's hardly room to breathe and the barrel of someone's semi-automatic pokes painfully into my back.

A group of Arabs, standing just beyond the tomb, are offering up prayers to Allah. They chant in loud voices.

The alcove empties as we move out to confront them. An anxious security guard hovers in the background. Nearby, the tourists are listening attentively as their guide drones on about the centrality of the patriarch, Abraham, to Judaism, Christianity and Islam. That sort of blasphemy might in itself set things off but today our attention is fixed elsewhere.

One of our Hebron brothers raises his weapon and noisily releases the safety catch. The Arabs watch us, seemingly unperturbed by the threat. He gestures at the nearest of them.

"Get out of here, Mohammed! You and your *towel-head* pals, now!"

"Mohammed" replies with no hint of irony in his voice.

"I trust that Jews and Moslems can share this holy place without ill will."

The Hebron pioneer is unimpressed.

"I won't tell you again."

The young Arab raises his eyebrows in mock bewilderment.

"There is no need for such hostility." He glances round at his comrades for the first time before continuing in the same affable tone. Although he is smiling, his dark eyes are cold. "Next thing you know we'll be rounded up and dumped in a concentration camp."

The words send a sudden, cold shiver up my spine. As if previously rehearsed, one of the Arabs feeds him an opportune line.

"You mean a refugee camp?"

"Is there a difference, my friend?"

The pioneer's finger tightens on the trigger – the slightest pressure and the thing will go off. Fear beats around us like startled birds. I notice the Yankee tourists are pressed against the rail surrounding the Cenotaph, suddenly aware that something is terribly wrong. My father, trying to look tough, is anything but. I recall mother telling him during one of their frequent, stormy rows that he was "all talk, and no action". I was furious on his behalf at the time, but maybe she was right. His face is a pale mask beneath its dark tan, and his legs are trembling. I feel ashamed and pray that no one else will notice. Fortunately, everyone is staring at the Arabs. Mr Katz's face is beetroot-red and slicked with sweat. My shame is swept aside by a sudden impulse to laugh. His swollen neck and bulging eyes remind me of the frogs we used to watch spawning in the early spring. At that moment the security guard intervenes.

"Break it up! What are you thinking? This is no place for confrontation!" He turns to the Arabs. "You'll have to leave now!"

They make no move to obey. Instead, "Mohammed" feigns surprise.

"Why are you picking on us, sir? We have done nothing wrong. These men and their brats are causing the trouble. They are the ones sticking their guns down our throats."

He stares straight at me with a mocking smile. I frown and stare back. Who the hell does he think he's calling a brat?

"Look, surely no one wants any trouble here of all places?"

The guard is trying to reduce tension by appealing to everyone's veneration for the ancient and holy site.

Again, the Arab smiles.

"Of course, sir. Your wish is our command. I forgot for a moment that our necks are under the Zionist heel. How foolish of me!"

He walks off, motioning his comrades to follow. The Yanks squirm out of his way as though he might suddenly explode in their faces. There is no doubt that "Mohammed" and his mates have won this round.

Shaking his head the pioneer flicks his weapon back to safety and frowns.

"That is what we have to put up with, day in, day out." Flecks of spittle fly into Mr Katz's face but he doesn't react in the slightest. He is fiercely intent on what the man is saying. "The *Canaanites* always cause trouble when they know it's hard for us to do anything about it. They're cowards, the lot of them!"

I have some trouble accepting such a branding but Mr Katz intervenes.

"You see how it is, boys! We are mocked and persecuted in our own temple by the agents of Satan. That is why there can never be any compromise with the Arabs while even one of their number pollutes our sacred land." Gad nods eagerly and my own unease dissolves as the words strike home. He's right! Why should we tolerate such blasphemy? "You boys are the future. Never forget that, and never forget your duty as righteous Jews. Then you will ride high when our Lord redeems his people."

I notice the concourse is now almost deserted. The tourists have fled. No one wants to be caught in the crossfire.

5

Outside things are also quiet. There is no sign of the Arabs who upset our prayers. Father and Mr Dayane seem to have lost their appetite for trouble and are anxious to depart. On the way home Mr Katz tells us that our persecutors will be punished for their latest act of sacrilege.

—⁓—

Gad phones me a few days later to confirm that things are heating up. He tells me that his father, as chairman of the locally affiliated Committee for Safety on the Roads, has come up with the perfect plan to punish the Arabs. The problem of children throwing stones at cars on the outskirts of Hebron has escalated recently so the Committee has voted to patrol the hotspots in force. This will provide the perfect smokescreen for our revenge outing.

"Father says that we can come along and observe."

"That's good!"

The idea of us "observing" is ridiculous, of course. Although we won't be armed, we'll definitely be in the thick of it. If mother finds out there will be hell to pay. She's only trying to protect me, I suppose, but we are fighting an enemy whose stated aim is to wipe our country off the face of the map, so there's no room for compromise.

I remember father once demanding to know why she condemned our just battle for survival when her own father had fought so heroically in defence of persecuted Jews. She gazed at him for a moment with what looked like pity in her eyes, but her words jabbed like daggers.

"How dare you bring my father into this? You and your friends are not worth the dirt under his fingernails! He laid his life on the line so many times fighting real evil. What you call a war of survival is a miserable excuse to occupy land and oppress innocent people."

Father tried to bluster his way out of it but he knew he wasn't getting anywhere. Mother just stood there glowering until he left the room. After that she slumped down on the couch, covered her face with her hands and began to cry. I couldn't decide whether to run after father or stay and comfort her. In the end, I just stood there like an idiot, staring at my feet.

"See you tomorrow morning, bright and early. We're picking you and your dad up at seven thirty."

"Great."

For a moment I have trouble shaking loose. Problems at home have been nagging away like a sore tooth recently. And, try as I might, I can't get these Arabs in the Cave of Machpelah out of my mind either. I sometimes think we're all reluctant actors in a film playing parts that none of us really understands. I can't explain it but that's how I feel.

"You okay, Sam?"

"I'm fine! See you tomorrow."

The phone clicks off and I slowly replace the handset. I really don't know what's going on inside my head. The last thing I want is for Gad to think I'm going soft on Arabs.

———⟋⟍———

The gathering is large. I recognise many of the faces from meetings at the Kiryat Arba Community Centre;

but there are lots of people here I don't know, including kids of my own age and younger, presumably from Hebron. One of their rabbis, a ball of a man with no neck and stocky shoulders, is mounted on the back of a pickup addressing the crowd. His voice, high-pitched and indignant, carries well.

"I am gratified to see such a large turnout today. Thanks are due to David Katz and our Kiryat Arba brothers for their help in organising an appropriate response to *Canaanite* profanity." I exchange glances with Gad and we both smile. A low growl of anger from the crowd shows how high feelings are running. "Remember to fill up your pockets with stones which we will need to provoke the reaction we seek. Under no circumstances fire your weapons until the *Canaanites* retaliate. It is important that we are seen as having been forced to use firearms in self-defence. If any among you have difficulty with such a deception, please remember that we are not dealing here with fellow-human beings. We, and we alone, are the true children of God, and the inheritors of the Land. Any method we choose to rid ourselves of vermin is acceptable."

The rabbi receives a rousing cheer as he steps down, and we set off. It's mid-afternoon and the sun beats uncomfortably hot on my neck and shoulders. We pass through a small olive grove where Arab labourers are resting in the shade of an ancient tree. They stare at us but we ignore them. Although these peasants are not our target today, they could be soon enough. Many such groves have been bulldozed recently because terrorists conceal their guns and bomb-making equipment among the roots of the trees.

We reach the first few houses at the edge of the district selected for the attack. The crumbling breeze-block walls and rusty corrugated iron roofs show how poor the residents are. Few of these hovels have electricity or running water. Our teacher, Mr Dayane, believes Arabs are animals who understand nothing better and that it would be a waste of money to attempt any improvements.

Father's hero, Rabbi Previnger, wrote in a recent article that:

"Although we live in close proximity to the Arab, we, the vanguard of the chosen, inhabit a separate universe of thought and feeling, and that is only right and proper."

Father cut it out of the local newspaper and told me to memorise the lines. Maybe he's worried that mother is having a bad influence on me.

I stoop to pick up some loose stones at the side of the road. Others are doing the same. Father tells me to stay close. This is really embarrassing. I can't believe he's treating me like a stupid kid. If the other men are happy to let their sons stick together, why can't he just let me be with my friends?

Things quickly hot up. Mr Katz grins as Arab women and children rush around us, trying to escape indoors. He hurls a stone which strikes an old women on the back of the head; she tumbles forward onto the road. The sound of breaking glass mingles with yells and screams as I throw my stones at a second-floor window. I hear Gad whooping in delight as he trips a terrified boy and boots him hard in the ribs. He doesn't look more than twelve years old. Father has vanished and I fight my way through the throng, eager to rejoin my friends.

At that moment, a crowd of yelling Arabs arrives. Just as I reach Gad, a bottle bounces off his shoulder and shatters on the ground. He grimaces in pain. Mr Katz rushes up firing his gun in the air. He suddenly levels it at an old man struggling to pull down a metal grid over his shop window. It barks once, twice and the Arab slumps forward onto the dirty iron slats.

Father is back, his face twisted in fear or fury, I'm not sure which. Bullets whine and ricochet among the buildings. Within seconds the street is almost deserted. I hear the wail of an approaching siren. A few metres away the old woman, felled by Mr Katz, is crawling sideways like an injured crab. The excitement has evaporated and more than anything I feel ashamed of what we've done here. I can't help thinking about the elderly shopkeeper sprawled in a puddle of his own blood, and the other casualties lying around me. I wonder if anyone will die before help arrives. Gad smiles through the pain in his shoulder.

"It'll be a while before they make trouble for us again. They had it coming."

Trouble is I'm finding it hard to visualise those who were injured as anything other than innocent victims.

Luckily, when we arrive home mother is out. Although I'm not hurt, my legs won't stop shaking. I strip off and take a shower. The water, swirling around my feet, is filthy. I hear the whir of the washing machine next door as father rinses away evidence of the street battle. It reminds me how strained things have become of late. I can't help wondering what life must be like in the Katz household where Gad's mother agrees with everything her husband says and does.

As I switch off the taps and step out of the shower, I think about Gad's latest 'war wound'. It was bad enough when he was bruised in a street fight last year, but this injury will make him stronger than ever. He has the knack of avoiding real damage while plugging his role as martyr for all it's worth. The funny thing is I wouldn't trade places with him. He struggles so hard to stay on top – to be the leader – that he's never able to let his guard down for a second. Maybe in that way he's like "Mohammed". I try to imagine his reaction if I was ever to make such a comparison to his face.

When I come out of the bathroom, cleaned up and feeling a little more normal, father calls me through to the lounge. He is sitting in his favourite armchair looking extremely serious.

"Samuel, we need to talk."

His behaviour is unusual enough to make me feel nervous. Maybe he's embarrassed about his behaviour earlier on today and needs to justify himself in my eyes. It won't be the first time.

"I asked you to stay beside me today, and what did you do? You ran off with your friends as soon as my back was turned. That is not what I expect when I give you an order."

I'm not sure what he's up to but I feel a slow throb of anger start to build.

"You disappeared. I couldn't see you anywhere, so I thought it would be safer to be with my friends."

The explanation doesn't help. Maybe he thinks I'm criticising him. He stares at me for a moment as if waiting for an apology. I don't see why I should back down – it's not my fault he vanished at the crucial moment.

"Nevertheless, Samuel, you disobeyed me."

Perhaps it's his high-handed tone or the pent-up emotions of the day. Before I can stop myself, words tumble out.

"Mr Katz doesn't treat Gad like a kid and he doesn't run off when things get tough either."

Quick as a flash he grabs me by the front of my tee shirt and slaps me hard over the face. Using physical punishment as a means of discipline shatters my illusion of adulthood and slices through my self-control. I wrench away and lash out with my right fist, catching him square on the nose. The gush of blood satisfies something deep inside while shocking me to the core.

Looking round I see mother framed in the doorway. She looks utterly horrified. Father sinks onto the floor moaning and clasping his face between both hands. The enormity of what I've done breaks over me like a huge wave. I lean down, wanting to help him, but he pushes me away, rises unsteadily to his feet and stumbles out of the room. Stepping aside, mother lets him pass and stares at me in disbelief. Then she follows him out, leaving me alone.

I feel physically sick. Our rabbi teaches that violence committed against a fellow-Jew is the most heinous of sins, unless the victim has consciously betrayed his people. I shudder to think how he would react to the sin of a son striking his own father. I feel tears trickling down my face. Once this gets out I'll be treated as an outcast – nobody will understand. I feel confused and frightened. How could I have lost control so easily, and lashed out so hard? What would grandfather think of me? Family meant so much to him. He would be appalled by such an outrage, despite his coldness towards father.

I hear mother's voice next door. Although I can't make out the words, her tone is harsh. She's probably trying to find out what happened while helping father clean himself up. He is saying nothing. Should I go and beg his forgiveness? I decide that would do more harm than good. Mother returns and stares at me again without speaking. My discomfort grows under her steady gaze. Finally, she breaks the silence.

"I never thought I'd ever witness a son of mine strike his own father. Your grandfather used to say that violence begets violence. It seems that the only way you can react these days is to lash out first and ask questions later. Is that how you were brought up to behave?"

"I'm sorry. I only wanted to... ."

"Only wanted to what? Teach your father a lesson he would never forget? Is that what things have come to in this family?"

"I didn't mean to... ."

"Don't insult me with your half-baked excuses, Sam. There can be no justification for what you did."

I bow my head. I know well enough that there is nothing I can say or do to make things better.

After a long pause, she continues, this time speaking a little less harshly.

"Try to understand why you would do such a thing. Has hitting your father made you feel any better?"

The answer is clear. I feel ready to listen to what she has to say, but, at that moment, father reappears. I want the ground to open and swallow me up. He is pressing a bag of ice against his face, and, to my amazement, smiling through his pain. He pats me on the shoulder with his free hand.

"I'm sorry I slapped you, Sam. I can offer you no excuse for that. And, I'm sorry I embarrassed you in front of your friends this morning. I've been treating you like a child and I have paid the price for my stupidity." I gaze at him in disbelief. I thought that he would never speak to me again, but instead he's actually apologising. I rise and hug him tightly. He laughs and thumps me playfully on the back. "Where did you get such a right hook?"

It sounds as though he's proud of me. Instead of despair, I now feel as if I have stumbled through some kind of initiation test. The door bangs loudly as mother leaves. She must be disgusted by what is happening, but I only feel an overwhelming sense of relief. Father glances round for a moment.

"Don't worry about her! Women can never really understand the bond between father and son. But how am I going to explain this?" Father suddenly looks woeful and points to his swollen face. My guilt returns in a rush.

"I'm, I'm not sure."

He laughs again. "Don't worry – that's easy. I'll say I got in the way of an Arab fist and Mr Katz will be mad it wasn't him. You know what he's like, always trying to be the biggest martyr for the cause."

I nod.

"Gad's the same – always trying to keep one step ahead of the rest of us."

I can hardly believe we're having this conversation. Father has never ever criticised any of his friends in front of me – especially Mr Katz – and I would never normally dream of putting down Gad in front of him. This is something entirely new between us.

"I'm really sorry that I... ."

"I don't want to hear another word about it. What's done is done!" How could I ever have thought badly of him? Not only has he spared me terrible humiliation, he's actually showing new respect by speaking to me adult-to-adult. "Now, let's get out of here and show off my war wound. Do you think we can convince people that I was beaten up by an Arab mob?"

"You don't look that bad." I laugh guiltily. "Let's stick to something they're likely to believe."

"You're right. We'll work out the details on the way."

I pull on my jumper, briefly wondering what mother was going to say before father's dramatic entrance, and before relief blotted everything else out of my mind. His arm is around my shoulder and the icepack has been discarded. He proudly displays his new proof of Arab hostility to the world.

—⁓—

Two days later, Mr Katz calls round at the house. I hear father talking to him in the lounge. Their raised voices and whoops of laughter spark off my curiosity. The outside door slams shut and father comes into the room.

"Look at this, Sam!" He throws a cutting from a newspaper onto the bed. Unable to contain himself, he picks it up and thrusts it into my hands. "Read it! This is what we were hoping for –it's why we'll get rid of all these Arab scum in the end."

I smooth out the crumpled sheet.

"Seven hurt in Hebron shooting incident

Three Kiryat Arba residents were injured in a clash with a mob of Hebron Arabs yesterday afternoon.

A group of Jewish families, members of the Committee for Safety on the Roads, were passing through the dangerous Harat a-Sheikh district of Hebron when they were set upon by several hundred Arabs, and pelted with rocks and bottles from rooftops and alleys.

A woman and two children were injured.

To escape the unprovoked attack, the settlers fired in the air, and when that had no effect, they fired at the legs of the rock-throwers.

Last night, four wounded Arabs were brought to Mokassad Hospital in East Jerusalem. One, the hospital reported, was in a critical condition with bullet wounds in the back. Another was seriously wounded in the head and chest, and a third lightly wounded in the leg.

The IDF relayed a report on the incident to the Hebron police, who have opened an investigation.

The Committee for Safety on the Roads said it would continue to patrol Arab neighbourhoods, which Jews have previously preferred not to enter, until attacks on innocent people ceased."

I look up. Father's eyes are burning into me.

"People will see us as heroes fighting to protect our community. That bit about the two children and the woman being injured is excellent, although Gad won't like being called a child, I imagine."

I really want to share his enthusiasm but find it hard to feel joyful about a pack of lies being passed off by

The Jerusalem Post as fact. I know it's what we wanted but I can't help thinking about the man shot in the back – no doubt the victim of Mr Katz's shooting frenzy. And, as for the injured Jewish woman, there were none there – the only injured women in the skirmish were Arab women; and the only real children in the firing line were Arab children. I know the danger of thinking this way, but I just can't help myself. I force a smile for father's benefit.

"It's a good story."

"I can't wait to see people's faces when they read it. I'm off to see Mr Dayane. Do you want to come?"

"No. I've got some homework to finish off."

"Quite right. I'll see you later on then. Keep up the good work!"

He snatches the cutting and dashes out of the room. I feel sorry about lying to him but I really don't feel like celebrating.

Mother comes in from the garden, trowel in hand.

"What's going on?" She stares at my glum face for a moment. "No, don't tell me, I don't want to know."

I can't explain what's happening to me right now. Some days I'm up for the fight, other days I feel guilty about what we are doing. When we were walking around showing off father's black eye, I felt proud. For once we were the centre of attention – heroes of the hour. Gad and his father seemed particularly impressed. A part of father, shrunken by past failures, blossomed in the warm glow of their approval. At last he was the person he most wanted to be. Later, though, after all the excitement had died down, the significance of the lie grew in my mind.

I felt like the world's biggest fraud. The fact that father was exhibiting his bruised face, the result of my shameful blow, while our victims were lying in hospital, felt awful. What would grandfather have made of it all? His sympathies, I'm sure, would have been with those we attacked – his contempt for our lies and brutality absolute.

But, of course, we are a people set apart and our enemies are in league with evil powers. I hear this said over and over again. Grandfather always rejected such ideas. Maybe the fact that he shunned the synagogue accounted for his lack of faith. I know that's what father thinks, even if he never actually says so. Few dare to criticise Shoah survivors, especially those who fought in the Warsaw Ghetto. Here in Israel, such people are regarded as heroes and righteous Jews.

I really want to believe but maybe it's what grandfather went through – things father, Mr Katz and the rest of them could never begin to imagine – that makes me hold back. Or maybe it's because he wanted nothing to do with our cause, and never stopped condemning what he regarded as racist outrages in Judea and Samaria. I should probably find out more about his past. I've forgotten so much of what he told me. I remember bits from his 'ghetto' stories, but that's about it really. Mother is the only person who can help me put all of the pieces together.

CHAPTER TWO

Krasnow: Spring 1939.

Leo listens intently to the angry hiss and crackle of the radio. Suddenly, the static parts like curtains and a harsh, metallic voice fills the room. The alien language means nothing to him, but the strident tone increases his unease. After a moment or two, Heniek's uncle, Mr Prost, switches the set off, sighs, and covers his face with his hands. He is reluctant to give the grim news shape in his own language – afraid that once the words are uttered, the apprehension, which has been growing steadily in all their minds, will take on a new and terrifying reality. He finally speaks.

"The Germans crossed the border early this morning. It seems that France and Britain will declare war on them. We can only pray to God they do so. That is our only hope now."

His wife wails and rushes out of the room. The men stand silent for a moment grappling with the implications of the appalling news. Heniek is first to break the charged silence, his voice choked with emotion.

"Leo, we must join the army! They will be looking for men."

Leo is confused. He believes they should do something but knows that his father will disapprove. Heniek continues to talk.

"There are terrible stories about how the Nazis have been treating Jews in Germany." His uncle glances uneasily over his shoulder before rising to close the parlour door. "Thousands have been deported and they are the lucky ones by all accounts. Others have been stripped of everything they possess and sent to work camps. They say beatings and destruction of property are commonplace."

Leo frowns. Although eager to relieve the tension by challenging the rumours that have been scaring everyone for so long now, he is reluctant to repeat his father's stock response to reports of German anti-Semitism. His words, when they come, sound hollow and evasive.

"We also have our problems here in Poland with racists, but that doesn't mean... ."

Mr Prost impatiently interrupts him.

"Yes, we have. But what happens here is generally carried out by hotheads whose activities are illegal, even if many of our politicians turn a blind eye. In Germany the policy is official and sanctioned by the government."

"How much of this do we know for sure?"

Leo is dismayed to hear his father's scepticism rise up through the question. Mr Prost's voice assumes a flinty edge.

"I know for sure that Maric Goldwasser has not been permitted to export his eggs and chickens into Germany for the last four years, and Baruch Kempinski's brother, a doctor of medicine in Leipzig, was dismissed from his post at the university in 1934. Baruch has heard nothing from him, or any of his family, since that time."

There is a long pause. Leo knows he shouldn't push things any further, especially in light of the invasion. He is saved from embarrassment by Heniek.

"I'm off to the Town Hall to find out about the mobilisation. Are you coming, Leo?"

"No. I'd better get back home and tell my family what has happened."

Mr Prost smiles, his anger quickly pushed aside.

"Give your father my best, won't you."

"Yes, and thank you for everything. I'm sorry if I... ."

"Don't apologise! You have a right to ask these questions. Things may not be as bad as we think. Some of us older folks have positive memories of the Germans who were here during the last war."

Now it's Leo's turn to smile.

"Yes, father is always talking about the power station they built in 1917. He has much more sympathy for the Germans than the Russians."

"There I would probably agree with him."

Outside, Leo takes his leave of Heniek, extracting a promise from his friend to do nothing hasty until they have had a chance to discuss the options open to them. Walking home, he passes the cluster of dilapidated houses occupied by Krasnow's poorer Jewish citizens. Beyond the trees, bordering the muddy track, he catches glimpses of the Vistula winding its way through Squire Kreitser's fertile acres. The Squire, an enlightened Jewish landowner, is respected by Jews and Poles alike. With a rueful smile, he reflects that if others with such wealth were as open-minded and generous, things might not have become so polarised here in Poland. He knows well enough, though, that the impoverished majority will always seek a scapegoat – ignorance and fear fuelling the desire to pin the blame elsewhere. Unfortunately, the German power station has made little difference to the lives of those in the shtetl too poor to install electricity or running water.

His thoughts turn to his own troubled relationship with his father. Despite the old man's bravado, Leo knows that he is deeply worried. He conceals his fear behind talk of another benign German occupation where Jews will be treated with tolerance. Even if current rumours are exaggerated, Leo is fairly sure that things will not be the same this time round. Hitler's hysterical ranting against those he deems racially inferior leaves little room for optimism. The only citizens of Krasnow who might prosper are the small contingent of *Volkdeutschen* living on the edge of town. In common with his own people they have always kept themselves to themselves, only interacting with others when necessary. He fears what will happen if they are given the whip hand.

He finds Yitzhak in his tiny workshop adjacent to the finely furnished first floor room he uses for measuring and dressing clients. He is carefully cutting a length of cloth and doesn't look up as his son enters. Leo is struck by how much his father has aged over the past year: his long beard, once luxuriant, is now scraggy and greying; his back stooped as if weary from bearing a heavy load.

"Father, the Germans have invaded. We heard it on Mr Prost's radio."

Yitzhak carefully places his cutters on the table and stretches his stiff arms above his head before replying.

"You spend too much time listening to that cursed radio set! Anyway," he sighs wearily, "it's no more than we expected. There is little we can do."

Leo reacts impatiently. "They'll be here soon, father. Mr Prost thinks we should… ."

"Prost is a fool! Does he really think things can get worse for us in Poland? We can barely make a living as it is! The country is full of *Goy* thugs threatening anyone who dares do business with us."

"Nevertheless, I think we should… ."

"And what about old Moishe Kaplan? He's never got over his son's death in Warsaw. The lad was only pursuing his studies; he was no threat to anyone."

"There was no proof that anti-Semites were responsible for… ."

"For pity's sake, open your eyes, boy! The Germans might actually impose a little more order in Poland."

"That's ridiculous, and you know it! I'm not going to sit around waiting for the invader to crash in. Heniek and I are considering joining up."

Leo, although not at all sure he agrees with Heniek, hopes his statement will provoke a reaction. He's not disappointed. Yitzhak smashes his fist on the table and turns to face his son for the first time. His mouth is a hard, tight line and his eyes narrow in anger.

"Are you serious? Do you really wish to die so young? Nothing you can do will make the slightest difference. Listen to me! The last time the Germans were here, things weren't so bad."

"Yes, father, you've told me all this before, but these Germans weren't Nazis. Things will be different this time!"

"You don't know that! The ordinary soldiers who come here will probably be much the same as they were in 1916."

Leo struggles to control his frustration.

"We can't just sit back and do nothing. What if you're wrong? It will be too late once they're actually here."

"Don't do anything rash, boy! Poles, Russians, Germans, I've seen them all before. Things will carry on much the same for us, whoever is in charge."

Yitzhak picks up his cutters and turns back to his cloth, signifying that the conversation is at an end. Leo experiences a renewed bout of frustration. As usual, his attempt to engage the old man has ended in failure. He stalks out of the workshop and heads into town. Perhaps he should punish his father by joining up, but he knows he could never walk out on his family: Lola, fearless but naïve in the ways of the world; his mother, kind and gentle with never a bad word for anyone; even his father's infuriating stubbornness, a manifestation of vulnerability. They will all need his help in the days to come.

The streets, unusually quiet and deserted at this time of day, seem in hiatus. Leo shivers, not knowing why. Glancing round at the familiar houses and shops, he notices the harsh red colour of the bricks is softening in the evening light. As he passes the town's beautiful old synagogue, he wonders whether the building will remain untouched – inviolate in the days to come. He longs for some miracle – perhaps word that the invading army has been vanquished by a merciful God moved to deliver His people one last time; that Krasnow, Poland, and the world beyond, will be spared the approaching Armageddon.

If his father is right about anything it is the tide of anti-Semitism sweeping the country. The hostility etched on the faces of Polish peasants crowding the town on market days cannot be easily ignored. They buy from the Jews only because they must. He has heard them muttering many times about over-charging and substandard goods; about Polish traders, reluctant to fleece their fellow-Christians but forced out by their rapacious Jewish business rivals. He recalls the smashed shop windows and the terrified faces of children ridiculed and spat at on their way to *cheder*. It is clear that the Nazis, if so inclined, will have little problem recruiting Poles willing to pursue the ancient enmity between Gentile and Jew.

—⁓—

A week later Krasnow wakens to the distant explosions of artillery shells. The previous afternoon the under-strength company of Polish volunteers moved out to take up defensive positions around the town when news of approaching German units was reported. After days of listening to the wail of overhead bombers and discussing the dire rumours of Nazi atrocities in the west of the country, the occupation takes on a terrifying reality for the townspeople.

Leo and Heniek decide to remain in Krasnow for the present – Leo having convinced his reluctant friend that by staying put they will be able to do more to defend their families and friends.

The Tuesday market, normally crowded by eight o'clock in the morning, is almost deserted. Nothing moves on the streets. Yitzhak, trying to occupy himself, works to complete a suit ordered by a client who has since left town. He doubts whether it will ever be collected or paid for. Leo sits upstairs endeavouring to cheer up his mother and sister. No one knows what will happen next.

At one o'clock Yitzhak announces that he is going to the synagogue to pray. Leo advises him to stay put but the old man disdainfully ignores his son and sets off.

An hour later Leo leaves to find Heniek, and to ensure that his father has reached the synagogue safely. Outside, the late September sun is shining but he notices for the first time that the leaves are turning. Not a breath of air is stirring and droplets of sweat trickle down his neck.

The sound of an accelerating engine sends him running for cover. An armoured vehicle, with a soldier clinging precariously to a top-mounted machine gun, speeds past. Moments later a convoy of troop carriers, also travelling at speed, turns right towards the centre of town. He glimpses the grey helmets of the soldiers sitting in the open-backed vehicles.

He is about to risk a dash for home when a new sound freezes him to the spot. The growl of powerful engines accompanied by the squeal and clatter of heavy metal tracks are like nothing he has heard before. Leo presses as deep as he can into the dry grass, thanking God that the municipal workers haven't got round to cutting the grass or trimming back the trees yet. From his hiding place he watches five tanks advance, one behind the other. Their turrets and tracks are plastered with thick mud and soldiers stroll alongside. He hears laughter and glimpses one man urinating against a nearby tree. Despite the peril of his situation, Leo is able to think clearly. The German unit must have crossed the marshes three miles west of the town. The young and ill-equipped boys sent out to defend the town have most likely been annihilated. He experiences a sudden stab of guilt that he wasn't fighting alongside them. At least then he might have died an honourable death.

Thirty painstaking minutes pass. More trucks, followed by motorbikes and armoured cars lurch by. Soldiers patrol in force but he is not noticed. Luckily for him most eyes are focused on upper windows where snipers might lurk.

Finally, the throb of engines dies away and Leo cautiously rises to his feet. Only long oil slicks and massive slabs of mud, excreted here and there like elephant droppings, bear witness to the passing column. He darts from one tree to the next back the way he came. He must reach the relative safety of his home and do his best to protect his family. The Germans will undoubtedly impose a total curfew and arrest anyone they find out in the open.

Entering the small square, adjacent to his street, he is alarmed by the roar of an approaching vehicle. His luck appears to have deserted him at last. A heavy wooden door suddenly swings open and an out-stretched arm urgently beckons him inside. He makes it just as a squad of German soldiers piles into the square. His deliverer, a young man of about his own age, is already halfway up the stairs. He is skinny with long, greasy hair and a torn shirt. Leo doesn't recall having seen him before despite the fact that they live on the same side of town. Perhaps he is a newcomer to the area. People always seem to be on the move these days.

On the second landing Leo follows him through an open door and they enter a small, sparsely furnished room. Without exchanging a word, they drop to the floor and crawl over to the window. Peering through the grubby panes, Leo watches as the soldiers push a group of young men against the bricked windows of the baker's shop. They stand, heads bowed and feet wide apart, while two soldiers methodically search them. Leo remembers when Samuel Willenberg, the baker, had his windows blocked up in the early spring after they'd been smashed for a second time by anti-Semite thugs. Samuel told him he just couldn't afford to put in another set.

With a terrible start Leo sees that Heniek is among the prisoners. He begins to rise but his companion drags him down, hissing a fierce warning not to move. Outside, the soldiers are forming themselves into a line. A sergeant, standing beside the squad, barks out a command. The men raise their rifles, take aim and fire. The prisoners slump to the ground. One man, bleeding from the shoulder, struggles to rise. The sergeant pulls out a pistol, strides over and shoots him point blank through the back of the head. The squad quickly departs, making no attempt to remove the bodies or cover up evidence of the cold-blooded massacre.

Leo bounds down the stairs and out into the square. People are slowly emerging and gathering around the corpses. He squats down and turns Heniek over. His friend's face is frozen in a final twist of agony – his lips drawn back and his eyes wide open. Leo brushes them closed and briefly rests his palm on the cold forehead. He rises to his feet, completely numb inside.

As Lola enters the square his stunned senses refocus in a heartbeat. He strides over and seizes her arm. She squeals and tries to pull away but he holds on, hustling her away from the scene of carnage. Outside their door he releases his grip and gazes stupidly at the deep, red finger marks etched into her white skin. His mother appears in the hallway.

"What on earth is going on? What is happening?"

Leo replies automatically, hardly recognising the harsh, staccato of his own voice.

"The Germans are here. They have shot Heniek. God knows what they will do next."

"My God, Yitzhak is at the synagogue! Would they have harmed those at afternoon prayer?"

Leo has quite forgotten his father. His heart skips a beat.

"Don't worry, mother, I'll bring him home."

"No, it's far too dangerous! You must wait until nightfall."

"By then it may be too late. Stay inside while I'm gone, and, and I'm sorry about your arm, Lola."

She shrugs, now too full of concern for her brother and her father to linger on something so trivial.

He knows a roundabout way to the synagogue and prays that the Nazis have not cast their net too widely yet. Maybe they will still be intent on securing and guarding their main lines of communication, but nothing is certain. They have already demonstrated ruthless efficiency in occupying the town. The thought of Heniek and the others dead at their hands fills him with anger and inconsolable grief.

Approaching the silent market, Leo spots something odd about the shape of the tall, ornate lampposts grouped round the entrance. Curious, he moves in closer, on the lookout for enemy patrols. He recoils in horror when he sees what has happened. Nine corpses – six men and three women – hang limply from lengths of rope slung over the tops of the posts. The nearest of them he recognises as an unfailingly cheerful Jewish fruit seller who managed a stall in the marketplace. His non-stop banter was popular with Polish and Jewish customers alike. The sight is more than he can bear and he hurries off, unable to look at the other bodies.

He enters the synagogue by a side entrance and stands for a moment peering into the dark interior. A circle of candles flickering in the far corner lends the place an air of perpetual mystery. Apart from his father kneeling next to the altar, the building appears to be empty – unusual for the time of day but understandable in the circumstances. Few people are as stubborn as Yitzhak.

"You must come home, father, now!"

His voice echoes around the domed ceiling. Yitzhak turns, his eyes narrowing in rage.

"What are you doing here, boy? Can you not see I am praying?"

"German soldiers are killing people all over town. They have murdered Heniek. We must get out of here while there's still time."

"No one with such intent shall dare enter the house of God."

As if in answer, the sound of raised voices and clattering boots on the cobbles intrudes from the outside world. Increasingly desperate, Leo grasps hold of the thick material of his father's prayer shawl and drags him to his feet.

"Take your hands off me! I will leave when I am ready and not before."

"You don't understand, father. The Nazis will most likely destroy the synagogue and shoot anyone who they find in here."

The doors suddenly burst open, shattering the fragile peace. A tall SS officer in a black uniform emblazoned with a red swastika armband enters. He is totally unlike the soldiers Leo observed earlier in the day. He gazes round him with undisguised contempt. Yitzhak twists in his son's grip and stares, open-mouthed, at this crude emissary from another world. He starts to remonstrate, a few words of protest escaping his lips, before Leo clamps a hand over his mouth. The officer strides over to the pair.

"What did you say, Jew?"

He addresses Yitzhak who is striving in vain to express his outrage.

Leo replies in a low, respectful tone.

"Forgive him, sir. He is a feeble old man who often speaks out of turn. He has become rather confused of late."

The officer slaps Leo hard over the face.

"How dare you speak without permission!"

The Nazi experiences a powerful urge to draw his gun and shoot both men at point-blank range. Instead, the red mist of anger momentarily lifts as a childhood memory filters through layers of savage indoctrination. He is sitting on his grandfather's knee in the farm kitchen back in Saxony. His face, wet with tears, is pressed against the old man's jacket. He has just been beaten by his father, but now feels safe and secure as he inhales the comforting aroma of pipe-tobacco smoke suffusing the rough material. Yitzhak bears more than a passing resemblance to the grandfather he dearly loved so long ago. Unaware why, the officer allows them a brief window of opportunity.

"Get out of here now, both of you, if you want to live."

He turns his back on the pair and barks orders at the soldiers pushing through the entranceway.

Leo pulls Yitzhak to his feet and they leave by a side door onto the street. Neither appreciates the closeness of their brush with death.

The first thing that meets their eyes is Rabbi Yoseph grappling with two soldiers; one is pinioning the priest's thin arms and forcing his head back while the other hacks at his beard with a short-bladed army knife.

"My God! What are these barbarians doing to the Rabbi?"

"There is nothing we can do! They will let him go when they have finished."

Leo is far from convinced of this, but is desperate to get his father away. The latter's ceremonial attire and long beard make him an obvious target.

"But what about the Scrolls and the Holy Ark? We cannot simply abandon these to destruction." His eyes fill with tears at the thought. "Let me go! God will give me the strength to resist this evil."

"No, father. You will be shot. Remember that you have mother and Lola to think about. Anything you do here may rebound on them later."

When they arrive home, Leo has to help his father up the flight of stairs to the flat. Just outside the front door, Yitzhak stops and grasps Leo's arm. He is deathly pale and breathing heavily.

"I apologise for my foolish behaviour at the synagogue. I could have got us both killed."

Choking back tears, Leo struggles to answer. The shock of what has happened, and his father's uncharacteristic vulnerability, are almost too much to bear.

"No one could have foreseen this."

"You must get your sister out of here."

"We must all get out of here."

Yitzhak shakes his head wearily.

"No, Leo. Your mother and I would only hold you up. You must both go to Warsaw and live as *Goyim*. It will be harder for them to identify you there, especially with new papers. I have put some money aside which will help."

"There must be another way."

He struggles to sound convincing but his father merely shakes his head.

"After what I have seen today, I do not think there will be anywhere for us to hide. It is possible, perhaps, that they may leave the children and the elderly alone. I cannot think they will see them as a threat."

"Nevertheless, I can't just leave you and mother here alone."

"For us this is probably as safe a place as any. But you and Lola must leave very soon."

—⁂—

Leo pauses for a moment and sighs. The memories still cause him pain but he feels an urgent need to pass them on before it is too late. Without understanding their meaning, Sam sees the mix of emotions flicker across his grandfather's tired, lined face.

"Drink your coffee, grandfather, before it gets cold."

The old man smiles, lifts the cup and sips to keep the boy happy. He then pulls out a cigarette, lights up and inhales deeply. Sam is uneasy knowing how upset his mother gets about her father smoking, especially since his health worsened. As if reading his thoughts, Leo smiles and taps his nose.

"Our little secret, eh?"

Sam, although willing to collude, feels a stab of guilt. A bout of coughing doesn't help and he hopes his mother has not heard the noise from the kitchen where she is preparing lunch.

Grinding the half-smoked cigarette into a tiny glass ashtray, Leo continues his narrative.

"After things had quietened down and they knew there wasn't likely to be any trouble, the Germans called for a census of all Jews living in Krasnow. We had to queue up outside the Town Hall to have our papers checked and provide information about where we lived, as well as the value of everything we owned. We were aware that this would not be used for our benefit, but there was nothing we could do. We now knew what these people were capable of – reprisals they called it – and we were too scared to openly defy their orders."

"What did your Polish neighbours do?" Sam is thinking about the young man who most probably saved his grandfather from the firing squad.

"Some were happy to provide information to the Gestapo. Others acted very differently, of course, and did all they could to help us. Maybe these were the ones whose relatives and friends had been executed during the first few days of the occupation. I don't know."

"What happened to the man who hid you in his flat?"

"I have no idea what happened to him or who he was. He could have been a *Bundist*, I suppose. There were many such left-wing organisations in Poland at the time with Jews in their ranks. The Gestapo was particularly anxious to get its hands on them. To be a Jew and a socialist was the worst possible crime in the eyes of the Nazis. I went round to thank him just before Lola and I left Krasnow, but the flat was empty. He may have been arrested. Who knows! I shouldn't have gone near the place. It was a risky thing to do."

Leo starts to tug at his cigarette packet again.

"Tell me more about the Poles."

The effort to divert his grandfather succeeds and Leo stops fiddling with the packet for a moment. Instead, he stares thoughtfully at his big, gnarled fingers, discoloured by yellow nicotine stains and dark liver spots, before continuing.

"The Poles proved to be our worst enemies and our best friends. The Shoah brought out so much that was good and bad in people. Even some of our own became informers, hoping, I suppose, to save their miserable hides. In this they were deluding themselves. The Nazis showed no loyalty to Jews, however co-operative they were. In the end they made the same journey as those they betrayed." He sighs before continuing, "I knew my father was right. Sooner rather than later, Lola and I had to get out of Krasnow."

"How could you leave them there like that?"

"We still hoped the Germans would leave the old people and children alone. We believed they were keen to get their hands on the young for slave labour. Rumours were racing round the town that after the census we were to be rounded up and taken into Germany to build weapons for their war effort. That's what spurred me into action. I'd no intention of helping the enemy defeat our friends and allies. I was terrified, of course. After what I'd seen, I had some idea of what might be in store for us."

—⚹—

Leo hugs his mother, feeling her tears on his neck. Yitzhak's hand is hard and dry in his own. The old man's rheumy eyes, set deep in their cranial hollows, are dark pools of sorrow. Outside, it is raining hard. He knows that in an hour or two he and Lola will be freezing and soaked to the skin. The distance to Warsaw is not so great but their journey across country in such conditions will be difficult. His main worry is what will happen when they reach their destination. With few friends, no relatives and an occupied city, he is not certain how they will survive. The money he is carrying might be enough to purchase forged papers and secure them lodgings for a month or two. But, apart from a Polish acquaintance of his father's living in the Jewish quarter of the city, there is no one they can trust. Even this man, one of Yitzhak's closest business associates, may not be able or willing to help them. The penalties for aiding and abetting Jews will be severe. Leo guesses that trying to assume a new identity, if possible at all, will be a highly dangerous and costly exercise. But everything depends on being able to do just that.

Leaving town they head towards the swollen river, and the thick cloak of forest which Leo hopes will allow them to go undetected. Alert for German patrols, he leads his sister across a muddy field, over a wall and deep into the dripping trees. The layer of needles beneath their feet is thick and slimy but they quickly reach the path running along the west bank of the river.

They meet no one. Perhaps people are hiding away from the foul weather. The wind is rising and driving the rain so hard that the trees provide little shelter. Lola, struggling along in her brother's wake, grits her teeth and lowers her head against the stinging drops. She is determined not to utter one word of complaint.

Three kilometres out of town, just as they are about to leave the river and strike across country, Lola slips and twists her ankle. Their luck is compromised for a second time when Leo almost collides with an old peasant bent double under a load of kindling. His eyes narrow suspiciously as the pair hurry past. Leo knows he must be wondering why they are out so late in the filthy weather and dwindling light. He may well report them.

As the darkness thickens they can see virtually nothing under the cover of the trees. Leo fears his sister will slip again on the wet pine roots, twisting like petrified snakes beneath their feet. Suddenly, the trees shuffle aside and he spots a few stars blinking above their heads. The rain has finally ceased and the air is cold against his cheek. They are beside a dirt road heading more or less in the direction they wish to go. He decides to risk staying with it. Although Lola is not complaining, he knows she must be in pain. Perhaps they will find somewhere to hole up at first light.

Freed from focusing on his feet, Leo allows himself to consider the terrible impact of the past few weeks. All rumours regarding German anti-Semitism have much underestimated the brutal reality. Krasnow's synagogue was burnt down – probably on that first terrible day of the German invasion. Several houses in the vicinity also caught fire and were left to burn; the blackened gap near the town centre remains a potent threat to anyone disposed to defy the occupier. The Germans also issued an edict suppressing all Jewish festivals, probably because of the imminence of *Yom Kippur*. Nonetheless, Yitzhak donned his religious robes and recited the *Kol Nidre* throughout the day. Although nervous, Leo couldn't help feeling proud of his father's refusal to be intimidated.

Several hideous images swim unbidden into his mind as they hurry along. Heniek's terrified eyes, frozen at the point of death; the fruit-seller's limp corpse hanging on the lamppost outside the marketplace; and the brutal soldiers hacking Rabbi Yoseph's beard off. In the first few days of the occupation some orthodox Jews were paraded in their traditional garb, lined up for photographs beside their grinning tormentors, then shot. Informers must have helped the Nazis find their victims. Leo worries that his father will be next. Again, he feels guilty about leaving his parents to their fate. Mr Prost was right. Racist thuggery without official sanction is nothing to this.

Distant barking returns him to the present with a jolt. Could this be a patrol, alerted by the old peasant, already on their tracks, or merely a dog reacting to some local disturbance? They strive to detect the slightest hint of pursuit. Another series of barks and yelps, definitely closer this time, confirms their worst fears. They leave the path and plunge down a steep slope. Fortunately, they find a rivulet swollen by the recent rains and blindly splash their way over the slippery boulders. Buoyed up, the pair run like hunted deer, Lola forgetting her sprain as her skilful feet find precarious footholds in the stream bed.

The water suddenly becomes swifter and deeper. Realising their danger, they clamber out and listen again for sounds of pursuit. Over the pounding of his heart, Leo hears another bark, much fainter this time. It seems as though their pursuers are still on the road. Perhaps they consider it too dangerous to risk a headlong rush over unknown ground in the darkness. Leo understands their reluctance. They have been remarkably lucky. Lola is bent double trying to control her breathing. She straightens up and smiles desperately at Leo. Although trying to be brave she is clearly struggling.

—ɯ—

"In the end, we managed another two or three kilometres before we were forced to halt. Lola couldn't continue without rest and I wasn't feeling much better. We just lay down next to each other on some sodden brushwood and fell asleep. I had to shake her awake a couple of hours before dawn. There was still a fair way to go and most of it had to be done under cover of darkness. The nearer we got to Warsaw the more chance we had of running into patrols. The woods were full of fugitives, mainly remnants of the Polish army and refugees fleeing the city."

Leo stops and gazes at his grandson's rapt face for a moment. "Many people were shot. We came across a family: a father, mother and two daughters lying where they had fallen, and we heard distant gunfire. Lola was very brave. Even though I knew she was frightened to death, she showed no sign of it."

Sam considers for a moment the strong, young woman he never knew.

"We rested again at daybreak under an overhang on the river bank. The perfect hiding place really. We lay there not daring to move. Weak sunlight warmed us up a little, and we managed to get some sleep. I went out for a look around just before dark, hoping to find some way to ford the river. I spotted an old red brick factory on the opposite bank and a power station half a kilometre downstream, but nothing that would help us to cross over. Bridges were out of the question, of course. I knew those that had survived the bombing would be heavily guarded. Anyone without proper papers would most likely be shot on the spot. Swimming was our only option, though it was a long way against a strong current with the water so cold. Luckily, we were both strong swimmers, but I wasn't sure if we could make it across in the dark."

Sam sits spellbound, imagining the terrible anxiety as the pair hesitated on the edge of the great river. He wonders if he would have been able to summon up the courage to strike out for the distant bank

—꿈—

Leo gasps as he launches himself into the water. The cold immediately numbs his limbs. Just ahead he can see Lola's dark head bobbing on the surface, and hear the rhythmic splash of her arms as she attempts to make some headway. They are swept downstream but manage to keep going. Exhausted and barely able to move his legs, he crawls up the opposite bank and flops on the grass alongside his sister. He knows they must keep going but the desire to fall asleep is exerting a powerful appeal. Urging his body into motion, he hauls Lola up into a sitting position. She pleads with him to let her rest. He wonders if they have made the right decision in leaving home. At least in Krasnow they were protected from the harshness of the early Polish winter. It is likely they will either die from exposure, or at the hands of a patrol. Shaking his head, he struggles to cast off these enervating thoughts; wallowing in a pit of despair is the surest road to ruin.

Once they are moving again things rapidly improve. By dawn they are entering the outskirts of Warsaw. Leo knows they must reach his father's business associate, Mr Lebinski, as quickly as possible. The address is lodged in his memory. The problem is that he doesn't have a clue how to get there. He only knows that the flat is located within the city's traditional Jewish quarter. According to his father, Lebinski, although a *Goy*, is agent to a number of wealthy Jewish businessmen and finds it beneficial to live close to his clients.

The streets grow busier. People, wrapped up against the cold wind, are making their way to work through the bomb-blasted city. They both feel a little safer now and less conspicuous among the hurrying commuters, many of whom are as shabbily clad and down at heel as themselves. Fortunately, it hasn't rained since they crossed the river and, despite the cold wind, their clothes have dried on their backs.

"What a mess the bombs have made. A lot of people must have died during the raids." Lola points to a building where an entire gable wall has been blasted away exposing six identical flats to the world's gaze. "Look at the top one!" Leo glances up and sees paintings and undamaged furniture still in place. "I wonder if the people got out."

"They may have done. Apart from the outside wall the place looks intact."

"I hope they did."

Leo is paradoxically dismayed and moved by her compassion for people she does not even know.

Spotting a German patrol ahead his heart lurches. The soldiers are checking the papers of workers queuing at a tram stop. Brother and sister cross the street trying to act as casually as possible. One man suddenly breaks away from the queue weaving in and out of startled pedestrians. Undeterred, a soldier drops down on one knee, takes aim and fires. A woman in a black trench coat, a few metres ahead of the fleeing man, throws up her hands and tumbles over. The fugitive dives down a small side street and vanishes. The Germans force their way along the crowded pavement in hot pursuit. People, unable to get out of the way in time, are clubbed aside with rifle butts. They pass the woman's motionless body without a sideways glance. Lola stares and stares until Leo pulls her away.

"What sort of beasts are these soldiers?"

"You surely know the answer to that question already! You were there when Heniek died. You saw the bodies in the square. If we are to stand any chance of surviving you must understand what we're up against." Leo knows he must purge his sister of her sentimental attachment to the idea that people are basically kind and generous at heart. "The best you can expect from the Nazis is that they will shoot you without a second thought; the worst, that they will work you to death in some appalling labour camp."

Lola's face twists in disbelief.

"They can't all be like that!"

"Perhaps not, but you must assume every German in Poland feels that way about Jews."

"We must ask for directions soon."

"That could be dangerous. Father told me if we can get to Okopowa Street, on the edge of the Jewish quarter, we should be able to find Mr Lebinski's flat on Leszno Street. We must keep going and trust to our luck."

Luck, however, doesn't appear to be on their side. After wandering for what seems like hours, they become totally disorientated. The streets appear identical: all badly bomb damaged with rubble strewn everywhere. Finally, they find themselves back where the shooting took place. Lola bursts into tears. She pulls herself together quickly enough but Leo knows she is exhausted and hungry.

They enter a shop advertising the sale of spirits and general food products. The interior is shabby and the stock meagre – a few tins and boxes perched forlornly on the shelves. Leo feels for the oilskin purse his mother made to hold their money, and the few other valuables they have brought along. The old man behind the counter packs their simple purchases in a brown paper bag and hands over the change without a second glance. Believing that their innate 'Jewishness' would attract unwanted attention, the shop keeper's indifference boosts Leo's confidence.

As they consume their frugal meal on a park bench, he finally makes up his mind to risk asking directions to the Jewish quarter. The man they approach stares at the pair for a moment before replying in *Yiddish*. The sound of the familiar tongue puts brother and sister at their ease. They are not so far from Okopowa Street and should be able to get there quickly enough. The man blesses them and promises to pray for their safe passage. Leo feels a lump gathering in his throat; hearing kind words in the midst of such desolation and danger moves him greatly.

Lola points to a poster plastered across a shop window. They both read what it says:

"In order to prevent impertinent behaviour by the Polish population, I order the following: Polish citizens of both sexes are to give way to representatives of the German nation. That is, step off the pavement into the road when passed by uniformed Germans. In addition, men are required to remove headgear. The streets belong to the conquerors, not the conquered.

By order of Dr Hans Frank: Governor General of Poland."

This, perhaps, explains the brutal disregard for human life they witnessed earlier in the day. It is clearly not only the Jews who should be worried for their future. Leo again ponders whether it would have been better if he and Heniek had joined up and died fighting the Nazis. In the wake of the Third Reich's total victory, life is rapidly becoming intolerable for the defeated. But, of course, he has his sister to look out for now; his death would have left her alone and vulnerable.

They pass a Jewish cemetery surrounded by ornate wrought iron railings, and spot other posters designating the entire area as subject to open quarantine regulations. They wonder what this means for those living here. The question is quickly answered. Every street running into the quarter has a checkpoint manned by armed police-men inspecting the papers of residents passing in and out. Although dismayed, Leo is not really surprised. Close supervision of the city's Jewish population is inevitable considering the German obsession with identification and designation. The quarantine situation is, he is certain, merely a ruse to exert control.

They spot Leszno Street, running at right angles to Okopowa, and watch the comings and goings at the checkpoint for a moment. The two Polish policemen on duty are clearly overwhelmed by the sheer volume of people moving in both directions and are making little attempt to check papers. Leo wonders how long it will be before the Germans plug this gap.

Minutes later they are outside number forty-five gazing at the surnames inscribed beside each brass-topped bell pull. Lebinski is halfway down and Leo tugs hard on the lever. They hear a faint tinkling in the heart of the building. The door swings open and they enter a wide stairwell. Five floors up a massive glass cupola floods the well with light. On the third landing an elderly man is staring down at them. He is small and squat with grey hair straggling untidily around his ears. He leans over and calls out.

"What can I do for you young people?"

Managing to sound anxious, irritated and curious all at the same time, he waits for the strangers to introduce themselves and state their business.

"My name is Leo Infeld, sir. Are you Mr Lebinski?"

"I am, young man."

"I have come here with my sister, Lola. My father said you might be able to help us."

"You are Yitzhak's son? Yitzhak Infeld?"

"Yes, sir."

Mr Lebinski visibly relaxes and smiles at the young couple standing shivering and dishevelled below.

"I am glad you have made it here. It must have been difficult."

Leo nods.

"We had to leave Krasnow in a hurry. Father thought we would be safer in Warsaw."

"I'm sorry to tell you that he may have been mistaken. But come up and we will see what can be done."

As they make their way up the stairs, Leo is in no doubt that Mr Lebinski will try his best to help them, but the city has the feel of a trap about to be sprung.

—⁓—

"My father was right about Mr Lebinski. He helped us in every way he could. He insisted we stay in his home until he could fix us up. His advice to us to remain in the Jewish quarter and not pass ourselves off as 'Aryans', seemed sensible enough at the time. He couldn't have known what was going to happen."

"What are 'Aryans' and why did Mr Lebinski think you should stay in the Jewish quarter?"

Sam's interest in the smallest details encourages his grandfather to a fuller explanation than he intended. "The Germans believed the 'Aryan' people to be the master race – superior in every way to other 'primitive' races. But for us, 'Aryans' became anyone who was not of Jewish origin living outside the ghetto or as we later called it – the Aryan side. In answer to your second question, Mr Lebinski believed that when the fuss had died down the Nazis would leave us alone. You must understand, Sam, that no one knew at that time what was meant by the 'final solution' to the Jewish problem. I guess even Hitler himself hadn't worked it out yet. Mr Lebinski was convinced that once the Jews and Poles were separated, the occupiers wouldn't have the will or the resources to do much more. After all, they, the Germans, would soon be embroiled in a life-or-death struggle in France. Most people still believed that the

British and French were going to thrash the Nazis, so it was only a matter of time before we were liberated. He arranged papers and new identities for us. He also found us a small, top-floor flat in a house on Gesia Street, at the edge of the quarter. Lola and I became a young married couple from Plock who had moved to Warsaw the previous spring searching for work. I remember Lola laughed a lot when Mr Lebinski suggested it."

Leo smiles at his grandson sitting cross-legged on the carpet. The boy is entirely captivated. This time he barely reacts as the old man lights up another cigarette.

"The money our father had given us was running out but at least we were safe for the time being, with our new identities and the rent on the flat paid up six months in advance. Mr Lebinski was sure we would both find work and live comfortably enough until the Allies arrived. He was one of the kindest men I have ever known. It's what I told you about the Poles, they were either our best friends or our worst enemies."

"Weren't you scared to death the Nazis would find you? And what happened to Mr Lebinski?"

This time, Leo laughs outright at the boy's intent face staring so expectantly at him. Although amused, he feels a great weariness settling over him.

"Your questions will be answered soon enough, lad, but I've had enough for today. Your mother will be wondering where you have got to. It's probably not such a good idea if she comes in here looking for you."

He holds up the cigarette and screws his features into a suitably terrified expression.

"Oh, grandfather, please."

"Sorry, but it's more than my life is worth. Come back tomorrow and I'll tell you more. But, if you say anything to your mother about me smoking, my lips are sealed, understand?"

Sam nods and rises reluctantly. He lifts the tray from the bottom of the bed.

"I won't say anything, I promise."

"Good boy. Now, off you go and give me some peace."

As the door closes Leo drags deeply on the remainder of his cigarette before leaning back and resting his head on the pillows. Not for the first time he wonders what he is trying to do here. He knows that by persisting with these stories he might inadvertently convince the boy to accept a version of stereotyped heroism battling an equally stereotyped evil. On the other hand, his desire to encourage an affinity for truth, and what it is to be human in a testing situation, might just provide the antidote needed to counter the Zionist poison being fed to the boy by his zealous father. The question is, whether Sam is old enough to make the necessary distinctions. He knows, however, that time is not on his side. The speed of the cancer's rampage through his body has dismayed him.

He ponders the disaster of his daughter, Miriam's marriage while recalling the pleasure he experienced when his son-in-law, Benny, first asked for his blessing. His restless thoughts turn to the children of the ghetto, many much younger than Sam, so streetwise, so courageous in the face of starvation and imminent death. Once again, he glimpses their emaciated bodies littering the filthy cobbles of Gesia Street as people hurry past trying to blot out the end of innocence.

CHAPTER THREE

Kiryat Arba, West Bank – February 1994.

Father rushes into the kitchen. It is just after one o'clock and the festival of *Purim* is well underway. He has been out drinking with his friends all morning and his face is bright red and wreathed in smiles. This is unusual enough for me to sit up and take notice. Mother stares at him in amazement.

"It's a miracle, a *Purim* miracle. I didn't believe it at first but then we saw it on Marek's TV: all the police cars and the ambulances; and the Prime Minister explaining what had happened."

Mother holds up her hands.

"Slow down, Benny. What miracle are you talking about?"

"Our doctor, Baruch Goldstein."

"You mean the fool at the clinic who refuses to treat Arab patients, or, for that matter, Jews who don't share his insane ideas?"

"Yes, and thank God there are some among us who respect the *Halacha*."

He glares at her for a few seconds – good humour vanished and old tensions flaring up.

"What has the good doctor done to make you so happy then?"

"He has shot dead twenty-nine Arabs in the Patriarchs' Cave, and wounded many others."

Mother's mouth falls open. She swallows hard, as though trying to force down a huge lump in her throat. It's a few moments before she can speak.

"So, you are actually celebrating the death of innocent people at prayer?"

Father strikes back, incensed by her reaction.

"Innocent! These are not innocent people. We are talking about Arab thieves and murderers who were violating one of our most sacred places. They have received numerous warnings to stay away. Only last year we punished them for their sacrilege."

He stares at me, seeking validation.

I nod.

Mother ignores me.

"If you cannot understand the true nature of such an act, husband" – mother spits the last word out – "think how it will be viewed by those who value human life and the rule of law. We will all pay the price for your madman's act."

I sit stunned as my parents' words batter on my head like angry beaks. The vision of a righteous Jew clearing a nest of vipers from such a sacred site is sullied by mother's description of them as innocent victims. When father finally speaks, his words are laboured. It seems he can scarcely believe such profanity is possible.

"Why should we worry about creatures whose views are utterly irrelevant? Why are you not praising Dr Goldstein for his heroic act? We are not talking about the murder of human beings! When the Messiah comes, these *Goyim* you esteem so highly will matter nothing.

Do you not understand, woman? Muslims, Christians, unbelievers alike, will be swept from our sacred land like chaff." Shaking his head, he turns to me.

"A special session has been convened by the municipality to condemn the deed. Rabbi Previnger is drawing up a counter-proposal and requires our support. We must be there within the hour."

As we leave the house father fires a parting shot over his shoulder.

"Perhaps you would like to come along and cheer on our municipal secretary, Uri Aron. You may find you have much in common with such a fool."

Mother's reply is swift and unrepentant.

"I have better things to do with my time, Benny. Murder is murder however much you and your friends try to spin it!"

Despite everything she says, does mother really believe that Dr Goldstein was insane? That the executions were carried out in a moment of madness? As we approach the municipal centre we find ourselves caught up in a milling throng of revellers. I remain troubled as Gad rushes over. His eyes are shining and he is too emotional to speak. He hugs me tightly. This is bizarre behaviour for him, but since he is so happy I don't really care. Elation kicks in as we enter the crowded hall.

Rabbi Previnger, Secretary Aron and the Mayor of Kiryat Arba are already seated on the platform. I also notice Rabbi Dov Levin deep in conversation with an *NRP* official. I gaze in awe at the man whose hatred of Arabs is legendary – even here in Kiryat Arba. The fact that he missed the opportunity of being elected to the Supreme Rabbinical Council of Israel due to his recommendation that medical experiments be performed on the living bodies of Arab terrorists, continues to be hotly debated. Grandfather was furious when these views first hit the press. He was so ill by then that I didn't want to say anything to upset him. Father told me if the previous generation had resisted the Nazis before they became so powerful, the Shoah might never have happened. "That is why, Samuel," he said in the solemn voice reserved for when he had something really important to say, "we must never display weakness in the face of our enemies again. Rabbi Levin is the man of action Israel needs."

The excited babble in the hall dies down. The meeting is about to begin. Uri Aron has wasted no time. Perhaps he wants to offset the mood of celebration on the streets, fearing how journalists and left-wing politicians will interpret it. Mr Katz has often said that the secretary is a weakling and an appeaser. Aron stands up to address the crowded hall. He looks ill at ease and hesitates before speaking. "When word came to me of Baruch Goldstein's deed at the Patriarch's Cave this morning, I knew I must put aside personal feelings and call for an unambiguous condemnation from... ." That is as far as he gets. We are all on our feet, yelling and shaking our fists. I can see beads of sweat glistening on his forehead under the harsh, fluorescent lights. He tries to wipe them away but the gesture is as futile as his appeal for our support.

Finally, Rabbi Previnger rises and lifts his arms, appealing for quiet; instantly the outraged commotion dies away.

"My friends, my friends, please allow the good secretary to continue. This is a debate where both sides of the argument must be heard."

Rabbi Levin leans forward in his seat and whispers something to the mayor. The latter chuckles in response. In the meantime, Aron struggles on, his words withering away in the hostile silence. He sits down heavily and it's Previnger's turn. He stands and gazes into space for a moment as if conscious of some unearthly presence in the room. When he finally speaks, his voice is low and measured.

"I must thank my friend, Uri Aron, for making certain facts clear to us. Baruch Goldstein was the victim of a relentless campaign which forced him to compromise his most sacred duty in accordance with the *Halacha*. For many years insidious pressure has been applied from above in an effort to compel him, and other righteous Jewish doctors, to abandon their faith and treat Arab patients. In the process, his army career was shattered and his transfer to a civilian clinic, a calculated attempt to discredit him. When Baruch entered the Patriarch's Cave early this morning, his action was the direct result of years of frustration and humiliation created by those who have no respect for our holy texts or the religious significance of Hebron; by those who have abandoned the sacred duty of righteous Jews to occupy the entire extent of *Eretz Israel*; and, perhaps, worst of all, by those who have betrayed their brothers to Arab terrorists and their foreign sympathisers."

Shouting and stamping threaten to drown out the rabbi's words but he merely slides up his internal volume switch.

His voice, now charged with emotion, soars easily over the din.

"My friends, we are at present witnessing the actions of a government not only guilty of striving for appeasement with alien powers at any cost but guilty of selling our birthright to those who would thrust a sword through our hearts."

The din rises to a crescendo. Everyone is roused by the blistering attack on traitors and unbelievers in the land. Gad's face is almost purple – his voice hoarse with yelling. Previnger waves his hand and the noise dies back. He is like the conductor of a symphony orchestra, unleashing power then pulling it back to a thrumming intensity.

"As Secretary Aron explained, some accommodation must be sought with the outside world which understands nothing of our long struggle and will naturally draw all the wrong conclusions from what has happened here today. You may ask why we should care about *Goyim* sentiment, or waste time and energy differentiating between unbelievers at home or abroad."

Someone cries out "Why indeed?" while others stamp their approval. I remember father's words earlier on. Previnger merely smiles and wags his finger in mock protest.

"We must placate national and international opinion during the *Time of Redemption* for our own ends. When our Lord reveals Himself, nothing said nor done by presidents or prime ministers throughout the world will make the slightest difference. We in *Gush Emunim* have learned the value of pragmatism over the years and our successes speak for themselves. The settlements we have built, and continue to build, are a constant reminder of what has been achieved. They tell everyone that we are here to stay. And, most importantly of all, they are making it tough for the traitors amongst us to negotiate an Arab state in the midst of Judea and Samaria. All such attempts will fail as we slowly but surely drive out Satan and his cohorts, and repopulate our sacred land."

Mr Katz leans forward, his eyes shining with tears. Previnger has worked his magic; his words are manna from heaven.

"Pragmatism does not, of course, apply to our core principles – only the methods by which we attain the end we seek. Therefore, although all of us in this hall understand that no murder, in the real sense of the word, was committed by our brother Goldstein this morning, care must be taken in the wording of our resolution. Instead of condemning the act we must condemn the government and the media for placing him under such appalling strain. Some expression of sorrow for the dead Arabs might also be included, although all of us here being compassionate folk will surely feel a degree of sympathy for the flies that have perished in this hall over the course of the week." A ripple of laughter at that. "In the weeks and months to come we will demonstrate our true appreciation of what our holy martyr has achieved through his courageous act. Such selflessness shall reverberate down the years and point the way forward. The funeral and the shrine erected in his memory will honour a righteous man and hero of Israel."

The final applause almost lifts the roof. Afterwards, before the next speaker takes the stand, a few people mutter against the need to placate the *Goyim*, but most have been powerfully swayed by the rabbi's argument.

A vote is taken and support for Previnger's counter-proposal is overwhelming. The hall empties and we spill out onto the street. Talk is now of the approaching funeral and the shattering impact the Messiah's coming will have on *Goyim* and Jewish heretics alike.

—⁂—

Next day I meet up with Gad and a few friends. Gad points approvingly at a rash of new posters that have been plastered on the whitewashed walls of a block of flats across the street from the elementary school. One contains a grainy image of Goldstein's face with the words: "Dr Goldstein cured Israeli ills. Praise be to the holy martyr" inscribed below. On another, an Arab face is cross-haired through gun sights alongside the caption: "More will follow. Our sacred land will be freed."

"These are being posted in every town in Judea and Samaria, as well as in Jerusalem. Father says we will all get special badges for the funeral."

Gad can barely contain his excitement as his eyes flick from face to face.

Paul Horowitz, a tall, pale-skinned boy whose uncle was ambushed and shot dead by Arab terrorists a few weeks ago, suddenly pipes up. His lips are curled back over his teeth like a snarling dog; and his normally mild eyes are blazing with fury.

"This is just the beginning, I tell you. There are going to be a few surprises at the funeral. My father says that any Arabs or Goy-loving Jews who get in the way will be sorry they did."

This doesn't sound like Paul at all.

It was only a month ago that Gad caught him reading a glossy magazine filled with photos of half-naked models cavorting at a fashion show in Tel Aviv. He promptly informed the headmaster who spent the best part of an hour the next morning reviling Paul in front of the entire school. I felt sorry for him as he stood there looking mortified and miserable. I had pored over the same magazines myself, furiously masturbating in an attempt to ease my secret lust. I knew for certain that all of us, including Gad, infuriatingly smug and self-righteous on the day of Paul's disgrace, were concealing similar secrets from the world. I wondered how he could have so cold-bloodedly reported Paul knowing that he was guilty of the same thing. We are taught that God condemns the sinner and the sin whether other people know or not. As I listened to the headmaster condemning the delinquency of self-abuse, I couldn't help thinking that even he must once have rubbed at the stiffness that refuses to budge. I shivered with disgust at such a thought. Strangely enough, Paul didn't seem to hold a grudge against Gad. Instead, he appeared to accept that it had been Gad's duty to report his sin to the authorities. He had been caught in the act and thus deserved punishment. Will he ever masturbate over such dubious material in the future? Definitely!

Gad's voice intervenes as I try to suppress images of the voluptuous female curves so candidly snapped on the catwalk.

"Paul is right. We all need to be at the cutting edge. Don't forget that we'll soon be serving our country while the *Haredi* and *Hassidic* cravens hide away in their classrooms chanting prayers."

I recall the press photograph of Paul's uncle sprawled beside his bullet-ridden car. In class next day, Mr Dayane explained that the murder was no different from the Nazi atrocities committed against Jews. "No Arab," he said, "can be assumed to be innocent when such things happen."

As we discuss the approaching funeral and our determination to continue the struggle, even in the face of death, Gad hammers home the point.

"We must prove worthy of martyred heroes like Baruch Goldstein and Paul's uncle. It's up to us to maintain the pressure, especially here with the Arabs all around us." Gad is expressing the frustration that all settler pioneers feel. "The trouble is we are always forced to compromise. That's why the route of the funeral procession has been changed – just because a few cowards worry about what the Arabs might think. Who cares what they think?" He stares at us, clearly expecting some expression of approval. We nod and grunt supportively. "The authorities say they want to avoid trouble in Hebron but I say that is the wrong strategy." Gad now sounds just like his father delivering a speech to the Kiryat Arba Committee for Safety on the Roads. "We need to show them that we mean business. Only when they realise that there is no hope will they ever pack up and leave." Another dramatic pause. "Maybe the older generation are just not up to the task. The sooner we're in charge the better."

He's right, of course, but why must he always sound so pompous, like a teacher talking to a bunch of stupid kids? We all know what has to be done! Glancing round at the others – so excited and enthusiastic – it seems that nobody else is the slightest bit bothered by his infuriating condescension.

—⁓—

The day of the funeral arrives. We are driven to Jerusalem on a chartered bus hours before the event kicks off, but already the square where the tributes and eulogies are to be delivered is awash with hundreds of cheering students, mainly *Chabad Hassids, Satmar Hassids* and young *Kahane* supporters. The atmosphere is electric, with everyone, for once, united in common cause.

I find myself talking to a cross-eyed *Haredi* youth with dirty ringlets and a straggling beard. He's wearing a thick black coat and a hat which bobs continuously as he talks. It gets progressively hotter as the sun beats down on the square, and the smell of stale sweat hangs on him like an invisible vest. I wonder how often he changes his gear. The *ultra-orthodox* make no concession to the weather, wearing their heavy garments all the year round. I struggle to rid myself of the usual stereotype responses.

He introduces himself only as Tsvi, and praises Dr Goldstein.

"He may have been a *knitted skullcap* but he was a righteous Jew." The derisory term reminds me that we are not the only ones to indulge in stereotypes. Tsvi continues, oblivious to the fact that he might have caused offence. "I am glad that we have all come together today to praise such a heroic deed. It's right that we put our differences to one side. The more cautious amongst my people say it was the wrong moment to act, that Jewish lives might be put at risk, but I believe this to be misguided! Nothing will ever be the same again."

I tell him that it's time for religious Jews from all backgrounds to unite against the common enemy. He nods vigorously, the hard rim of his hat perilously close to battering my forehead.

"We must make a stand. The *Time of Redemption* is close at hand. I do not know how much more punishment we must endure because of the godless among us who delay the advent of the Messiah."

I'm not quite sure who he's referring to, but, despite the scraggy beard, the ringlets and the battered hat, I feel we are connecting.

Nearby, Paul and his father are in deep conversation with a gang of *Kach* supporters. If things get ugly today this bunch will be behind it, I'm sure. Many of them are ex-jailbirds who strut around flaunting their notoriety like a badge of honour.

The crowd has now swollen to thousands. When the coffin arrives the applause is deafening. I stand shoulder-to-shoulder with my new *Haredi* friend listening to a succession of eulogies praising Goldstein and commending his martyrdom. Emotions intensify: people yell out while others openly weep and pluck their beards. Passions beat around the square on countless wings. The *Kach* contingent chant "Death to the Arabs", as Ben-Yehuda, recently released from prison for terrorist outrages against Israeli Arabs, rises to his feet.

Ben-Yehuda's amnesty incensed mother. She said she had no idea how such a vicious killer could possibly be considered for release after only serving two years of a life sentence.

"What sort of a society are we living in anyhow? Truth is he wasn't in prison at all – more like an honoured guest of the government living in the lap of luxury."

He certainly doesn't look any the worse for his short time in jail. His youthful face is lit up, and his deft handling of the microphone makes him look more like a pop star than a freedom fighter.

"Brothers and comrades in arms, may I first of all say how good it is to be a free man once more. Things are surely improving when I look around and see so many different sects and parties gathered here today. My hopes for the future quicken as I contemplate God's people speaking in one clear, strong voice. The time is approaching when a man will be rewarded, not punished, for acting in the interests of his country. Baruch Goldstein, a good and honourable man, made to suffer for so many years, has shown us the way. We must not falter in our duty to act with similar courage and conviction when our time comes. We have been given an extraordinary example to follow and have only ourselves to blame if we fail to live up to it. Let us raise the bright sword so bravely unsheathed by the martyr Goldstein and never lower it again till we have secured our birthright. Let us take the fight to those who would betray our dearest principles and subvert the laws of God as entrusted to us through all the ages."

Even the police and border guards are cheering. Excitement boils over and froths around the square.

Finally the cortège moves off, winding out onto the usually busy streets now cleared of traffic. I wonder what will happen if any Arab strays too close. The unit of guards at the front, and the police walking alongside, look nervous and are clearly anxious to avoid trouble. I sense in the present situation, with feelings running so high, that the *Kach* "boys" from East Jerusalem may be planning an action of some kind. Maybe this is what Paul was talking about. Arabs, mainstream media reporters and their camera teams, lefty politicians, *Goys* – any or all of them could be the target today. The terrible image of a Jewish market seller strung up by the Nazis and left to slowly strangle suddenly springs into my head. Perhaps grandfather told me such things not from a desire to shock but to focus my mind at moments like this. Marching along in the middle of the chanting crowd, I experience a strange conversion. It's not that I'm any less committed to the cause, or unmoved by Dr Goldstein's martyrdom, but I feel confused and increasingly jumpy. I pray to God that no outsider will stumble across our path; that no one will have to die the lonely, wretched death of that poor soul in Krasnow.

A few tourists are watching as the cortège slowly winds its way through the streets. They seem blissfully unaware of their danger and peer through the lenses of their fancy cameras, probably believing that the procession is just another bizarre religious outing by the natives. The mood quickly changes when some of the mourners start to spit and scream at them. One man has his camcorder wrenched away and smashed to pieces on the pavement. Unsurprisingly, they beat a hasty retreat, leaving the streets to the mourners.

Arab street sellers have deserted their posts, and shops along the route are boarded up. Most of them have wisely decided to avoid trouble, or been moved on by the police. I doubt that Baruch Goldstein's action at the Patriarch's Cave will cause them to flee the country as father believes. More likely the death and injury inflicted on their kindred will stoke up more hatred. I know it doesn't help to think like this but I just can't help myself.

I spot an Arab woman with two young boys watching from behind a low wall. Too late, she realises that she has been trapped on the wrong side of the cortège. In an instinctive attempt to protect her boys, she pushes them behind her, clearly willing to shield them with her own body if need be. A policeman leaps the barrier and bundles the trio round the front before the bulk of mourners turn the corner. They vanish into a maze of alleyways off the main drag of the avenue. The more extreme elements miss an opportunity to vent their spleen thanks to the quick-thinking officer. I feel relief quickly followed by guilt at my concern for the Arab family. When I try to tease out these contradictions, all I can see are grandfather's sad, grey eyes staring at me out of the darkness.

Gad suddenly appears at my side. He's sweating and breathless.

"Where have you been? I've been looking for you everywhere."

I smile and point to my *Haredi* companion.

"I got talking to my new friend here."

"Him! He's not one of us!"

Gad has obviously been unaffected by the various appeals for unity and remains unmoved by the significance of such a mixed gathering of mourners. I try to explain but he impatiently interrupts.

"I don't want to talk about that weirdo! I came to tell you that Mr Horovitz is screaming for blood. Everybody's going crazy back there." He points towards the rear of the cortège. "you should come now if you don't want to miss out on the fun."

With that he's off, weaving his way back through the crowd. I certainly wouldn't mind missing out on the "fun", as he calls it. I know that Gad has hard-line views on almost everything but surely even he can see how awful this is. It's been good to get away from the Kiryat Arba bunch for a while, though I can't help feeling anxious. Maybe my absence will be commented on, especially if Gad comes back without me; then father will be under pressure. Reluctantly, I slip away, following, as usual, in my friend's footsteps.

I soon discover that he wasn't exaggerating the ugly mood. The mourners are rapidly cohering into a violent mob with only one thing on its mind. Disturbing images flicker through my mind like an old film reel. I see a crowd of Nazi thugs kicking an old gypsy to death. The raucous laughter and the vicious thud of boots are as clear as if I'd actually been there. At that precise moment, an elderly *towel-head* stumbles onto the street – perhaps curious or confused about the din outside his home. He stands gawking, oblivious to his danger. I look around in vain for another helpful officer but none is at hand.

Paul's father is first to pounce. He violently shoves the old man onto his back and aims a kick at his head. Luckily, the press of bodies knocks him off balance and his foot swings wide. The Arab tries to crawl away but is dragged back by several pairs of hands. He is completely surrounded and instinctively doubles up. Paul, standing close to his father, looks scared and upset: his legs are shaking and his face is ashen. I know what he's going through – any idea of avenging his dead uncle swept away by the vicious irrationality of an attack up close and personal.

Someone produces a length of thick rope and waves it in the air just as a group of policemen force their way through the screaming mob. They form a cordon round the injured man now motionless on the pavement. Mr Katz tries to break through but is hurled to the ground by a burly police officer who raises his baton in warning. A perverse pleasure at the sight is immediately replaced by guilt as Gad helps his father up and screams abuse at the policeman. Other mourners throw themselves at the cordon but are quickly repelled by the swinging batons. One man clutches his head as blood oozes between his fingers. Unnerved by the determined police presence the mob breaks up and people hurry off after the funeral procession, now almost out of sight. The blare of an ambulance siren suggests help is on its way. In the meantime, one of the officers administers first aid. I suddenly feel the helpless old man's welfare to be the most important thing in a world gone crazy. Goldstein's victims jostle with the Krasnow ghosts for my attention. I see them kneeling at prayer as the rattle of the machine gun shatters the peace of the Patriarchs' Cave. None of this makes sense anymore.

A hand grasps my shoulder. I leap out of my skin and spin round. It's father.

"Sam, where have you been?"

He sounds more worried than angry. I try to sound unconcerned.

"With some people. Is there a problem?"

He backs off. "No, no, it's just that Gad was asking where you were."

Mention of Gad's name releases a flood of anger and frustration.

"I'm really sick of hearing about Gad! He's not my keeper, you know. I don't have to be running after him all the time like a little boy!"

He throws up his hands. "Okay, okay, I'm sorry I mentioned him. Taboo subject. Let's get out of here. Mr Dayane said we could follow the cortège in his car."

I nod, already sorry for my outburst. What's the point of lashing out at father when my frustration has nothing to do with him, or even Gad?

Leaving Jerusalem, we by-pass the usual road blocks on the edge of town. Arabs, waiting to be checked through by Israeli border guards, stare at us. I wonder what's going through their minds as they wait and wait, delayed in an endless queue of traffic. If they know who is being accorded such respect their impassive faces give nothing away. The state of disorder, predicted by General Yavin, is certainly not apparent here. The mayor complained so vigorously about the Hebron commander's lack of consideration for the Goldstein family, and the sensibilities of Jewish residents, that the present compromise was offered. By agreeing to avoid some of the more heavily populated Arab districts, we were permitted to celebrate

Dr Goldstein's martyrdom in Jerusalem itself. Not a bad outcome really!

Gad and his father, who have also cadged a lift in Mr Dayane's car, are busy discussing the likely impact of the celebrations.

"We can only hope that the funeral sparks off a reaction in the country as a whole. It's high time people were stirred up. We need to act now before the furore dies down."

Gad listens attentively, hero worship shining in his eyes. I can't help wishing sometimes that I felt the same way about my own father. In the meantime, Mr Katz pursues the logic of his argument.

"Baruch Goldstein might have lit the fuse that ignites the entire country. Imagine a popular uprising against the common enemy!"

Mr Dayane shakes his head in disagreement.

"The unbelievers hate us more than they fear the Arabs. We have nothing in common with these godless sinners who call themselves Jews."

"Don't be so sure. Goldstein's act may be the catalyst that finally wakes people up. A little more trust in God would do no harm, Yoel! *Redemption* might be closer than you think."

As usual, Gad tosses in his views.

"I think a lot of young people in the country will respect Dr Goldstein's sacrifice. They may act even if others are reluctant." A side swipe at Mr Dayane.

Mr Katz gazes admiringly at him.

"That's right. The future of our nation lies with the young. It's what I've always said. God will speak to his children and show them the way."

Back in Kiryat Arba, we park near the hall of the Nir Military Institution and push inside to hear the final eulogies of the day. As Rabbi Dov Levin begins an impassioned tribute, I think again about his proposal to carry out medical experiments on Arab terrorists. Could such terrible punishment ever be truly justified?

At home father is brimming over with confirmations of Dr Goldstein's new role as saint, martyr, divine intercessor and hero of the Israeli people. Luckily, mother is out. We sit down and stretch our legs, thankful that the day is over at last. Father probably expected more trouble and is relieved that a major confrontation was averted along the route. Liberated from fear, he expands on the wider significance of the "Patriarchs' Cave Operation", as people are now calling it.

"We will build a lasting memorial to Dr Goldstein and Jews will come from all over the world to Hebron to pay their respects. They will light candles for the intercession of the new holy saint and martyr."

He smiles at me. Although his eyes are puffy and tired, they glow with undiminished pride.

"I hope you appreciate how fortunate you are to be living through such times. The tide is turning! Mark my words, Samuel!"

I nod, eager to fend off the doubts that have been plaguing me all day. I still can't help thinking about the contradictions in father's life. Although his passion and commitment are real enough so is his fear. Is this because he doubts what he says, or is he a coward whose actions will never match his words? I really don't know what to think. Sitting here, away from the reek of violence, I want to believe in him, to share his enthusiasm.

He stares hard at me for a moment before continuing. Has he somehow read my thoughts?

"Many people will never understand the meaning of such events. They simply dwell on outward appearances without appreciating the deeper significance."

This veiled attack on my mother doesn't help. I know what she will think about our celebration of a man who has slaughtered so many innocent people. She, at least, can never be accused of contradicting herself or backing away from a fight. I change the subject.

"You remember these IDF forms I was telling you about? Maybe you can help me with them."

"Yes, of course. Now is as good a time as any."

I've been worrying about my call-up papers since they popped through the letter box last week. Father is very keen on service, though poor eyesight kept him out of the action in the Sixties and Seventies. He constantly grumbles about being forced to sit out the *Seven Days War* behind a desk. He believes that the more right-minded people who serve in the army, the less likely it is the government will be able to implement such despicable policies as clearing settlement outposts or delaying the construction of new homes and roads in Judea and Samaria. Apart from the various *ultra-orthodox* factions, most religious Jews believe in active participation in all branches of Israel's armed forces, and many battalions are made up solely of religious recruits. Father hopes I will be drafted into one of these elite units. I'm not really sure what I want but the forms must be attended to. Gad received his last week and has already sent them back.

—ᵐ—

Returning from school a few days later, I notice a scrap of newspaper lying on the bed. It has been carefully cut out and parts of it highlighted in yellow.

"Compared to the giant-scale mass murders of Auschwitz, Goldstein was certainly a petty murderer. His recorded statements and those of his comrades, however, prove that they were perfectly willing to exterminate at least two million Palestinians at an opportune moment. This makes Dr Goldstein comparable to Dr Mengele; the same holds true for anyone saying that he (or she) would welcome more of such Purim holiday celebrations. Let us not devalue Goldstein by comparing him with an inquisitor or a Muslim jihad fighter. Whenever an infidel was ready to convert to either Christianity or Islam, an inquisitor or Muslim jihad fighter would, as a rule, spare his life. Goldstein and his admirers are not interested in converting Arabs to Judaism. As their statements abundantly testify, they see the Arabs as nothing more than disease-spreading rats, lice or other loathsome creatures; this is exactly how the Nazis believed the Aryan race alone had laudable qualities that were inheritable but that could become polluted by sheer contact with dirty and morbid Jews. The *Kach* Party, and their leader, Meir Kahane, learned nothing from the Nuremberg laws, and hold exactly the same notions about Arabs."

Laying the paper aside, I sit staring into space trying to come to terms with what I've just read. In a strange, worrying way these views relate to how I felt on the day of Goldstein's funeral. Mother obviously feels I need a counterblast to the opinions expressed by Goldstein's many admirers. Although annoyed that she is so blatantly attempting to manipulate me, I want to read more and commit the names of the newspaper and journalist to memory.

In the meantime, I resolve to say nothing to either father or mother. I will keep my own counsel.

CHAPTER FOUR

Warsaw: December 1940.

Leo scrapes the frost away with his fingernails and peers through the chink he has created in the window pane. In the grey light of dawn he spots a mounted German officer riding along Okopowa Street on the Aryan side. A white sea of mist, swirling around the horse's withers, seems to bear the rider over mysterious depths. He shivers violently as if icy fingers have clutched his heart.

The ten-feet-high wall, surrounding the entire ghetto, passes directly below the flat where he and Lola live. It is stoutly built, and appears impossible to cross without being spotted. Appearances are deceptive, however. The newly built barrier is already riddled with boltholes where bricks have been loosened, removed, and carefully replaced after use. These are the main supply lines through which food and other essential items flow. Part of Leo's job, as an officer in the internal Jewish police force, is to curb such criminal activity, but he turns a blind eye. The same cannot be said of the German auxiliary police, or their Polish lackeys, who routinely shoot smugglers on sight.

Stricter regulations have recently been enacted by the Nazi authorities. Jews caught beyond the ghetto boundary without the requisite passes are now likely to be shipped to labour camps, or thrown into the overcrowded prison on Pawia Street. Penalties have also been stiffened for Poles aiding Jewish runaways.

With only half an hour to go before his shift begins, he pulls on his uniform, tightens his belt and fixes the regulation star of David onto the right arm of his greatcoat, just above the official police insignia. He dons his peaked cap and glances round at the bed where Lola is sleeping after her late shift at the Sztuka nightclub. The blanket has rumpled back, exposing her neck and shoulders. He gently readjusts it. She sighs and turns over. He is dismayed by how thin and careworn she looks. Recently turned eighteen, she looks much older. He opens and closes the door quietly so as not to waken her. The flat is silent. The Shreibermans are not up yet and Leo hopes his sister will be left undisturbed for another hour or so. He wistfully recalls the months when they had the place to themselves. Now they are confined to a single room, and share a toilet with the thirty or so residents living on the stair. While Mr Shreiberman is easy to get along with, his wife, embittered and resentful at the hand fate has dealt her, gives everyone a hard time. The situation could, of course, be a great deal worse. The vast increase in population, and the relentless pressure on living space means that at least one more family, and perhaps two, could have been squeezed into the flat.

Outside the cobbles are slick with ice and he slips, almost landing on his back. Gesia Street, crammed with stalls offering a plethora of useless articles, is already busy. It seems as though people have been up all night, waiting patiently for the moment they can resume their endless bartering. No doubt they congregate here to simulate a sense of community. Away from their tiny, overcrowded rooms, and a gnawing hunger never satisfied, folk gossip and forget their troubles for a while. The many beggars, sprawled at the sides of the packed thoroughfare, are ignored, probably because their presence provides an uncomfortable reminder of the thin dividing line between subsistence and penury. Although the atmosphere on the street is charged with fear, he experiences a sudden stab of nostalgia for the social buzz of market days in Krasnow.

When Mr Lebinski suggested that Leo apply to the newly formed *Juedischer Ordnungsdienst,* he at first rejected the idea. To help the enemy do their dirty work seemed a betrayal of everything he held dear. After a few weeks observing German auxiliary policemen humiliate and beat up Jews in the ghetto precincts, he changed his mind. A shopkeeper recently told him how proud she was to see Jews policing the streets in uniforms adorned with the star of David. Such a thing, she said, would not have been possible before the occupation. Although flattered, he knows how absurd the sentiment is. If the Nazis believed for a moment that the Jewish force existed for any reason other than to facilitate the occupation, it would be disbanded immediately. He also appreciates that while some of his colleagues are less liable to brutalise their people, and more likely to ignore petty misdemeanours, many others have succumbed to bribery and corruption. When Lola tells him about the highly placed police officials slurping in the troughs of the Sztuka, and other up-market nightclubs still functioning within the ghetto, he wants to tear off his badge and walk away. The thought of a wealthy elite carousing alongside poverty, disease and death on a massive scale, disgusts him. Yet, believing that he might be of some value to the beleaguered community, he delays the moment of truth.

The central station is full of officers reporting in for their morning shift. Some are sipping hot, sugared water, their bare hands wrapped around the warm mugs, while others stamp their feet and beat their arms in an effort to stave off the biting cold. The duty sergeant takes the roster. Men shout out as their names are called and are assigned various duties. Leo is teamed up with Paul Zalman, an officer he knows of old and detests. They are instructed to maintain order on Grzybowska Street, where vendors sell hot drinks and bread to those who can afford such luxuries. Inevitably, the street has become a magnet for beggars desperate to obtain a few morsels of food. From past experience, Leo is aware that his colleague takes pleasure in dealing harshly with such unfortunate folk – all too ready to lash out with boot and baton.

On the way to Grzybowska, Zalman talks non-stop about the need to keep on the right side of the occupation forces.

"The Germans are here to stay. Surely no one would seriously dispute that now! Talk of help from the outside, or a general uprising, is wishful thinking. We've got no choice but survive the best way we can."

It seems that Zalman's personal quest for survival has extinguished any empathy for his fellow-Jews. Even when they spot a heap of corpses, stacked like logs, at the corner of Chlodna Street, he seems reluctant to investigate. The overnight dead, shrouded by a grey blanket of hoar frost, have been dumped for collection and burial. The fact that they have not yet been uplifted gives Leo cause for concern. Normal procedure, if anything can be deemed normal these days, is to remove piles of cadavers before people are up and about.

One woman, lying on top of the pile, is clasping a baby to her naked breast. Even though her body must have been dragged a considerable distance after death, the infant has somehow remained attached to its mother. On closer investigation, Leo is appalled to see that the tiny, blue lips are still clamped to its mother's teat, held fast by a froth of frozen, milky ice. This time, Zalman's voice proves a welcome distraction.

"Most likely someone will be along soon to dispose of this lot. There's no point in hanging around."

"But what happens if no one turns up? We can't just leave them here like this!"

"It stands to reason somebody will be back for the clothes. Even these filthy rags have some value."

Leo stares for a moment longer at the human detritus, trying not to imagine the bodies stripped of their last vestments of dignity.

At Grzybowska, a miniature fog, created by rising steam from boiling kettles and pots, hangs over the street. People, clad in every piece of clothing they possess, stand around sipping beverages from chipped enamel mugs and dirty glass tumblers. The fortunate few, with a little extra money in their pockets, nibble on thin slices of bread. The close proximity of food, and the warmth from the red brick stoves, have inevitably attracted a crowd. Although unable to afford the few groszy required to make a purchase, they huddle close by.

Zalman pushes his way through the crush. Clearing a space, he orders up two glasses of steaming tea and some thicker slabs of bread. He then produces a small pot of jam from inside his greatcoat, pours it over the bread and motions Leo forward to join him in the impromptu breakfast. The latter shakes his head but suddenly changes his mind and accepts a share. Zalman sneers. Maybe this prig with his infuriating air of moral superiority is finally climbing off his pedestal. With the right attitude they could easily skim off a layer of cream for themselves. After all, without a police presence, half the vendors' profits would be pilfered each day. Turning to discuss the possibility, he finds that Leo has disappeared. Scanning the sea of squalid humanity, he spies his colleague's peaked hat bobbing around among the crowd. He gasps in astonishment when he sees that Leo is breaking his bread into pieces and handing it over to the beggars. Such behaviour is not only in breach of regulations, but downright foolhardy. He must speak to the duty sergeant to ensure he never has to share a shift with this fool again.

Leo carries the last morsels over to a grubby blanket. Kneeling down, he gently pulls back the covering. Two pairs of eyes, abnormally large for their pinched faces, stare up at him. A third, belonging to a tiny girl curled up between the others, is tightly closed. Her hair, once carefully brushed each morning by doting parents, is now a filthy, matted pillow. She may be dead or merely asleep.

As he places pieces of bread into the children's open mouths, he recalls long ago trying to save a brood of blackbird chicks after the hen bird had been killed by a neighbour's cat. His mother allowed him to rehouse the nest in a corner of the kitchen where he diligently fed the fledglings a diet of chopped-up worms and milk-soaked bread. The sense of hopeless despair as they died one by one, despite his best efforts, returns to him now.

Glancing round, he notices the tall, slightly stooped figure of Albert Freidman smiling at him from a nearby doorway. They met recently at a Courtyard Committee meeting, convened to organise the setting up of soup kitchens in the ghetto.

"Do you know anything about these children?" It has begun to snow, and the large, feathery flakes are transforming the grimy landscape. The gentle drift of white eiderdown seems to have little connection with the mass of dark clouds crouched ominously over the chimney tops. "I asked them where they came from but they seemed to have no idea what I was talking about." Freidman stares at him for a moment as flakes settle on his black cap – one perching precariously on the tip of his nose before melting away. The cut of his jacket and the quality of his badly worn boots suggest he has seen better days. The impression of former gentility is reinforced by his unpretentious eloquence and the ironic smile playing on his lips.

"The idea of home, like the word itself, means little or nothing to these children." He smiles bleakly. "I only know that they have been begging here for a few days now. They do get some food from the smuggling gangs, but it's never enough. God knows where any of us would be if it wasn't for them! They may yet force the Nazis to think up another strategy for our extermination."

Leo frowns and purses his lips.

"I don't believe we are being deliberately starved to death. It's just that they haven't worked out what to do with us yet."

Freidman smiles gently, as if indulging a naïve but well-meaning child.

"The last part of what you say is probably true, but it changes nothing. The Germans know exactly what is going on here. To them we are a bacillus which they are eventually bound to eradicate for the greater good. Believe me, it is only a matter of time before they find a way to do just that. Our conquerors are an efficient and determined people." The ironic smile is now fully accentuated. He waves his hand in the direction of the snow-covered blanket. "In the meantime, in ghettos all over Poland, we are forced to watch our children die. It is curious, is it not, that we simply stand by and let it happen."

Leo struggles for an answer but can find nothing meaningful to say. He shakes his head, more a gesture of futility than disagreement, and moves away to break up a group who have moved too close to one of the steaming boilers lining the street. The stall-holder is shouting furiously at them in a vain attempt to ensure her customers are not impeded or harassed. Many of the beggars are shaking with cold and Leo asks the woman if they might at least be allowed to stand between her stove and another nearby. She reluctantly agrees – the charitable nature of her concession belied by a grimace of disapproval. He can see that she wishes he was more like Zalman, willing to use his baton to clear space. Her sullen mouth and glowering eyes tell him that in Poland there is not only the racial divide between Pole and Jew but the gulf of wealth and status separating Jew from Jew. The ghetto elite might just as well be living on another planet.

—⚬—

"Why did people stand by and let the children die? Father said it was one of the worst things that happened during the Shoah."

The old man raises his eyes to the ceiling, wondering how he should respond to a question so naïve but, at the same time, so apt. Not for the first time, he inwardly curses his son-in-law's crude representation of history. This is one of the reasons he feels compelled to persevere with his painful testimony.

"I'm not sure if I can explain it, Sam." His voice reveals nothing of the turmoil seething inside. "One of the most dreadful things about living through those times was the sense of helplessness, sapping our will to resist. When you are stripped naked and beaten down, it is all too easy to despair and do nothing. You feel scared all the time and you cling to the hope that things are not as bad as they seem. We clutched at straws until they crumbled in our fingers. Rumours and lies, deliberately circulated in the beginning, I guess, convinced us that the Germans were about to deport us to some part of the world where we would be allowed to organise our own affairs and live in peace. I hoped this might be Palestine, and so held back from doing anything too drastic. What was the point of dying if we were about to begin a new life, or if the children might be saved?"

"But when you saw all these starving people, did you not think your friend was right about the Nazi plan?"

"Yes, Sam. There were times when I saw it as clear as day. But, I just didn't want to accept the evidence of my own eyes."

"Father says that Jews must never be tricked into believing *Goy* lies again. He says that if we hold true to God, He will give us victory over our enemies."

This all comes out in a rush. Leo, furious that Benny has been spoon-feeding the boy such vitriol, restrains himself with difficulty. He cannot openly repudiate the father to the son. Taking a deep breath, he tries to answer calmly.

"There may be some truth in that, but no one can know how they will react in times of crisis. It is easy to talk, though much more difficult to live up to the high expectations we have of ourselves. Your father is, of course, wise to treat much that is said about Israel by outsiders with scepticism; but not all they say can be dismissed as lies. People on both sides are good and bad, according to their natures. Not all *Goyim* are bad simply because they are not Jews. I have encountered good Germans and bad Jews along the way."

Sam is bursting to interrupt, but, in deference to his grandfather, holds back. The latter continues, intent on alleviating some of the damage already done.

"Many people blind themselves to the truth, believing what they most want to. During the Shoah, Jews desperately wanted to believe that the persecution would end in their relocation to another country. And most Germans, I guess, even those who had swallowed the propaganda lies, wished for the very same thing. Few Jews, or Germans, were willing to face up to the reality of the "final solution".

"But father believes that Jews must... ."

Leo interrupts, determined to push home his point.

"Here in Israel, many think we are invincible. This myth arises from the humiliations and failures of the past, and an idealistic notion that we can fight off everyone and everything sent against us. We cannot take on the world and win. Nor can we cut ourselves off; no nation can do that and survive! Do you see?"

He stops, realising he has gone too far. Moderating his harsh tone, he searches for a simple, less hostile way of expressing his fears for the future.

"The very last thing I want to see us becoming is that which we have most cause to fear: another racist state persecuting the weak and grabbing territory we have no right to. Treating our Arab citizens and neighbours unjustly will bring us nothing but hatred in the Middle East and beyond."

"I, I don't really understand, grandfather."

He senses that Sam is close to tears. How can a lad of twelve be expected to grasp the complexity of self-delusion, combined with a highly selective view of history? His father says one thing, his grandfather another, and the boy's loyalties are divided. This can only lead to confusion and, perhaps, in the long run, radicalisation. He regrets his outburst. Leaning forward, he gently ruffles the boy's hair.

"I apologise for raising my voice, Sam. Call it an old man's foolishness. Shall we continue or have you heard enough for today?"

"No, I mean yes, please. I want to know what happened next."

Sam wipes his eyes with his sleeve and tries to smile. Leo takes a deep breath before attempting, once more, to bridge the gulf between the sunny Jerusalem bedroom and the bleak Warsaw streets of January 1941.

—⁓—

It seems that nature and the Nazis have entered into an unholy pact. While more and more people are forced into the ghetto, the homeless freeze to death on the streets or succumb to the ravages of cholera. God does not spare the firstborn, or anyone else. Each family gives up its dead and undertakers work round the clock. Piles of corpses, awaiting burial, now become a common sight.

One morning Leo is sent to Mirowski Square where a new 'aktion' is to be launched. These raids are becoming ever more frequent – useful to the Nazis as a means of seizing hostages or simply terrorising the population. As the end of his shift approaches, he begins to hope. Maybe the information, like so much else channelled through the *Judenrat*, will prove worthless. Seconds later, the roar of engines shatters any such optimism. His heart sinks as soldiers pile out of four trucks, and residents are driven onto the street while their houses are ransacked and decontaminated. Forced to strip naked in the freezing temperatures, they are hosed down in accordance with German disease control procedure. Their tormentors laugh as they shift the excoriating spray from one traumatised victim to the next.

A German officer motions him over and orders him to stand guard while his squad search a residential block. Leo, although deeply reluctant, has little choice in the matter. The lorries are already filling with prisoners. One man, bleeding from a deep, head wound, lies motionless on the floor of the nearest vehicle. Leo wants to staunch the relentless flow of blood but knows what will happen if he tries. Harsh voices echo in the stairways above, and rifle butts thunder on doors. The sharp crack of a pistol shot is followed by the crash of shattering glass, and a body thuds onto the pavement beside him. He is close enough to hear the sickening crunch of bones, and air bursting from the victim's lungs. Glancing up, he sees a soldier grinning down at him from a top-floor window.

"Next time I'll improve my aim, Jew!"

The last group of captives are bundled out of doors into the trucks, and the raiding party departs as quickly as it arrived. Residents return home to pick through their stinking, saturated belongings. Leo makes his way back to police HQ, rage building inside him like steam in a pressure cooker. He yearns for revenge – a way to strike back at these devils in human guise.

As luck would have it, he is granted his wish. Less than a block away from Mirowski Square, he stumbles upon three Polish policemen torturing a group of young Jewish captives. The *blueys* seem motivated by nothing other than the wish to while away the time to the end of their shift. The boys have been forced to stand on tiptoe, arms raised behind their backs as if rehearsing crucifixion. They hold a brick in each hand, which adds greatly to their suffering. Their emaciated limbs quiver as the *blueys* bet on who will give way first. They continually lash out at anyone showing signs of weakness. One of them, turning to glance up the street – perhaps in response to a reflexive feeling of guilt – receives a shattering blow on the face from Leo's baton. He screams in pain, and clasps his splintered cheekbone. The violence is contagious. The remaining policemen, stunned by Leo's intervention, are set upon by their victims who use the bricks to good effect. Within seconds, their captors are either dead or unconscious.

Leo knows that he must dispose of the evidence without delay. He winds his thick scarf tightly around one of the captured pistols, pushes the barrel against the first *bluey's* head and pulls the trigger. The shot is sufficiently muffled not to attract any unwanted attention. He repeats the process twice, then, with the help of the others, drags the corpses into a bomb-damaged building. Out of site, they scrabble desperately with their hands to dig a hole large enough to contain all three bodies. As the floor is already torn up, and piles of loose rubble lie heaped around them, the task is completed quickly enough. Leo's initial satisfaction is soon replaced by a deep sense of foreboding. The stench of death pervading the ghetto might mask the evidence for a while, but the policemen will soon be posted missing and an extensive search carried out. His outburst, fuelled by fury and revulsion, will most likely lead to serious repercussions for innocent people – perhaps even the hostages he watched being loaded onto the trucks barely half an hour earlier. It is too late for regrets, however. The deed speaks for itself.

He picks up the pistols and stuffs them inside the pockets of his greatcoat. They will be needed if Freidman's assessment of Nazi long-term strategy is correct. Recalling their recent conversation, he realises he must stop deluding himself. Not until he is able to confront reality will he be of any use to those who need him most.

He swears his companions to silence before hugging each of them in turn. On the way home, he wonders if he has struck a blow at the barbarity stalking the ghetto streets or merely tightened its bloody grip.

—ᗰ—

Sam's eyes are shining. Leo, knowing how this part of his story would be received, internally debated whether or not to relate the events of that terrible January afternoon. Having done so, he is now faced with the task of explaining the consequences. It is vitally important that the boy realises that cause and effect are indissolubly linked.

"Of course, if I'd considered for a moment what my foolish intervention would lead to, I would have slipped by unnoticed."

"I don't understand, grandfather! Surely these men deserved what happened to them."

"That may be true, but I acted without considering where my own lack of restraint would lead."

"What do you mean?"

"Simply that in the ghetto any resistance was met with a response out of all proportion to the original act."

"Did other people suffer because you killed the Polish policeman?"

"Yes! When the bodies were discovered a few days later, twenty hostages were executed, and fifty others rounded up to take their place. Mr Lebinski, who all this time had refused to leave the ghetto, was one of those arrested. A week later he himself was shot because another foolish young man threw a stone at a German guard patrolling the ghetto perimeter."

"So, any move against the enemy led to something much worse happening. Should you have done nothing at all then?"

"That is a good question. I should certainly have considered what I was doing and the consequences others would face as a result, instead of acting in the heat of the moment." Leo pauses to see if he is getting through. "When we eventually rose up against the Nazis, we understood that there was nothing to lose. By then most of the people living in the ghetto had been removed to the death camps, and the rest of us knew we would soon be making the same journey. So, forcing the enemy to pay dearly for our lives was the only positive thing to be done. When I killed these *blueys* nothing was so clear cut."

"If that's true, why didn't you step forward and admit what you'd done?"

Sam sounds uncomfortable and disappointed, but Leo knows he must try to be honest.

"To tell you the truth, I was scared to death, and I knew the hostages were going to be shot whatever I did. These are not good reasons, although I was aware that I'd probably be tortured and forced to implicate my friends and colleagues. Perhaps that alone was worth remaining silent for."

"So, if an Arab kills a Jew, should we not seek revenge?"

Leo has been expecting something of the sort. It was only a matter of time before the boy would conflate the two things.

"Again, it depends on the circumstances. People have a right to defend themselves, or fight for a cause they truly believe in, but, if in the course of seeking revenge, innocent people die, that is surely wrong. Here in Israel the act of revenge has become an end in itself, and peace slips ever further away."

"Father says there is no such thing as an innocent Arab, and no treaty with terrorists is possible. He says the Arab only understands the language of the gun."

"Perhaps they say the same about us. Have you considered that? It is very easy to forget we are the ones who now live on their land. I have little doubt they view us as I once viewed the Germans."

"But the land belongs to us!"

"And that is what the Germans also said."

"But it is surely not the same thing."

"No, perhaps it isn't, but it is always wise to learn the lessons of history. It is surely in everyone's interests to reject the way of force and strive to resolve things peacefully."

"What if that is not possible?"

"Have we really tried here in Israel? Could we not have done more to convince our Arab neighbours that working with us was in their best interests? Making friends of your former enemies is often the only way to create the conditions for peace.

Although the lad looks sullen, Leo fervently hopes that he is breaking down some of the barriers built to safeguard the prejudices and downright lies pedalled by Benny and his orthodox brothers-in-arms.

—⚊—

Leo is patrolling along the inside of the wall between Krochmaina and Chlodna Streets. Sharp frosts have throttled the recent thaw. He gazes up in awe at the incredible brightness of the moon and stars, wondering if somewhere out there, in that huge expanse of space, other intelligent beings are tearing their hard-won civilisation to pieces. The penetrating cold keeps him moving, and he beats his arms against his body to induce some sensation of warmth.

A scraping noise brings him to an abrupt halt. Someone on the other side of the divide is pulling away loose bricks. Rubble falls at his feet and the dusty head of a child fills an impossibly small hole in the wall. Nevertheless, the shoulders and arms of the miniature Houdini twist their way through. As Leo hurries forward to help, the boy's pinched face contorts in pain and he is hauled back the way he came. Leo grabs at the flailing arms, only just missing. He hears a ripple of laughter, a muffled scream, and several harsh thwacking sounds like a carpet being beaten. He backs away from the wall and moves swiftly on. Although appalled, there is nothing to be done; it would not do for him to be discovered anywhere near the newly exposed bolt hole. He marvels at the courage of the youngsters who keep these lifelines with the outside world open at so much risk to themselves.

Lost in thought, he is tripped from behind and falls heavily. Strong hands pull him onto his back, pinning him to the ground. A knife glints in the bright moonlight, its sharp edge scraping against his throat. A voice hisses in his ear.

"One sound and I'll cut your fucking head off!"

He wonders if he will be given a chance to talk. There are many in the ghetto who despise Jewish police officers every bit as much as their German and Polish counterparts.

Again, the menacing hiss, so close that his ear hurts.

"How did you signal the Nazis that Paul was coming through the wall?"

"You've got it all wrong." He knows he must choose his words very carefully as he may not get a second chance. In a strange sense, he is glad that the moment of truth has arrived. "I had no idea the boy was coming through. I was patrolling when I heard a sound. I tried to grab him but the *greens* were too quick. There was nothing I could do for him."

"Do you really expect me to believe that?"

"Believe what you want – it's true. The fact that I was passing at that particular moment was pure coincidence."

Why should we believe a Jew who has sold his soul to the devil?"

"I joined the police to help the cause. Check my papers. People will tell you I do what I can, when I can. I hate these murderers as much as you do!"

The knife is withdrawn, and the weight on his chest shifts a little. A whispered discussion ensues. If he wants to fight back, now is the time, but he lies still. Something tells him he has nothing to fear and much to gain from the encounter. A hand slips under his greatcoat and inside his tunic. His identity papers are removed and handed over to the unseen accomplice who scurries off. Judging by the lightness of the footsteps pattering on the cobbles, the messenger must be another child. Perhaps the young are the only ones with courage enough to take risks these days.

"Keep quiet and don't move."

His interrogator climbs off him.

Finally, after what seem like hours shivering on the ground, the runner returns.

"Axel says he's all right and we should let him go. He also said to ask him to come and talk, if he wants to."

"You can get up now. I'm sorry about the knife, but we can't be too careful. A lot of you people belong to the Nazis."

Leo brushes at the white fuzz of frost clinging to his overcoat.

"The boy who was killed tonight – was he a good operative?"

"Paul was one of our best." The man's voice is tinged with a mixture of anger and sadness. "Someone must have tipped the bastards off. There's no other way they could have known about that bolt hole."

"Maybe I can help. Up till now I've only been able to act on impulse, so to speak."

"Yes, I recognised your name. We heard about those *blueys* who got in your way." Leo blushes. It was inevitable that the incident would come back to haunt him. "It led to serious bother. Some say it was downright foolish." The operative's tone suggests that he believes otherwise. "Do you want to speak to Axel? That's his operational name. We all have them. Mine is Janus and the lad here is Angel. You'll have to choose one for yourself, if you join us. We don't know anyone's real name, of course."

"I'd like to talk to him."

"Fine. Then come back here tomorrow night and Angel will take you to him."

The pair melt into the darkness.

—⚹—

"It is good to meet you at last, my friend."

Leo studies Axel's lean face, while the latter, in turn, gazes quizzically at him over a scratched old table. They are sitting in a small, uncomfortably cluttered room where a single light bulb glares harshly above their heads. Where they are or how he got here remain a mystery. Behind the blindfold, he tried to work out where he was being led but soon lost track. He is fascinated by his inquisitor's piercing blue eyes and the aquiline nose poised as if to strike. He imagines an eagle pinning its living prey to the ground, and hopes he will never be such a victim.

"You could be very useful to us but the risks are high. If you are linked to our organisation, the Nazis will show no mercy. You would have to exercise a great deal more caution than you have so far. While some regard your recent action as heroic, I consider it foolish. Two of our own people, among others, were shot as a direct result of what you did. Do you understand?"

The eagle's talons are raking perilously close to his flesh. Although being offered an opportunity, he is under no illusion what will happen if he puts his fellow-operatives at risk in the future.

"Yes. I know I was out of order, it was just that I… ."

"Explanations are not necessary. I simply need an undertaking that nothing of the sort will happen again, unless properly sanctioned, of course. It is vital that all of our people remain disciplined in the days to come."

"All I want to do is help in any way I can."

"Very well. We will contact you soon. Further checks will be necessary before we are able to make the final arrangements."

"Thank you and, and I'm sorry about your colleagues."

"Just ensure your future conduct is exemplary, and their deaths will not have been in vain."

"It will be, I promise."

Axel thumps loudly on the wall. Angel returns with the blindfold.

Back at the flat, he considers the fate of the hostages who died as a result of his rash behaviour. There is little comfort to be derived from the knowledge that they were doomed the moment they were arrested.

—⚌—

Leo is once again patrolling Grzybowska Street. Last night word arrived that his bid to join the Resistance had been approved. He feels buoyed up by a new sense of purpose. Everything has taken on a fresh significance. His efforts will now be properly directed; his conscience, such a burden over recent weeks, eased.

He spots Freidman supping tea at one of the many stalls and strolls over.

"How are you today?" he smiles warmly as his friend looks up. Maybe spring has come a little early this year."

Everyone is trying to extract maximum significance from a recent easing in the temperature. Since it is only the third week of February, however, the chance that spring has arrived is as likely a prospect as that of the German's packing up and leaving Poland. Understanding the motivation for such optimism, however, Freidman joins in.

"You may be right. I heard a blackbird singing this morning in the park beyond the ghetto wall. Another little bird told me that a certain Rudolf had decided to throw in his lot with the Resistance."

Leo stiffens at the mention of his operational name from such an unexpected source.

"How do you... ."

"Do not worry, my friend. I was the one who first suggested your suitability as an operative. I knew you were to be trusted, and that your insider's knowledge of the ghetto police might prove useful to us."

"But, but I thought only a small number of people knew about... ."

"Of course, and I am one of the group you will be working with." He smiles encouragingly. "Freidman is not my real name, you know."

What? But I thought... ."

"Say no more, my friend! Very little is as it seems in these troubled times. All that matters is that we're proper comrades now in the fight against tyranny."

Freidman's cheeks, although heavily bearded, seem to have sunk in even further. Remembering their previous conversation, Leo inwardly shudders. His new comrade-in-arms appears to be the living embodiment of how well the German strategy of starving ghetto inhabitants is working. Yet, there remains something in his ready smile and precise articulation that confirms he is no victim. Here is a man who will struggle against the iniquity of the occupation to his dying breath. Leo suddenly realises that it is this shared quality which has drawn them together. They shake hands, the power of his friend's grip belying the impression of physical frailty.

"Have you seen the children who were camped outside the shop across the road?"

Freidman lowers his eyes.

"They died a few days after we spoke. We tried to help but they were too far gone. We should die a thousand times ourselves before we allow such things to happen."

"The time for self-sacrifice will be when we can make a real difference."

"Yes, I keep telling myself that, but it doesn't help much when you see the future slipping away before your very eyes."

Leo falls silent. The death of so many children does not bode well for the future. He is forced to contemplate an enemy too powerful to defeat in battle. Perhaps all he and his comrades will ever be able to do is to make their own passing as costly as possible.

—⚓—

"That's enough for today, Sam. I think we may have overdone things a little. Miriam will be furious if she finds out you've been up here for so long. She thinks I should sleep for most of the day."

"Are you going to die, grandfather?" The question pops out before Sam can stop it. He is shocked at himself and hopes the earth might swallow him up. "I, I didn't mean to.... I'm sorry, I, I... ."

Leo smiles to put him at his ease.

"Don't be sorry, lad, we all have to die. And don't worry so much. I'm not ready to leave you just yet. Certainly not while so much remains to be told." He smiles and reaches for his cigarette packet. "Tell your mother you've been reading in your room for the past hour, and that you dropped by to collect my breakfast things to save her the trouble. She'll appreciate your thoughtfulness, I'm sure."

Sam rises to his feet, pleased to be in league with his grandfather against parental authority.

"I'm glad you decided to take a stand against the Nazis. Father says that we must all be willing to fight for what we believe when the time comes."

He collects up the dishes and leaves the room, flashing a smile over his shoulder as he closes the door. Leo sighs. It is painfully obvious at times like this that Benny's ideological influence over his son makes any attempt to redress the balance a hard struggle indeed. He wonders whether he will be able to summon enough strength to slacken the strands of paternal hubris enmeshing the boy. Only time will tell.

CHAPTER FIVE

Yeshivat Nir Kiryat Arba: Autumn 1996.

"And the strangers shall stand and feed thy flocks."

Rabbi Sharburgh smiles benignly and scratches his fuzzy white beard. His eyes catch mine and hold them for a moment – their intensity at odds with his easy manner. A prominent *Chabad Hassid Kabbalist,* and an authority on the writings of the *Lubovitcher Rebbe*, the rabbi is very popular in Kiryat Arba. My father thinks highly of an article where he provides religious justification for the murder of thirty Arabs at prayer by Baruch Goldstein.

"Why did the *Lubovitcher Rebbe* bring this line from Isaiah to our attention? You may also wonder who these strangers are and why they should serve us. Those who are not divinely ordained, whose souls do not spring from holiness, are strangers in the truest sense of the word, entirely dissimilar to ourselves in both a physical and a spiritual sense, thus, "strangers" in the eyes of God and His chosen people. Their existence is to serve – hence, "feed thy flocks" – and nothing more. In the *Time of Redemption*, this will become clear."

I am itching to ask when the great moment will come, but the rabbi keeps talking.

"Maimonides wrote that a non-Jew must be kept in his place and not permitted under any circumstances to challenge his master. If he refuses to obey then he must be punished or expelled from the Holy Land for ever. Maimonides went on to tell us that under certain circumstances – and I quote his words so there can be no mistake – "we are forbidden to let an idolater among us: even a temporary or itinerant trader shall not be allowed to pass through our land" Therefore, how we treat aliens is simply a question of our status, or our need, if you will, at any given time. I repeat that while a Jewish life has infinite value and purpose, a non-Jew's existence is in vain. When one understands this, many pieces of the puzzle slip into place. In order to clarify the situation let me ask you a question. If you came across two people drowning in a river – a Jew and a non-Jew – what would you do?"

Gad's hand shoots up. The rabbi smiles and motions him to answer.

"Save the Jew's life, of course!"

"Quite correct, but why?"

"Because the Jew is superior in the eyes of God."

"Of course, now let us expand on the idea of the Jew's innate superiority. If a Jew is dying because his heart is defective, is it permitted to replace that faulty organ with the heart of a non-Jew, even if the latter is alive and perfectly healthy?" The rabbi ignores the twenty hands waving in the air, preferring to answer his own question in his own way.

"The need of the Jew must always take precedence over that of the non-Jew. Every cell in the Jewish body is suffused with divinity, and even the inferior cells of a *Goy* are capable of transmutation when placed inside such a holy vessel."

Everyone nods.

"I have made reference to the *Lubovitcher Rebbe*, the foremost interpreter of truth in our own times, and to Moses Maimonides, whose twelfth-century teachings form the nucleus of much contemporary wisdom. Let us now consider for a moment the *Lurianic Kabbalah*, named after its founder, Rabbi Yitzhak Luria. His influence on the teachings of Rabbi Kook the elder and his son – both of blessed memory – was profound. He deciphered the *Kabbalah* in order to reveal to us the true nature of the world God has planned for his chosen people. He told us that the role of Satan is embodied in the persons of all non-Jews, while those chosen to join the four divine worlds are the Jews who elect to embrace their great destiny." Sharburgh points to himself, then slowly extends his arms in a wide, inclusive gesture. "In other words, we, all of us here, and those of our tribe, scattered like seeds throughout the world, are the reason for creation – the physical emanation of pure divinity. We must simply recognise what we are and join together in a cause greater than any other. God requires us to open our hearts and feel his power flowing like lifeblood through the sacred temples of our bodies. Rabbi Luria warned, however, that we must be on guard at all times against the wiles of Satan, who fills our ears with subtle arguments designed to confuse and deceive."

Once again his eyes catch mine before moving on to the next student and the next. I feel myself part of something overwhelming – linked to forces which will soon rock the foundations of the world. When Sharburgh continues, his voice is hushed.

"Rabbi Luria often referred to the *Time of Redemption*. He cautioned that any shrinking on our part, any weakness in our resolve, might delay that time – delay, not halt! What has been written will come to pass, but not without the just punishment of those who fail to act at the appropriate moment."

I feel excited and terrified at the same time. I hope that I will not be found wanting and suffer the chastisement of a wrathful God. Another of our guest lecturers recently explained that the punishment of Jewish sinners over the centuries, who either denied or ignored God's covenant with his people, was entirely justified. He didn't actually say so, but it was clear he was suggesting this as a reason for the Shoah. I applauded with the others but afterwards felt sick at heart and guilty of some ultimate betrayal.

"I am often asked what will happen during the *Time of Redemption*. Much was revealed by Rabbi Kook the Elder regarding the advent of two Messiahs. The first will not be one being, but many – a collective, divinely ordained manifestation who will prepare the way for *Redemption* itself."

The hairs on my neck are tingling. This is mind-blowing stuff. It is surely, as Rabbi Sharburgh says, the transforming spiritual quality unique to our people that counts.

"And the Messiah will enter mounted upon an ass and upon a colt."

What does this mean? How can the Messiah be mounted on two such beasts at the same time? Again, we turn to Rabbi Kook the Elder for enlightenment. Righteous Jews who have chosen to embrace their great destiny are the collective riders of the ass. The ass itself is the nation, or, put another way, the majority who lack the necessary wisdom to advance and must therefore accept the guidance and authority of a divinely inspired master. The rider of the colt, however, is a being of incredible power whose coming will herald a time of spectacular miracles. The Holy City will be cleared of *Goys* along with their false gods, and God's Chosen will come into their rightful inheritance. But before this ultimate cleansing, we, the riders of the ass, must prepare the way. Already we have wrested Jerusalem from the enemy. We are now required to continue this process and ensure, above all things, that the government does not weaken or give ground. In time, if we follow the appointed path, Al-Aqsa will be swept from the Temple Mount, and the Temple itself rebuilt."

Gad's hand is up again. Sharburgh smiles indulgently and nods in his direction.

"I admire your questing spirit, young man. How can I help?"

"What will happen to those ignorant Jews who carry us forward on our journey? Are they to be used for our purposes?"

"No, far from it! The seeds of divinity lie dormant within them and may germinate in their due season. It is taught that the rider, or riders, have the power to redeem those Jews who have wandered from their true path."

"And if this does not happen?"

Gad is relentless but the rabbi merely smiles. No one else in the room would have dared speak out like this.

"Then, young man, some force may be required to ensure that the ass does not stray too far from the path. This is the responsibility of righteous Jews. The ass has great power, but is largely ignorant of its purpose. If you wish to think about the ass in concrete terms, consider the IDF or, indeed, our elected government." A new note of sarcasm creeps into Sharburgh's voice. "We must ensure that these mighty engines of power are properly harnessed. That is one of the priorities of our mission, and the main reason why you are all sitting here today! We do not hide away like others, making a virtue of exclusivity. We immerse ourselves in society, in all of its vital institutions, transforming from within. Such changes are the key. Never forget that Jews, however unenlightened or stubborn they may appear, can be redeemed – *Goys* never can. They are not for *Redemption* and are at our disposal. Rabbi Kook the elder once said that "the difference between a Jewish soul and the souls of non-Jews – all of them in all different levels – is greater and deeper than the difference between a human soul and the souls of cattle."

Without waiting for permission, Gad intervenes.

"What happens to a Jew who knowingly breaks God's commandments and betrays his people?"

There is a long pause. Everyone present knows to whom he is referring. The assassination of Prime Minister, Yitzhak Rabin last year is never very far from our minds. Although the mood of celebration persisted in Kiryat Arba, and Hebron for weeks after the Prime Minister's death, a vague unease regarding the consequences of the murder remained.

"What is your name, young man?"

"Gad, sir. Gad Katz."

"Well, Gad, the Jew who knowingly sins against his own people, or behaves in a manner deemed contrary to their best interests, is the worst of all possible heretics – a person deserving of the most severe punishment. Chastisement has always been meted out to such evil-doers throughout the Diaspora where our religious laws have been allowed to function without interference. The worst heresy any Jew can commit is ceding sacred land to Satan. Consider carefully the terrible retribution such transgressors will ultimately face."

"You mean those Jews who signed up to the Oslo Accords?"

"I will comment no further on the matter."

I understand the rabbi's reluctance to discuss recent events, knowing the sensitivities surrounding them. *Goys* and most of our own people believe that Rabin's murderer was a madman with no popular support in the Holy Land. Those in the know insist that outsiders, especially Americans, must be kept ignorant of the truth and encouraged to perceive Israel as the victim, never the oppressor. For the time being, their good will is to be carefully nurtured in order to make common cause against the Arab menace. In the *Time of Redemption* I don't suppose it will matter what any of them think.

"If you will allow me"– Sharburgh smiles at Gad for a moment – "I will return to the key notion of *Redemption*. Not only can ignorant and obdurate Jews be redeemed, but animals or even objects possessed by the enlightened being. You may recall the story of the duck that is consumed by the holy rabbi."

A ripple of laughter runs through the class. Everyone recalls the comic-book version of this popular tale where a fat, smug duck waddles into a hunter's concealed net. On the next page the bird sits smiling on a holy man's plate, waiting to be eaten. Despite the fact that it has been plucked and roasted to a crisp, the duck still looks very pleased with itself. Rabbi Sharburgh is intrigued by our mirth.

"What do you find so amusing?"

I raise my hand, as much to stop Gad monopolising the session as anything else.

"We read the story in a picture book in elementary school. In one of the illustrations the duck is smiling as it waits to be eaten by the rabbi."

"Ah, I see. I think I have seen that children's book myself" He beams at me. "Yes, very funny, but it is an accurate, if somewhat crude, reflection of the duck's condition. Consumed by the rabbi the creature will indeed be redeemed, and attain the divinity it previously lacked."

He pauses for a second to let the meaning sink in. "Not only can animals be redeemed but even material objects such as tanks, guns and houses. The most important thing, of course, is the *redemption* of the land itself. There is no question of stealing territory from Arabs, as they claim. We are required by God to redeem the sacred soil of Israel from those who have poisoned it. In spiritual terms, this means that the land must be transferred from the Satanic to the Divine sphere. That is why the occupation of the entire extent of *Eretz Israel* is so vital to the process of *Redemption*. Remember God's promise to his people in Deuteronomy: "Every place on which the sole of your foot treads shall be yours: our border shall be from the wilderness, from the river Euphrates, to the western sea." This does not entail some temporary military operation to occupy territory or provide limited security. It is a God-given directive to purify those parts of our land defiled by Satan and his cohorts."

Sharburgh's smile has been replaced by a frown, emphasising the seriousness of the struggle ahead. It seems that there is much to be done before God's promise to his people can be fulfilled. As if reading my thoughts, he tunes into the fear churning inside all of us.

"Never lose faith, my young friends! Final victory is assured, and we will all be part of the annihilation of our enemies. Only make certain your hearts are pure and your commitment to the cause absolute. This alone may shorten the time of waiting. Thank you for listening so attentively today, and" – he glances over at Gad – "for asking such relevant questions. I will be available to answer any further questions you might have after prayers. Only through increased understanding can any progress be made."

As the lecture theatre empties, I feel elated. Despite previous doubts, everything now seems so much clearer – our mission, a crucial part of the divine process. I turn to find Gad at my side. For the first time in ages, I'm glad to be his friend. His eyes are shining with new-found confidence.

"He's the best so far! They've all been good but he's in a league of his own. It's funny, but I never really understood that duck story before. Did you?" I shake my head. "He makes me feel that someday we will push that stone right up to the top of hill." Gad hesitates for a moment, as if unsure whether to continue. "Sometimes I wondered whether we were doing the right thing. You remember, the patrols in Hebron, and all the other stuff we did back then. When Dad shot that Arab, I was really shocked; I don't mind admitting it now. It's sometimes hard to get your head round the fact that they're out to destroy everything we stand for."

I smile, realising that I am not alone in my doubts. It's good to know that even Gad, normally so self-assured and focused, is human after all.

—⁓—

The guest speaker today is Colonel Yosef Rubenstein – a senior officer at Staff Headquarters and veteran hero of the *Yom Kippur* War. In preparation for the session, our tutor explained to us that the colonel was highly influential in establishing the *Yeshivat* link with the armed forces. His dedication to the cause is legendary, and, as his steely eyes sweep the room, it seems to me that he is already assessing the raw material sitting in front of him. Will any of us match up to his exacting standards?

He waits for total silence before speaking. There is no outward sign that he requires our undivided attention, nor does he indulge in the usual small talk to put us at our ease. It's as if he's granting us this one opportunity for enlightenment before moving on.

"I wish to focus on two questions today: the first concerns how we shape military strategy based on our understanding of past events and the current situation in Israel; and the second is how you, the elite of the nation's youth, can become the best soldiers possible in these challenging times."

I suddenly recall Jeff Schiff, expelled from the Yeshivat a few weeks ago. Certainly a promising candidate – one of the elite the colonel is talking about – Jeff was seen cavorting with a woman in an Arab neighbourhood in Hebron. Fellow-student, Tsvi Shach spotted him and immediately reported the matter to Rabbi Goldberg. The fact that Tsvi was lurking in such a dubious area himself was pointedly ignored, so keen was our religious tutor to make an example of someone in the class. Rumours of sexual delinquency had been circulating for a while, and we knew that it was only a matter of time before a scapegoat was found. And who better than a candidate without immediate family or connections in the area.

Three rows in front of me, Tsvi shifts uncomfortably in his seat. I wonder, not for the first time, if Jeff's fate was really determined by Gad's ill will against him. The rivalry between the pair was not a secret, and Tsvi's reputation as Gad's willing lackey would suggest a set-up of some kind.

In the meantime, the colonel is warming to his theme.
    "The waging of war in the Holy Land has been correctly identified as a process of purification – or refinement, if you will. Think of it as a brush, sweeping away spiritual detritus accumulated over millennia. Rabbi Shmaryahu Arieli once described war as a "metaphysical transformation" –the key to our salvation, and the issue on which all of us will be ultimately judged. The *Yeshivot Hesder* to which we all belong, were established to revolutionise the armed forces from within. We look to lead by example, and already we have impressed many of

our citizens disillusioned by political corruption and military incompetence. While some Jews passively accept the alien culture which threatens to destroy the country, many others begin to doubt the wisdom of government policy. We are here to encourage that doubt – to channel dissatisfaction and open the eyes and hearts of our people to the greater destiny that awaits."

And, presumably, to pass down the decrees of an established hierarchy where officers like Colonel Rubenstein exert such a powerful influence. This seems to be the way of things at every level, with people only too willing to accede to the authority of those who cajole and threaten their way up the ladder. Gad is that sort of leader, only tolerating minor criticisms from me and a few others because we defer to him on all the important issues, never daring to step beyond the mark.

It was clear from the beginning that Jeff would never bow to the status quo. It just wasn't in his nature. His easy charisma pulled others into his orbit. Like a bright star in a crowded firmament, he attracted lesser bodies all bent on basking in his reflected glory. It was a natural talent, as powerful and thoughtless as gravity itself. As things began to unravel, I marvelled at the thought of such a shift without any conscious effort on Jeff's part. But Gad was never going to give way that easily – any under-estimation of his ruthlessness, a serious error. The colonel's raised voice interrupts my consideration of Jeff's rise and fall.

"The need to exert pressure on those who might otherwise falter has never been more necessary. In Ariel Sharon or Benyamin Netanyahu, we have leaders who, although strong and decisive, require the guidance of those blessed with a deeper spiritual understanding. Sharon, for instance, can be extremely effective if his talents and ambitions are properly harnessed. Without a proper focus for his energies, however, he often stumbles from the path and loses his way. I have worked with him and know better than most his strengths and weaknesses."

Gad's success has always been his ability to manipulate those closest to him. When I asked him if he knew anything about Jeff's expulsion, he smiled inscrutably.

"Jeff should never have been allowed into the Yeshivat. You must have known he was up to no good, Sam. You didn't have much time for him, surely."

"I... ."

"I wasn't surprised in the least when he was caught with that Arab whore. He was always boasting about friends in high places, and his winning ways with women. No one really wanted to listen to such a pack of lies."

Not true given the numbers of people hanging on his every word, but his popularity was, of course, the reason for Gad's enmity.

"I was still a bit surprised when Tsvi... ."

"It was no surprise at all. Tsvi simply confirmed what we all knew about the guy. He was a phoney right from the start. And sinful too with that stack of filthy magazines he lent out to the fools he took in. After he got the boot, Rabbi Goldberg asked me to find and burn them." He shook his head. "You're such an innocent, Sam. It never occurred to you that Jeff was out to corrupt us all."

I felt strangely flattered and threatened at the same time. As usual, Gad was at the helm, forcing me along in the direction of his own choosing.

Gad and his thugs did a lot more than collect the magazines, of course. The beatings he handed out were nothing to do with punishing immorality, but all about reasserting his authority over those who had dared to shift their allegiances. I knew there was no point in pursuing the matter any further. Gad's star was firmly in the ascendant, and the last thing I needed at that moment was for him to think I doubted Jeff's guilt. I felt bad but what could I have done? Gad could just as easily have arranged my disgrace, or even a beating. Our friendship may be skin deep, but for old times sake, he probably doesn't want to lose my respect by revealing his own selfish motives. Wherever the truth is, it's clear that Gad will be very effective at exerting pressure to get his own way when the time comes. He fits the description of Colonel Rubenstein's ruthless manipulator at the centre of power. I tune back into the relentless monologue.

"When discussing the formulation of military strategy, I always return to the "48' campaign. I have studied the operations in much detail and conclude that this was truly our finest hour. Why? Because ideology merged with practical, down-to-earth tactics, and, because our plans were watertight and their implementation flawless. Religious leaders, politicians and soldiers worked together to rid the land of those who defiled it. General Yigael Yadin, responsible for devising the *Tochnit Daleth,* was the driving force behind the seizure of twenty thousand square kilometres of territory, as well as the wholesale expulsion of Arab squatters. As a direct result of this great victory, the Jewish nation state was securely established, and the UN forced to acknowledge the reality on the ground. The government of the day was also successful in convincing its allies that war was necessary in the face of Arab hostility – not only that of local bandits, but of surrounding Middle Eastern countries such as Egypt and Syria. When these nations eventually rode to the rescue of their uprooted brethren, we drove them back to their borders and beyond. There was no diplomatic fudge, no prevarication; we were united and resolute in our action. Everyone worked for the common good and no account was taken of bleeding-heart sentimentality. The Arabs were given no quarter and no one wavered in the execution of the plan to win back our sacred land. General Yadin's plans were simple but effective. He advocated, and ultimately executed, the destruction of local villages by fire, explosives and mining. I remember his exact words when describing the operation."

The colonel doesn't falter for a moment, speaking without notes:

"The gaining of control will be accomplished in accordance with the following methods: encircling enemy villages and searching them, and, in the event of resistance, destroying the resisting forces and expelling the population beyond the boundaries of the state."

"The official version, claiming that many Arabs ran away due to fear of instability, and that their leaders ordered out those remaining to make way for the invading armies, proved highly successful in deflecting international criticism. We were thus granted the opportunity to consolidate our victory."

All this is news to me. I knew from the history books that the campaign in 1948 marked an important turning point, but never imagined it as a shining example of unity and efficiency for future generations. It's hard to conceive of Jews ever uniting to redeem Israel, and expel the enemy. Could it all really happen again? Maybe, but only with a ruthless efficiency that has been lacking in the last few years. That is why we are here, of course. The colonel is clearly intent on working us up to a fever-pitch of passion. With such religious fervour we could achieve anything. Watching Gad lean forward in his seat, I know that he would relish the opportunity to rid the land of all Arabs.

The colonel seems aware of the powerful effect his words are having on us. When he resumes, he speaks quietly but with no less intensity.

"In the wake of this remarkable success, other campaigns have not fared so well. Although limited objectives have been achieved, the dedication and unity of 1948 have never been repeated. The '67 War, which you all know about from your history books, although invested with an extraordinary degree of courage and resourcefulness at the cutting edge, was undermined by those who shamefully traded land for what they called peace. Although we secured Jerusalem and Judea and Samaria, a great victory in itself, we allowed the unique opportunity of annexing and settling vast tracts of *Eretz Israel* to slip through our fingers. The *Yom Kippur* campaign, in which I had the honour to serve, also started well but became quickly mired in diplomacy directed by the United States and its allies.

But it was the invasion of Lebanon that undermined our best hopes of winning back sacred territory from the enemy. Once again, the operation got off to a promising start but quickly lost direction and coherence. We all believed that the spirit of ''48' had returned when the invasion began. After all, we were fighting a pitiless enemy sworn to wipe us from the face of the earth – the inheritors of those who had originally driven us from our land. It is impossible to say how much our defeat – for make no mistake that is what it was – has delayed the *Time of Redemption*, and how many Jews have suffered or will be forced to suffer as a result of the cowardice of our leaders during that ill-fated mission."

The mention of divine punishment reminds me again that grandfather, his family and millions of others, may have been forced to endure the Shoah because of similar dereliction in the past. Is God truly capable of inflicting such harsh retribution on those who had no part in shaping the events that ultimately led to their suffering? And, if so, is anyone free of blame for the terrible things that happen during their lifetime?

The colonel suddenly changes tack.

"So, how do we create the kind of elite unit to which all of us aspire? The answer is that we strive to become the best soldiers we possibly can be in the service of our Land and our Lord. Firstly, we must eradicate all doubts about what is required of us in the line of duty. Righteous Jews must show no mercy to those they are ordered to fire upon or remove from their homes. Pity, remorse and doubt are emotive weaknesses we cannot afford to indulge in. Those of us who have some experience of war, know where such things inevitably lead. So, learn to concentrate fully on the task at hand, obey orders without question and respect the chain of command."

All my life, everyone, apart from mother and grandfather, has warned me to reject any positive feelings towards Arabs. Father ordered me never to speak to Arab children, or entertain any notion that they might be like us. The strangest thing was that grandfather, despite his harsh treatment at the hands of the Nazis, didn't appear to hate Germans. He once told me that he had met a few after the war, who, in their willingness to help him and other victims, reaffirmed his faith in humanity. I suddenly feel another memory tugging deep down inside me – something that grandfather once told me. I experience a powerful anxiety and swerve away from further efforts to remember.

I'm suddenly aware that I'm doing exactly what I resolved not to do – allow the past to deflect my attention from the present. How will I be able to properly function as an army officer if I'm so undisciplined on such a basic level? How much have I already missed of the colonel's practical advice on how to become an effective warrior? I refocus, determined not to miss another word.

"Recruits from *Yeshivot Hesder* colleges often end up in special ops or elite units where it is possible to make a significant contribution. To succeed in that arena, it is vital to show extraordinary devotion to duty and excel in training. The challenge lies in becoming better than the best by eclipsing the achievements of secular recruits, no matter how able or motivated they might be. But most importantly of all, you must accede to the authority of your spiritual leaders, and be guided by them in all things. Then, as I have said, those who do not as yet share your faith may be moved to do so by your devotion and dedication to the cause. For, make no mistake about it, your career in the IDF is a calling – no mere job or duty. Keep this in mind and you will not go far wrong. Our war is unlike any other war in history. It is directed by God through His people with the sole purpose of vanquishing evil forever, and establishing His Kingdom on Earth. As the cutting edge of the divine sword, we must be honed to perfection. I look forward to seeing many of you in the years to come. May God bless you all. I will now take any questions you may have for me."

As Gad's hand shoots up, I see Jeff's distraught face on the day Rabbi Goldberg assassinated his character in front of the ranks of silent *Yeshiva* students. This journey is leading me in unexpected directions.

—⁊⁊⁊—

"So, how should we Jews treat the Arabs who live among us, here in Judea and Samaria? Many of our fellow citizens, and our allies in the west, believe that we must learn to live in harmony and share what we have with our… ."

"Do we really care what *Goys* and traitors think? Are we bound by their codes and conventions? I don't think so!"

Gad glares round the room, daring contradiction.

"That is a fair point, Gad." Rabbi Goldberg smiles indulgently. Perhaps because Yeshiva students are actively encouraged to question what their tutors say, the rabbi doesn't seem even mildly irritated at having been interrupted in full flow; or, indeed, care that his question has been so rudely cast aside. "We are not, of course, bound by the alien ideologies which apply to non-Jewish societies, and which have so badly infected many of our own people. But what of the *Haredi* rabbis, who believe that little can be done before the *Time of Redemption*?"

A new voice suddenly breaks in.

"Since we are in the period of transition before *Redemption*, these prevarications are surely of little importance to us."

Students twist round in their seats to stare at the sullen outsider, who joined the class a fortnight ago, and has remained silent until now. His massive shoulders and blunt head give him the look of a heavyweight boxer. Although the statement is unlikely to stir much controversy, his tone is menacing. Perhaps he's attempting to impress us and push his way up the pecking order. Recalling Jeff Schiff's fate, I hope he has the good sense to work out who is who before going any further down that road.

His comment irritates me, though, almost as much as Gad's attempt to hijack the session, and I decide, on the spur of the moment, to challenge the accepted wisdom.

"How do we know with any degree of certainty that the *Time of Redemption* is about to begin?"

Rabbi Goldberg positively beams with pleasure, clearly delighted by the way the discussion is developing. He appears blissfully unaware of the emotional undercurrents sweeping the room.

"Yes, of course. Sam makes a good point. How do we know that this is indeed the time of transition predicted by the prophets?"

Gad smiles at me. Maybe he thinks I'm deliberately feeding him good lines. I realise, too late, that my intervention has provided him with yet another spring board. I have no idea why my feelings fluctuate so wildly. How can I feel close to him some days, while on others he irritates me so intensely?

"Precisely because we are now the most powerful force in Judea and Samaria. Our success in occupying this land is no accident. The Arabs are on the run; our roads, our settlements, our security forces show them who's boss. That's why we must never concede a centimetre of land, but consolidate and add to our gains."

"Are you saying that facts on the ground are proof of the period of transition and the transformation of the land?"

The rabbi's loaded question allows Gad more scope to expand on his pet theme. It's hardly surprising really since these discussions, despite the pretence of being open, almost always stick to a tried and tested formula. The emphasis may change from time to time, but the conclusions never do. My occasional attempts at playing devil's advocate – normally a ploy to fight off boredom – always fail, but not usually as quickly as this.

"You would have to be a fool not to see what has been achieved over the past fifteen years. Look at the number of settlements established here and in Gaza. Gush Emunim and the NRP have prompted the government whenever it falters, and dictated the pace of change. The facts on the ground are all the proof we need that *Redemption* is at hand."

"Well said, Gad." I tighten up inside. This is ridiculous! Teachers should at least attempt to be a little more objective. "Anyone questioning the resettling of Judea and Samaria must surely consider what has been accomplished. But if we accept, as I believe we must, that the Messianic Age is almost upon us, how should we treat those aliens living in our country?"

I can't help feeling a little impressed as Rabbi Goldberg manoeuvres us back to his original question. Maybe there is some underlying plan at work in these chaotic sessions.

"The only relationship there can be is that of master and servant. As Rabbi Sharburgh said, the Arabs are here to do our bidding until we can be rid of them."

Again, the brusque outsider.

For the first time the rabbi looks a little irritated.

"Very good, eh… . Sorry, but I seem to have forgotten your name."

"Paul, Paul Ben-Hagai."

Ah, yes, you joined us a fortnight ago, Paul, did you not?"

Yes, Rabbi."

"Let us attempt to deal with specifics." Our tutor is clearly anxious not to get bogged down in too many generalisations.

Annoyed by my earlier failure, I try a different approach.

"If the Arabs are the agents of Satan, corrupting the sanctity of the land, should we be treating with them at all? When Rabbi Sharburgh talked about 'strangers feeding our flocks' should they be? I mean, what if they attempt to poison our animals or sabotage what we have built here?"

"How many goats do you have running around your garden, Sam? Maybe the Arabs are poisoning them as we speak."

Unfortunately, my somewhat archaic reference to livestock has allowed Tsvi Shach a jibe at my expense.

There's an infuriating titter of laughter. Tsvi smiles broadly, pleased at his success."

I pounce, determined to restore my injured pride.

"I was speaking figuratively, Tsvi – if you know what that means – you billy goat! Maybe the Arabs would poison you if we asked them nicely; that at least would be something in their favour."

To my intense satisfaction, the return laughter is louder and more sustained. Gad is grinning from ear to ear and wagging his finger at his acolyte. Tsvi frowns, desperate to come up with an appropriate retort, but the rabbi denies him the opportunity.

"Come, come! Please try to remain focused, if you will. Let us consider Sam's question for a moment. He is correct in the sense that, ideally, we would love to be rid of the Arabs, and not have to rely upon their labour at all. However, from a purely practical standpoint, is that possible in the short term, or must we learn to be a little more pragmatic? Many would argue that our economy relies heavily on Arab workers. We provide them with special permits to enter and carry out assigned tasks in our territory, intended, of course, to spare our people degrading and mind-numbing labour. Any of them caught sabotaging equipment or stealing, is subject to severe punishment and barred from further employment. Remember that Arab families rely on the wages they receive and will literally starve without an income. Surely there is a strong case for… ."

Gad butts in again.

"Maybe the system we operate does help the economy, but many of the Arabs use their passes to smuggle in guns and bombs. Sam is right in the sense that they should never be trusted. They have stolen and corrupted our land, even though you say they are motivated by wages."

Rabbi Goldberg looks thoughtful for a moment before replying.

"Perhaps, but you will remember that Maimonides himself justified the use of *Goyim* labour if they "accept paying a tax and suffer the humiliation of servitude."

I notice he is now leafing through a copy of the *Kivunim*. Father once told me the *Kivunim* was an invaluable document containing the collective wisdom of great visionaries exhorting the expansion of Israel and the inherent superiority of the Jewish people.

"He also said, and I quote: "a non-Jew may be held down and not be allowed to raise his head against Jews. And that: non-Jews must not be appointed to any office or position of power over Jews and if they refuse to live the life of inferiority then this signals their rebellion and the unavoidable necessity of Jewish warfare against their very presence in the land of Israel." Is this a compromise we can all accept vis-à-vis the present situation in Judea and Samaria? Remember that we are living through a period which many would argue necessitates a degree of flexibility. Although warning as to remain vigilant, Maimonides clarifies a means of exploiting crucial economic factors while remaining true to the law."

Out of nowhere I recall a stray dog my father once shot when we first moved to Kiryat Arba. The half-starved creature – probably from one of the nearby Arab villages – had wandered into our garden when father burst out of the house, yelling and brandishing his semi-automatic. I rushed round to see what was happening. It was during *Purim* and he was more than a little drunk. The creature was desperate to escape, but he wouldn't let it, eventually shooting it as it cowered down in submission.

Having rounded off the debate, at least in his own mind, Rabbi Goldberg changes tack.

"I would now like to turn out attention to Shlomo Aviner's, *Book of Responsa,* written during the first *Intifada* to provide pious Jews with a response if threatened or attacked by Arabs, or their children. I trust you have all managed to read the text. Would anyone like to comment or ask a question?"

David Nisson – one of the few intellectuals in our group – raises his hand. Although not generally inclined to push himself to the fore, *Halachic* law is David's particular preserve and he rarely misses an opportunity to air his knowledge on the subject.

"Maimonides asserted that while Jewish children under the age of thirteen are exempt from statutory punishment, whatever they do, Arab children of a similar age are subject to the same penalties as their parents."

"Not necessarily." Tsvi unwisely moves to correct David. "Maimonides advised that such children must have sufficient understanding of their wrong-doing before being punished."

David's response is swift and contemptuous.

"As anyone who has bothered to read the *Responsa* knows, all pious Jews can make that judgement, and mete out punishment on the spot."

"You're quite right, David." Just in time, I manage to stifle a laugh – turning it, instead, into a cough. Gad sounds just like Rabbi Goldberg. "We can't afford to pussy-foot around. If Arab kids throw stones at cars, as often happens around here, there is no time to debate whether they know what they're doing or not. We must assume they intend to injure or even murder the occupants. We know that if a Jewish life is threatened in any way, the assailant must be neutralised immediately."

What the hell does he mean by neutralised? Without thinking things through, I jump in again.

"It's not always that easy to know if someone is out to kill you, especially in Hebron. Arabs get shot all the time, even when they're unarmed or not actually threatening anyone. And what about when they try to harvest their olive trees? We either rip up their groves, spoil the olives, or shoot at anyone trying to work."

As soon as the words are out of my mouth, I know I've gone too far. Maybe there is no hope for me. I have this burning need to question everything, even when I know I'm verging on heresy; and even when I swore to myself that I wouldn't get involved today. If I'm not able to control myself at such a basic level, my army career will be over before it has rightly begun. Officers like Colonel Rubenstein would dump me in a heartbeat for uttering such blasphemy – and then what? As everyone in the class gapes in disbelief, I realise that friend or no friend, Gad is going to make an example of me.

"What are you talking about, Sam? Have you lost your mind?" I grind my teeth in fury at his tone. "All Arabs are tarred with the same brush. Why should we care if any of them gets killed or injured? What's the difference? It's probably better that we put them out of their misery sooner rather than later. If you want to grieve, then grieve for our own people – blown to pieces by terrorist bombs. If we consider the rights of Arabs in a risky situation, where will it end? Colonel Rubenstein explained what we must do. You're going to have to stand up and face the world as it is!"

I squirm in mortification. The trouble is he's right. There is no possible excuse for my outburst.

Rabbi Goldberg intervenes.

"Let none of us forget the reality of the world we live in. We are surrounded by a hostile population, who, from childhood, have been taught to hate and defy us. As we struggle to redeem the land, they fiercely resist our every move. Gad is correct. If we allow pity to enter in, all will be lost. The number of *Goys* killed along the way is not going to blight us. If we can deter their murderous intent, we will be rewarded in the days to come. And never forget, Sam, that this is our land to do with as we will. The Arab farmers who claim the olive groves belong to them speak falsely. It is the soul of the land, the soul of the people of Israel for whom we fight."

I know, for sure, that an explanation for my outburst is required. In a few months we will begin our eagerly anticipated army careers, whether as officers or as ordinary soldiers is yet to be determined. After this, my chance of being considered as worthy officer material is probably zero. Everything else has been going so well; written exams, leadership qualities, physical fitness, have all been favourably commented on. Father wrote only last week to express his delight at my progress. Gad, a dead certainty for officer selection, said he was looking forward to training alongside me. Now, his black scowl suggests otherwise.

The others are trying to pretend nothing's happened, but their strained looks, and efforts to ignore me, belie the charade. My heresy has undermined the confidence which unites righteous Jews against a host of enemies. A strict taboo has been breached. What could I have been thinking? Suddenly, all feelings of resentment, anger and doubt vanish. The vacuum is filled by a powerful desire to repent. I rise to my feet without the slightest idea what I'm going to say. I cough loudly to attract everyone's attention, though the action is superfluous given the situation. The immediate hush reveals the brittle atmosphere. What I say now could make or break my reputation as a righteous Jew, and, with Rabbi Goldberg listening, determine my career prospects.

A reel of images flickers through my mind: grandfather, propped up in bed, rubs his tired old eyes. Is he wiping away tears? Mother turns her back on me, as if unwilling to listen to what I have to say. Father, his brow wrinkled, waits for me to put things right.

"I just wanted to say, to say that I'm sorry. I was wrong." – in a flash of inspiration, I see the only way out of this maze. "It's strange, but just after Rabbi Goldberg was talking about the devil working to undermine us, I heard a voice in my head telling me that all efforts to secure our homeland were misguided and wicked, and we were bound to fail in the end."

My classmates are sitting rigid in their seats. I sense their fear of an unseen evil stalking the inner sanctum of God's *Yeshivat*. Could the devil really be here, probing for weakness? My ploy is turning into something completely different. An extraordinary power suddenly possesses me. Lies and excuses are transforming themselves into a need to express the truth – to place the blame where it really belongs. Evil writhes inside me. I fight to speak, desperate to expel the serpent, but my tongue is sluggish.

"I couldn't help but say the things I said, even though I knew the words were not my own. It happened before when I... I... ."

A wave of terror crashes over me; I feel sick and disorientated. Tears blind me and I sway on my feet. I don't understand what's happening. Is this divine intervention? Rabbi Goldberg grabs me as I fall, easing me back into my chair. I see Gad swim up close, his face brimming with concern.

"Be calm, my boy, be calm!" The rabbi's words bring me back to myself. "The devil has no power to hurt you here. He has tried and failed! Do you understand – he has failed!"

His voice is charged with emotion. Someone pushes a glass of water into my hands, and I gulp it down. This was real. What a fool I've been! The weakness quickly passes, and I find the strength to shake the hands of my teacher and fellow-students. Gad takes me in his arms and hugs me until I think my back will break. It's as if I've stumbled through a minefield and somehow survived. I feel renewed as I bask in the warm glow of approbation. We live in a dangerous, unpredictable world, but I'm safe – finally returned to myself and my friends.

I hear the rabbi exhort vigilance as the key to salvation –
that, and faith in a glorious future for those Jews who
remain true to the laws of God. As if in a dream, I find
myself lifted high in the arms of my comrades and
carried through the doors, out onto the wide parade
grounds bathed in bright sunshine.

CHAPTER SIX

Warsaw: August 1942.

The ghetto bakes while the roundups continue. Dazed survivors emerge from their hiding places in the cool of the evening when operations have ceased for the day. Horizons shuffle closer, hemming the dwindling population into an ever tighter space. Few think beyond tomorrow's replay, and the desperate struggle to evade capture. Since the edict for resettling the Jewish population in the east was first posted, fear, like the fierce summer heat, has become an omnipresent, palpable force.

The *Judenrat* continues to work with the Nazis, even though its officials are aware that promises of resettlement are being offered as a means of precipitating the deportations. Few deny that the trains shunting out of the *Umschlagplatz* each day are transporting their pitiful cargo to certain death. Leo's shadowy superiors in the Resistance are working with the *Bunds* to uncover their ultimate destination.

Leo remains in the puppet police force only because he has been ordered by the Resistance to do so. Over the past few months, he has done much to help the cause.

From monitoring high-ranking Jewish officials, to participating in dangerous missions on the *Aryan side*, his value as an operative has become increasingly recognised. He puts up with the contempt of the local populace with a surprising degree of equanimity; those who count know the risks he takes. One day when the nightmare is over, he is confident the truth will emerge.

Today, his unit has cordoned off the end of Francisz Street, at the crossroads with Nalew and Gesia Streets. They are forced to stand in the broiling heat while a squad of German policemen search every building in the neighbourhood for fugitives. The stench of death, pervading the ghetto at all times, is particularly strong today – a combination of rising temperatures and the corpses rotting on the streets. As usual, he suffers the intense frustration of being forced to assist in the round-up of his own people. One elderly man approaches the police cordon and spits contemptuously.

"How can you stand to do this job, eh? You will be next, never fear. We will all make the same journey in the end."

Hands on hips, he stares round, attempting to establish eye contact, but no one cares to oblige. The tension is broken only when a young woman – his daughter, Leo guesses – hustles him away. There is little doubt that the reputation of the *Juedischer Ordnungsdienst* has dipped to an all-time low.

Fellow-officers look on curiously as Leo sways on his feet. Having been involved in a round-the-clock surveillance of black marketeers operating inside the ghetto, he hasn't slept for over twenty-four hours and feels faint under the torrid sun. He removes his cap and wipes his soaking forehead with the back of his sleeve. The officer next to him hisses out a warning without turning his head.

"Watch Captain Zalman doesn't spot you. Any excuse and he'll have you on a charge for being drunk on duty."

This is undoubtedly true. Since his promotion, Zalman has been waiting for any opportunity to act against Leo. Unless something is done, the captain's antipathy will most likely lead to his arrest, torture and death at the hands of the Nazis.

The prisoners are ordered to pick up their belongings and begin the short march to the *Umschlagplatz*. Flanked by units of Ukrainian soldiers, specially recruited by the SS, there is no chance of escape. These thugs are notorious for their barbaric treatment of Jews. One woman, near the front of the line, suddenly drops her case and runs back towards the cordon, screaming something unintelligible. A young officer, directing his men from the pavement, steps out onto the road, draws his pistol and shoots her in the back. She crawls on, crying out two names over and over again which Leo guesses must be the children she has lost during the round-up. The plea is cut short when the officer stamps on her head. He presses the barrel of his revolver against her exposed neck while her arms and legs flail helplessly. One of the Ukrainians mimics the thrashing limbs, and his mates guffaw. Two shots end the entertainment. Blood, brains and melting tar merge into a strange, purple hybrid.

Leo stands dumbfounded. Even by the appalling standards of the ghetto, the incident is shocking. What he finds most disturbing of all is that neither the German policemen, smoking and chatting nearby, nor the prisoners, shuffling past on their way to certain death, appear concerned about what they have just witnessed. Tormentors and victims appear united in common apathy. He struggles to accept that the middle-aged men recruited into the German reserve police battalions, and largely responsible for guarding and clearing the ghetto, can be so utterly indifferent to the brutality demonstrated here day after day. What sort of men were they before the war? Hard-working fathers, loving husbands, loyal friends? They are surely capable of human tenderness. Perhaps recent events have inured them to the horror, but the explanation seems somehow inadequate.

Amongst the victims themselves, few appear capable of decisive action. People so stunned, so reduced, will apparently go passively to their deaths – any last-ditch attempt to break away from the herd lining up at the slaughterhouse, the exception rather than the rule.

Leo mutters a prayer for the Shoah's latest victim, wondering what has become of the two children she believed were so much more important than her own life. He pictures them crouching terrified under the floorboards of their derelict flat, perhaps hidden by their mother before the death squads ripped the delicate fabric of their lives in pieces.

—ᨠ—

Watching the boy sitting cross-legged on the floor in front of him, Leo knows he must sound just like his son-in-law, touting resistance as infinitely preferable to capitulation. He finds it surprisingly difficult to make the distinction between persecuting people in the name of freedom and resisting those determined to eliminate your freedom. The facts must be allowed to speak for themselves.

—⁂—

The raids become ever more frequent. Thousands of families are being deported from the ghetto each day. Talk of death camps spreads like wildfire, stoked by rumours that the trains are not travelling far from Warsaw before diverting onto local lines. Only a tiny band of optimists keeps alive the dream that the Polish Jews are being shipped out to a new homeland created in Palestine.

Leo is desperate to quit the force, which, following the suicide of the incorruptible *Judenrat* chairman, Adam Czerniakow, has fallen under the control of toadies and traitors. His requests are firmly rejected, and he is ordered to remain where he is – his usefulness as an inside operative too valuable to relinquish. He struggles to find a way of helping victims without compromising his strict instructions to stay inconspicuous. He knows there are many among his colleagues who feel the same, but fear of officers like Zalman prevents them coming forward.

The Resistance finally approves his appeal for Zalman's execution, but only if the deed can be done without exciting suspicion and reprisals against hostages. Leo agrees to the conditions and lays his plans carefully.

—⁂—

Leo waits in the darkness of a tiny alleyway. He knows, after weeks of surveillance, that Captain Zalman will soon pass this way to a shop on Zamenhofa Street where black-market goods can still be purchased by high-ranking Jewish officials. The bound cloth handle of his knife is damp with sweat. When it comes to it, he's not sure whether he'll be able to stab a fellow-Jew – even one as odious as Zalman. The circumstances are totally different from the savage encounter with the *blueys* last year. Then he had no time to think – pure rage overwhelming any doubts or moral considerations.

In his present mood, he experiences a odd mix of confusion and despair. News that Lola has spurned the clumsy advances of a drunken SS major at the Sztuka nightclub has deeply unsettled him. Although the officer was persuaded to leave by his two companions, it's hard to say what will happen next. The attitude of Germans towards Jews throws up strange contradictions in behaviour. In the context of late night drinking and entertainment at such a sophisticated establishment as the Sztuka, relations can appear almost normal – wealthy Jews mingling freely with the Nazi officers who choose to come there. The fact that strict protocols regarding fraternisation with inferior races appear to be suspended is misleading, however. After the drink wears off, the officer might very well view rejection by a Jewess as a humiliating affront to his dignity and have Lola transported. Leo is aware that the man has only to sign a piece of paper to seal her fate. Trying to refocus, he wonders how his associates in this grim undertaking will dispose of Zalman's corpse. It's more than likely he'll make his final journey out of the ghetto in a handcart, buried beneath rotting vegetables.

The click of approaching footsteps jolts him back to the present. Even off duty, the fool marches along as if he's on parade. Leo's head suddenly clears – all doubts dismissed in an instant. It is this ability to act coolly under pressure that is so valuable to the Resistance. Suspecting nothing untoward, Zalman passes the alleyway without a sideways glance. The next thing he's aware of is a violent backward jerk, a sharp pain in his lower back and a rapid draining of energy. He has no time to reflect on the rectitude of the justice meted out, or regret collusion with the mortal enemies of his people.

Leo leaves the body slumped against a wall, and turns homeward. The death of one more Jew, even a ranking police officer, is unlikely to create many ripples. What Jews do to Jews is hardly worthy of Gestapo attention. A sudden rush of apprehension for the safety of his sister squeezes everything else out of his mind. He knows she'll be agonising whether or not to turn up for her shift at the Sztuka in two hours' time. If a warrant for her arrest has been issued, it won't matter what she does. The flat will no longer be safe, and Leo, posing as her husband, will also be hunted down for interrogation.

As it turns out, all the worry is for nothing. Perhaps the major woke up next morning having forgotten the entire incident, or more likely keen to avoid any official attention being drawn to the incident. Whatever the reason, the crisis blows over and Lola returns to the Sztuka. At police headquarters word has it that Zalman has quit his job and been allowed to return to his home town of Konin. Although the explanation is flimsy, no further questions are asked. Perhaps high-ranking Jewish officials, themselves tainted with accusations of corruption, have decided not to pursue the matter. The prospect of summary executions at the hands of the Resistance is no longer treated lightly by collaborators and freebooters.

—w—

January 1943.

There are now fewer than fifty thousand Jews remaining in the ghetto. The streets are virtually deserted, especially at the times of day when round-ups are likely. Leo and six fellow-officers are despatched to a block of flats on Mila Street where it is reported that Jewish fugitives are hiding out. It's pitch black and freezing cold. David Levi, one of Leo's most trusted colleagues, knows exactly where the residents are concealed as he lives in the block himself. On the first landing he pulls Leo aside.

"We must convince the Germans that we've carried out a thorough search and found nothing, otherwise they'll most likely shoot us and do the job themselves. There are more than twenty people hiding behind the cavity walls in the attic so we've got to be persuasive. God alone knows how long they can survive up there."

On the top floor, David unlocks the door at the end of a narrow corridor, pulls out a ladder, props it against the wall and ascends through the trap-door in the ceiling. Leo follows him up. The space between floor and roof is less than two metres and feels like the inside of a freezer; the concentrated cold easily penetrates their police-issue greatcoats. David motions towards the wall at the other side of the attic.

"Our people are hiding behind that partition. I don't really understand why the builder put in these false walls in the first place, but it's lucky he did." David manages a wry smile. "It's also fortunate that most of the structural plans for Warsaw buildings were destroyed by German bombs. One of life's little ironies!"

Leo is encouraged by such a twist.

They cross over, taking care to tread only on the well-spaced joists. David knocks four times on the wall. The tapping is immediately repeated like an echo.

"Keep absolutely quiet." His voice, although little more than a whisper, sounds loud in the confined space. "The Germans will be here in a few minutes. We'll do what we can to divert them."

A muffled reply confirms that the warning has been understood. Leo can barely imagine the distress of the people, crushed together in the freezing darkness.

"Let's go."

David leads the way back to the hatch and they quickly slide down the ladder. David pushes it inside the storeroom and locks the door.

"There's a chance, if they can keep the children quiet."

Back at ground level, their colleagues have begun a half-hearted search of the flats. Most of the rooms have already been emptied, apart from some worthless junk and soiled bedding. The reek of human waste permeates everything – sewage disposal and running water having long since vanished from the ghetto.

The roar of engines and squeal of brakes on the street freezes them. The beating of Leo's heart feels like hammer blows in the pit of his stomach. The thought of the people crouched upstairs in the attic – their collective fate in his hands – calms him, and he reviews the available options. Is there any way the fugitives can be saved without putting his own life and the lives of the others at risk? Leo desperately wants to be part of the uprising which he knows is fast approaching. If the Germans suspect that they are protecting fellow Jews, execution or transportation will quickly follow.

An officer enters from the street – his men quickly filling the hallway behind him. His haughty stare alerts Leo to the fact that he is probably the worst sort of German – one who will kill without a second thought. He addresses David who happens to be closest.

"Have you located the beasts who live in this pigsty yet?"

David doesn't falter for a moment. He doffs his peaked cap, snaps his heels together, salutes and bows before replying in respectful tones.

"We are conducting a thorough search, Herr Major."

Another salute and deferential bow. Leo knows that David is as eager as him to survive until the day of reckoning. He is doubtless committing every aspect of the man to memory, hoping they might meet again in battle.

The lieutenant smiles balefully, maybe flattered by the reference to his elevated rank, but most likely disappointed to find nothing wanting in David's demeanour.

"You had better find them or provide a good reason for their absence, otherwise it will go very badly for you and your men. You understand? I will fill my quota list today with any Jew. It matters not a jot to me who is transported as long as the figures add up."

Despite the provocation, David remains respectful.

"Yes, sir. Very good, sir."

"My men will wait down here until you are finished. If you want our help, ask the sergeant. I will return in an hour to pick up the prisoners."

The charade of searching the building continues. As they thrash around, Leo and David debate whether there is any chance they will be able to persuade the Nazis that the place is really deserted. There is still a chance that even if the German soldiers do take over the hunt, they will find nothing and leave.

True to his word, the lieutenant returns within the hour. As senior officer, Leo reports that he is satisfied the building is empty.

"It is possible the people living here received prior warning that a search was about to be conducted and fled before we arrived."

"I wonder how they might have received such helpful information."

Leo ignores the sarcasm and completes his report.

"Also, as you know, sir, the block was searched and cleared just over a week ago. It is therefore unlikely that anyone would still be here."

Although knowing he must avoid eye contact at all costs, he can't help stealing a glance at his enemy. The man's high cheekbones and square chin, criss-crossed with tiny shaving nicks, give away nothing of the evil inside. He reminds Leo of the greengrocer's son back in Krasnow – a lad he used to play with on the street.

"In that case, you and your men will be required to take their place. As I explained, I have my quotas to meet." The tone of mock pity suddenly changes. "If anyone is found, of course, I will have you all taken outside and shot, so you had better start praying to that useless God of yours that the building is truly rat free."

He orders his sergeant to initiate a new search, while Leo, David and the others are hustled downstairs into a wide corridor on the first floor. Armed soldiers rush past, enter the flats and begin to smash and kick down anything that might conceal a hideaway. Men with axes go to work demolishing floorboards and wooden partitions. The din increases as the sweep progresses from floor to floor. Leo hears the ladder being dragged out of the storeroom four storeys up. The moment of truth is fast approaching. The Nazi officer may be bluffing about replacing the cache of prisoners with Jewish policemen, but that won't matter if his men enter the attic and continue their demolition spree. Leo braces himself for action, determined not to go down without a fight. If their captors can be disarmed, the acquisition of their rifles and sub-machine guns would be a prize worth dying for.

Shouting and gunfire outside changes everything. The guards glance nervously at each other wondering what's happening on the street. So far there has been little resistance in this or any other Polish ghetto – a posting in Warsaw considered a dream alternative to the Russian front. Knowing it's now or never, Leo springs into action. He grabs the distracted soldier nearest him and delivers a crushing head butt. David kicks another guard in the groin as he attempts to level his gun. The third is quickly overpowered by the remaining policemen. Armed and desperate, they rush out onto the stairway. A soldier running full pelt down the steps is tripped up by Leo and unceremoniously tipped over the rail. The thump of his body on the floor below provides a moment of grim satisfaction. David waves Leo and the others away, raises the captured machine gun and fires with complete abandon into the stairwell. The din resonates painfully in Leo's ears as they reach ground level.

A man enters from the street, moving cautiously into the hallway. Leo gasps in astonishment as he recognises Freidman. His friend is brandishing a Luger. A brief smile is all that is forthcoming.

"Get a move on, Rudolf. This place will be full of Germans soon."

So great is his surprise that his pseudonym holds no meaning for him and he wonders who Freidman is talking to. It all returns in a flash.

"But what's going on?" he blurts out. "Has the uprising begun? I thought that… ."

"There's no time for explanations. You and your men must get out of here now."

"But David is still up there."

The thought of his friend struggling alone to hold back a dozen soldiers fills him with dismay.

"Go! We'll do our best to get him out."

Another burst of gunfire, and David staggers backwards into the hallway. The German CO appears on the landing above and shoots him twice in the chest. Leo leaps forward but Freidman is quicker. His Luger barks once, twice, and the Nazi tumbles head over heals down the stairs. Freidman turns, his expression grim but untainted with blood lust.

"For God's sake, get out of here, now!"

Leo and his colleagues run for their lives, leaving the main street at the first opportunity. Behind them, renewed gunfire pops like firecrackers. Soon they are racing through a warren of side streets and alleyways towards a hidden bunker where they will be safe. He wonders if his career as a police officer is finally over. Surely he will now be a marked man, hunted by every German soldier in Warsaw. If a general uprising is underway, it won't much matter. He fervently hopes the time for subterfuge is over and that he and his comrades will be allowed to take the fight directly to the enemy.

—⁂—

"As we found out later, this was not the beginning of the end but only the end of the beginning."

Leo smiles at the confusion registering on his grandson's face.

"The attack that day was simply a dress rehearsal, staged by the Resistance to make the occupiers feel less secure in their daily round-ups. It was also carried out to raise the rock-bottom morale of those remaining in the ghetto. These two goals were achieved, as well as the death of a handful of German soldiers and the release of prisoners being escorted to the *Umschlagplatz*."

"Were the people hiding in the attic shot?"

"No. They were very lucky. The German soldiers fled after their officer was killed, and Freidman managed to get them all out. I was ordered back to my police duties because the Resistance believed me to be in no greater danger than usual. Anyway, the Nazis had a lot more to worry about now that Mordecai Anielewicz was committed to the struggle."

"Who was this Mordecai Anielewicz person?"

Leo smiles at Sam's halting attempt to pronounce the name of the greatest Jewish hero to emerge from the horror and the chaos of these desperate days.

"I'm surprised you have not heard of his exploits in your history class."

"I think we have but I'm not sure."

"Mordecai was head of the Resistance, although few of us knew his real name at the time. He had been organising self-defence groups inside various Polish ghettos since 1940. It wasn't until 1942 that he was appointed commander of the Resistance in the Warsaw Ghetto itself. That was when things really began to get hot for the enemy. He managed to link up with the Polish free army and persuade them to supply us with some of the weapons we needed to mount an effective defence. The Nazis had grown too confident in our weakness. They weren't ready for any resistance from such 'inferior' people. That was a big mistake. The idea of never again bowing meekly to the oppressor was born in 1943, and it wasn't the only place where we defended ourselves. The uprising in Treblinka, and some of the other concentration camps, also took them by surprise."

On a sudden impulse, Leo decides to challenge the simplistic link made by some Jews between defending the ghetto and promoting the Zionist philosophy of attacking the perceived enemies of Israel at every opportunity.

"You must try to understand the difference between fighting oppression, and oppressing others in the name of freedom and security. The mantra, 'never again' can blind people to the importance of behaving justly and even-handedly. Repelling a cruel invader is not the same as persecuting the Arabs who live amongst us, or occupying land that does not belong to us."

Sam scowls.

"The land has been given to us by God, and the Arabs are the agents of evil sent to destroy us all. How can they own our land?"

Leo knows that his grandson's loyalties are split down the middle, and, as his own voice weakens, Benny's grows stronger. Despair pricks at his determination to redress the balance. Again, he wonders if relating his experiences from long ago might be proving counter-productive. The emphasis on fighting and killing may only be confusing the boy. Human frailty, in particular the tendency to be seduced by an attractive ideology, is a major factor in all of this. The relatively small number of people predisposed to outright evil is dwarfed by those unduly influenced by fear and ignorance.

Somehow, he must increase the pace of telling. The significance of everything that has gone before is contained in the aftermath of the ghetto uprising.

—⚬—

Later the same evening, Freidman arrives at the bunker where Leo and his comrades are holed up. The two men embrace, each glad to see that the other has survived the day. Freidman is first to speak.

"I have some news that will please you. We managed to get the people in the attic out, so at least your colleague did not die in vain. And your sister was saved from deportation along with dozens of others on their way to the *Umschlagplatz*."

Leo gasps.

"How did she come to be…?"

Freidman smiles reassuringly.

"I do not have the full details yet, but apparently she was on her way home from work when a German patrol spotted her and bundled her into one of their wagons. There was absolutely nothing she could do, even though she had her work permit pinned to the front of her coat. As you know, the Nazis often ignore such trifling details. Nothing matters these days but their damned quotas! Anyway, the escort was attacked not far from the station, and the prisoners escaped."

"How is she? Where is she?"

"Back at the flat, and none the worse for her ordeal – just glad to be alive and free, I guess!" Freidman releases a long sigh. "This morning's operation has certainly livened things up, but there's a lot to be done before we can mount anything more serious. Getting hold of weapons is the crucial thing, and that will be harder after what's happened. Security is going to be tighter than ever on the *Aryan side,* and the Polish Resistance remains obdurate. We can only hope the Germans back off a little and give us some breathing space, but I don't know. We may have miscalculated. They might just as easily throw everything our way before we get any stronger."

"I want to be there when they come. When will I be able to get out of here?"

"Soon enough, but there is still work to be done on the streets. We've managed to alter the log at police HQ, which now places you at the other side of the ghetto at the time of the operation. With any luck, everything will be fine."

"I'd hoped that my stint with the police would be finished after today."

Freidman smiles wearily and shakes his head.

"I know how much you want that, my friend, but you're just too valuable to us where you are. When the fighting really begins you will be in the thick of things, never fear. Now, I must be on my way. You'll hear when it's safe to leave."

—⁓—

"I can't stop worrying about mother and father. We've heard nothing from them for so long now."

Lola and Leo are alone together on a rare evening when both are free from work. They are sitting in the front room of their flat which has once again become exclusively their own. It is just over six months since the Shreibermans were arrested and transported. And, with the population having shrunk so dramatically over the past few months, the prospect of another family moving in is unlikely. He attempts to reassure his sister.

"They're probably fine. Life in the smaller towns is much less dangerous than in the ghettos." He struggles to sound convincing. "There's no way they could have got in touch with us, especially after Mr Lebinski was murdered. The fact that we've heard nothing doesn't really mean much, one way or the other."

"I know, but it's all the rumours about the round-ups and the camps. It just feels so hopeless with no way of knowing what's happened to them."

"Father has a lot of contacts. He and mother might well have got out of Poland."

Although determined to be upbeat for Lola's sake, he doesn't hold out much hope that many Jews will have managed to bend back the iron bars of the occupation – especially the elderly and infirm. She continues as if he hasn't spoken.

"I think we all might meet up again, even after what's happened. Maybe God is watching over us."

This simple statement of hope, expressed without sentiment, moves him deeply. Lola does not cry or complain. She never has. Looking at her sitting there so resolute, Leo is once again amazed by the toughness of character that has sustained her over the past three years. Even more incredible, given that two days ago she was riding a Nazi tumbrel.

There is a long silence before she resumes.

"Where is it all going to end, Leo?"

Her clear, hazel eyes, gazing into his, demand candour, but also reveal an absolute confidence in his ability to keep them safe. He desperately hopes that he can live up to her faith in him. His wish to throw himself into battle, and annihilate as many of the enemy as possible before being killed himself, must be resisted. Lola, despite her strength, remains his responsibility. He recalls the oath he swore to his father on that final, dreadful night before they fled from Krasnow, to protect his sister through the dangerous times ahead. Although he and his father had grown apart, Leo is aware just how much he loved and revered the old man. This knowledge reinforces his determination to honour the promise, come what may. He answers carefully. Although his sister needs some reassurance, he must not cover up the grim reality of their situation.

"I don't know, to be honest. The Germans will never stop trying to kill us. They will take the ghetto apart brick by brick, if they have to." He pauses, gripped by a new sense of purpose. "But I will find a way out for us! Anyway," – he attempts to lighten the mood a little – "it looks like the Allies may be winning the war at last. You never know when they'll come galloping in to our rescue."

He smiles at her and she smiles back though her eyes seem far away as if she has passed beyond the present horrors to some haven untainted by fear.

—w—

Next morning the Germans withdraw from the ghetto, leaving the survivors to pick up the remaining pieces of their lives as best they can. In the wake of the uprising, the occupiers have apparently decided to pull back and take stock. No one doubts that this will only be a temporary assuagement, but it provides vital time to prepare for the last stand. Despite their unwillingness to enter the ghetto, the Nazis have effectively sealed it off from the outside world. Sometimes the odd individual escapes from a work detail crossing over into the *Aryan side,* or the Resistance pulls off a particularly daring raid, but starvation and illness are killing the survivors in ever increasing numbers. Even the ghetto elite recognise that their period of grace is almost at an end. The cushion of wealth which has permitted their privileged existence is all but spent. The need for huge bribes and the steep rise in black-market prices have fleeced even the richest of them.

Leo has been ordered to watch and wait. The first signs of a German change of plan may manifest itself in a re-ordering of police activities. The Resistance are keeping tabs on everything, the better to prepare for the final battle.

CHAPTER SEVEN

Ramallah: March 2002.

"Our target is the *Muqata*. According to intelligence, President Arafat, and his key ministers, are sheltering there."

"You mean cowering like frightened rabbits, sir!"

Standing on the other side of the table on which a street map of the centre of Ramallah is spread out, Gad winks across at me. He is adept at tail-pulling, especially those belonging to tigers like Major Shalom.

"I mean what I say, lieutenant! Might I be allowed to continue?"

The CO scowls, his thick eyebrows knitting into one hard, black line. Gad smiles sweetly.

"Of course, sir."

"The compound will be assaulted from two sides. Tanks on Irsal Street, here" – Shalom's thick finger jabs the map – "will concentrate their efforts on the western wall." We peer at the long artery beginning at the Manara roundabout, close to the town centre, and running over half a mile to Arafat's headquarters. "Another squadron will bombard the southern wall, here. When both walls are breached, we will enter and secure the Tegart building, systematically searching it room by room. Anyone found inside," he pauses and stares meaningfully at Gad, "is to be apprehended and removed. These are your orders. Are they clearly understood?"

He gazes round awaiting our acknowledgement. We nod.

"The remainder of buildings and annexes in the compound will be searched by other units. Our orders are to withdraw and rendezvous in the outer courtyard. There will be helicopters on hand to transport the prisoners back to HQ. Please take note of the precise coordinates, and familiarise yourselves with all available intelligence. Are there any questions?"

"Yes, sir." Undeterred by Shalom's earlier irritation, Gad doesn't hesitate for a moment. It's like we're back at military college. "If there is any resistance – I mean from armed militia within the compound – are we supposed to pat their heads and ask them to hand over Arafat like good little boys?"

"We will cross that bridge when we come to it. No one will open fire without a specific order from me."

As usual, Gad refuses to let go.

"But what if we come under fire? Are we not even being allowed to defend ourselves?"

Shalom refuses to be drawn – his face an impassive mask.

"You will take evasive action and await my orders. This briefing is over. Please instruct your men accordingly."

Outside, Gad grasps my arm.

"Well, here we are, at long last!" He seems positively gleeful. "The suicide bombers have played right into our hands. So, goodbye, Oslo Accords, goodbye, Arafat!"

His view that the slaughter and maiming of so many of our own people is an acceptable price to pay if it means an end to the faltering peace process is hardly surprising, but such unequivocal delight is harder to swallow. The suffering of the victims and their families seems of no concern to him at all.

—⚋—

The Manara roundabout in the centre of Ramallah is packed with soldiers, tanks and armoured vehicles. The din of revving engines and the stink of exhaust fumes fill the air. My eyes are drawn to a tattered poster of Yasser Arafat gazing serenely down on the square. His index finger is slightly raised as if in protest at the armed incursion about to be launched into his capital. The familiar features, displayed on wall posters throughout Judea and Samaria, although younger and less wrinkled than in real life, never fail to disgust me. His shrunken face with its thick lips and snake eyes; the pock-marked chin, sprouting sparse grey hairs; the spotted *kuffieh* hanging limply over his head and shoulders like folds of loose skin, rekindle my contempt for Fatah and the other terrorist groups. What should I feel for this barbarian who spends his waking hours plotting the extermination of my people while simultaneously plucking on international heart strings? I stare for a moment at the four ridiculous lions, placed in the square to celebrate recent moves towards Palestinian autonomy. For me, they symbolise the artificiality of the entire process. It seems appropriate that a bunch of soldiers are now busy scrawling obscene graffiti over their bullet-ridden torsos.

Arafat and his cronies will never be satisfied until the last Jewish settlement has been blown to pieces and its citizens murdered. Should we therefore not strike first, taking the war to the heart of our enemy? Father is surely right when he says that defending our people and rejecting the passivity that led to our undoing in the past is the key to Israel's survival. To my dismay, the petals of renewed patriotism wither as quickly as they blossomed. The deployment of a military juggernaut, bristling with the very latest in destructive technologies, against a bunch of poorly armed, half-trained militiamen, hardly seems heroic. Will we Jews finally be condemned by a world community sickened by our arrogant flouting of diplomacy and international law? My colleagues couldn't care less, of course. They have nothing but contempt for foreigners, living safe and secure lives, knowing nothing of our battle for survival in the centre of so much hatred and violence. As usual, I struggle with the ambivalence which has defined my life for so long now.

The moment of truth arrives. Tanks roar out of the square onto Main Street while helicopters beat overhead, their fast-moving searchlights illuminating buildings along the route. The first phase of the operation is intended to flush out hidden gunmen from three key buildings: the Natshe – a well known centre of terrorist activity; the locally named Arizona, containing the offices of FIDA, a faction of the PLO; and the Midan, housing one of the new Arab ministries. When all units have taken up position, the main task of securing Arafat's compound will begin in earnest. I glance up at the huge propaganda poster one last time. Perhaps I'll soon be face-to-face with the object of so much disgust.

In the total darkness of an unlit street, a stab of yellow flame and an ear-shattering explosion freezes the blood in my veins. The tanks have begun their deadly assault. The shelling quickly intensifies. I can't help imagining the plight of those huddled inside the *Muqata* as its walls vibrate and crumble around them.

We're on the move again. Waving my men forward, we follow close behind the squealing leviathans across a wilderness of blasted masonry – all that now remains of the perimeter wall of Arafat's headquarters. There is no opposing fire; no hidden machine gun nests. Like the newly-fledged Palestinian state itself, the building is disintegrating before our eyes. I wonder if Arafat is now regretting his collusion with the terror squads.

In a surprisingly short time we are inside the main complex and scouring the network of rooms and corridors. What remains intact is demolished. Furniture and equipment are toppled and smashed; hard drives are torn out of computers, and, along with hundreds of files, tossed into black bags. One soldier starts to rip posters off the walls until I remind him why we are here. He grimaces, opens his mouth, thinks better of it, and returns to the search. I can tell he wishes he was in Gad's squad where such 'initiative' would be commended, not condemned. Gad's leadership encourages the licence I attempt to subdue. I shudder to think what will happen to any poor soul we encounter, despite Shalom's express orders.

After half an hour's frenzied activity, we are forced to admit defeat. The place is empty of people. No one is home. Perhaps the staff got wind of our plans and fled before the bombardment began. The men indulge in wanton acts of vandalism as frustration sets in. Only Shalom's arrival quietens things down. Waving Gad and me aside, he wastes no time on preliminaries.

"Intelligence now believes" – he enunciates the last word in a manner conveying maximum contempt – "that Arafat and his people are hidden elsewhere in the compound. A further search is being initiated as I speak. Organise your men, we're leaving!"

The beat of a departing helicopter reminds us how sure our commanders were that Arafat was holed up in the *Muqata*. The longer it takes to find him, the less chance there will be of decisive action. The resolve of mainstream politicians, fickle at the best of times, may crumble if subjected to enough international pressure. In any event, the baton has been passed on.

The distant spatter of small-arms fire alerts us to the fact that our soldiers are meeting at least some resistance on the ground. Perhaps incursions against the Fida or the ministry offices have provoked a more determined response than anticipated. Suddenly, things look a little less rosy than they did during the planning stage. The formidable reputation our intelligence service once enjoyed is becoming a little frayed around the edges.

Shalom seeks to revive morale. Gathering the company together in the outer courtyard, he congratulates us on a "highly professional" sweep of the western compound. He is clearly prepared to turn a blind eye to the wave of destruction that has reduced the furniture and fittings of the Muqata to tangled wreckage.

"Your new mission is to breach a known terrorist hideout, and search for insurgents and weaponry. We have reports that a cache of arms and explosives is hidden there. Firearms will only be used in self-defence, or if resistance is offered."

Gad winks and smirks at me. I can almost see his report sheet now. Lists of people shot with the phrases "self-defence" or "resistance offered" at such and such a place, at such and such a time, scrawled beside each name.

Two troop carriers and a Jeep draw up outside the ruined compound. Dawn is breaking as the men climb aboard the lorries, and Gad and I get into the Jeep. As we speed along Main Street, I notice several bulldozers squatting motionless in the rubble like giant toads. A digger standing nearby, its serrated head thrust high into the air, triggers a childhood memory of a predatory dinosaur I once saw in a school picture book. I remember being terrified by the rows of sharp teeth, as large as carving knives. But most scary of all was the scale figure of a man inserted to show the size of the beast – the top of his head barely reaching its bent knee. The digger and its posse of thuggish bulldozers, however, conjure a dread more intense and immediate than any long-extinct monster ever could.

The tanks have gone quiet now, but the massive damage to nearby buildings bears witness to their awesome firepower. Mangled remains of cars litter the road beside mounds of blasted bricks and masonry. Soldiers, implementing a total curfew, patrol in the half light. I wonder if the resistance has been quelled. It's hard to imagine that a few men armed only with rifles, however determined, could withstand the formidable assault unleashed here tonight. The thought that many of these people regard themselves as freedom fighters, willing to die resisting a brutal occupation, increases my uneasiness. The terrorist label can surely not be applied to every Arab fighting in Judea and Samaria.

Our driver suddenly swerves off the road, accelerates up a side street and brakes violently. We lurch forward in our seats. The lorries squeal to a halt behind us. I am about to reprimand the fool for his appalling driving when Gad leans forward, squeezes his shoulder and thanks him for getting us to our destination so quickly. Predictably, I've failed to tune into the machismo which fuels such recklessness.

Gad addresses the soldiers lining up behind us.

"This is the terrorist stronghold we've been ordered to search. The *towel heads* living here won't be pleased to see us, for sure. If there is any resistance shoot first and ask questions later."

Appalled, but hardly surprised by Gad's interpretation of our orders, I quietly resolve to try and keep the situation as calm and professional as possible. The way things are, that will not be easy.

We smash open the reinforced glass door at the bottom of the four-storey building, and enter. Inside, the men move cautiously. The terrified caretaker is hauled out of his cubby hole; his keys are confiscated and he is forced to sit on the floor with head bowed and hands clasped behind his neck. Some of the men climb the stairs while others enter a lift, looking as though they expect armed terrorists to drop down on them from the ceiling.

The people living in these flats are clearly not short of a shekel or two – most likely professional, middle-class Arabs trying desperately to lead normal lives in abnormal circumstances. I imagine them equally appalled by the recent spate of suicide-bombing murders and the armed occupation of their city.

Upstairs, rifle stocks thunder on doors and children begin to wail. I wonder about the strategic importance of such a building and what we are really doing here. Maybe someone in authority considers it a worthwhile place to loot, or we might be involved in a tit-for-tat operation, intended to punish innocent civilians. This would certainly strike some as appropriate revenge for the recent spate of Arab outrages. Whatever the motivation, it seems unlikely that we'll discover terrorists or their arms cache.

No quarter is given. The unfortunate families are driven downstairs into the hallway. Women in dressing gowns, hastily pulled on in the face of jerking gun barrels and dire threats, huddle in groups clasping their children. This treatment flies in the face of Moslem modesty, and their husbands mutter and glower at us.

Gad motions to one of the men, demanding to know where the guns are hidden. The Arab is small and thickset with a neat moustache and flashing black eyes. As the interrogation hots up, he shrugs and refuses to answer the questions fired at him. Without warning, Gad punches him hard in the face. The force of the blow causes him to stagger; a second blow to the stomach brings him to his knees. Another resident starts forward to help his stricken friend, but a well directed rifle stock puts an end to his heroics. At that moment, a woman drops to her knees and emits a blood-curling wail. Others push their children behind them, clearly intent on using their bodies as shields against further violence. In an instant, the atmosphere is transformed – fear and dismay replacing the residents' initial anger. Despite everything I've been taught to believe about these people, I'm shocked at what is happening. Our men are wound up tight as watch springs, and Gad is too obviously intent on aggravating the situation for me to generate any kind of restraint. Unaware of my internal struggle, Gad removes the first victim for questioning. I consider going with them but decide to stay put. The man appears to have escaped serious injury, which is more than can be said for his comrade, who looks as though he might require medical attention.

While Gad is out of the room, I allow the other prisoners to tend him. He slowly comes to and sits propped up against a wall. His refined features, distorted by severe swelling, accentuate the vicious irrationality of the attack. The injustice batters with both fists against the fragile wall of my surviving prejudices. This man is clearly no murderer of innocent women or children. He is a family man whose wish to see an end to the current nightmare engulfing his country is not hard to imagine. Knowing how such heresy would be construed by Gad simply adds to my belief that fault does not lie solely with those on the opposite side of the conflict. Our religious convictions, reinforced by rabbis and politicians, justify almost any outrage against Satan's emissaries, but here, in the midst of terrified women and children, I find it hard to share such fervour.

The prisoner is returned a few minutes later. To my relief, he looks no worse than when he left. I wonder what new tactic Gad has in mind. I don't have long to wait. He picks out a woman with two children for interrogation. Several of the residents start to protest but cower down when threatened with raised rifles. While she is being removed, and her wailing children prised away from her, I motion to Gad to join me for a private word. He nods and we step out onto a balcony overlooking the main drag of the avenue below. Two large plant vases have been toppled and the jigsaw pieces of blue-glazed earthenware lie scattered like jewels among the soil and leaves. Perhaps one of the men thought he might discover guns or explosives hidden among the roots. I desperately grapple with the problem of how to protect these people from further abuse. I have no idea what I'm going to say. My sudden impulse to get Gad out here without a definite plan of action is plain stupid; the whole thing could easily backfire. A light-handed deactivation process will be required, and I've no idea where to begin.

Words suddenly tumble out of nowhere.

"This bunch seem more trouble than they're worth. Maybe we should just search the flats and report our findings to Shalom. My feeling is we're wasting our time here."

"Don't be so sure. Once we start questioning their women, the bastards might be more willing to talk. They must know where the arms are hidden."

"Do you really think there are any guns to find?"

"It stands to reason Shalom wouldn't have sent us here for nothing. Anyway, we don't want to give him an excuse to jump down our throats."

Gad sneers. As far as he's concerned, Shalom's obsession with orders and doing things by the book are signs of weakness, and worthy of contempt. It occurs to me that I might be able to utilise his antipathy in my favour.

"I forgot to mention that I got a letter from my father this morning."

Gad stares at me strangely, no doubt wondering why I'm bringing this up now.

"Oh yes. How is he?"

Fortunately, good manners prevail, although I can see he's itching to get back to the prisoners.

"Fine. He was telling me that he'd been chatting to your dad about the old times in Hebron. They were recalling our run-in with the Arabs after that incident at the Cave of Machpelah."

"Yes, I remember. That was the time I broke my arm. We all thought it was just a sprain but the X-ray showed a hairline fracture. Not much really, but I milked it for all it was worth. Do you remember how I kept that sling on for weeks after the arm had healed? Everybody at school thought I was some kind of wounded war hero. And then your father got that black eye when an Arab bastard punched him."

Gad sounds impassioned as old memories flood back. I realise that I might be onto a winner here.

"He said that your dad was hoping we were still in the thick of things, making a difference." I pause to let this sink in, then play my ace card. "It seems to me that we're being side-lined because we failed to grab Arafat. It wasn't our fault, but here we are, the finest commando unit in the entire bloody army interrogating a bunch of miserable *towel heads*! Even the rookie grunts are in the thick of things and what the hell are we doing? I don't know what I'm going to tell my father when he asks about this mission. It seems so pathetic somehow. We're supposed to be a special ops unit and… ."

Gad cuts me short.

"You're right! Even if we do find weapons, or even bombs here, so what? We're not exactly going to make the headlines. We were sent in to get Arafat, for fuck sakes! We need to get out of here and back into the real action!"

I breathe more easily. God knows where all that came from, but, hopefully, the families inside will be released.

"Let's get the men together, Sam. Thank God you're here to keep me right. Mind you, there will be hell to pay when Shalom catches up with us." He smiles mirthlessly.

I seize the initiative before he changes his mind.

"You organise the transport and I'll sort out the prisoners. I'm pretty certain there's nothing hidden here anyway." In an effort to fan Gad's wrath to a white heat, just to make sure, I push things even further. "Maybe this is Shalom's way of punishing you for interrupting his precious briefing last night."

His expression reveals the effectiveness of my strategy. If I can keep him away from the Arab civilians for the next few minutes, I might be able to get them back into their flats, and the men out of the building. I rush back inside shouting right and left.

"We have new orders. You two, bring that woman back here and escort these people upstairs. The rest of you, line up outside."

There's a ragged cheer. It occurs to me that more of the men than I thought have no stomach for this kind of work, only hardening their hearts in order to hide what they believe might be construed as weakness by their mates. The relief on many faces allows me to see them in a different light.

As husbands and wives embrace and the weight of their fear falls away, I experience a surge of elation. For once, I'm doing the right thing. The unease I've felt for so long doesn't altogether vanish, though. I can't help wondering what other dubious missions will compel me to wrestle with my conscience in the future. There is no doubt that the anger which once sustained my devotion to the cause is trickling away like sand in an hour glass. My earlier reaction to Arafat's poster, and the struggle with patriotic sentiment, are nothing to the revulsion Gad's behaviour has provoked. While father's influence diminishes, and the baggage piled up along the way slips further behind, other matters clamour for my attention. Everywhere I turn these days, grandfather's ghost seems to be watching me, monitoring what I do, assessing the merit of my every decision.

A Jeep pulls up outside. A corporal leaps out and bounds up the flight of steps. What now? I pray his arrival will not interfere with my efforts to help these people.

Seeing me, he snaps to attention and salutes smartly.

"I have orders from Major Shalom, sir."

I tear open the sealed envelope and scan the contents. The major wants us to drop everything and prepare to storm the Arizona building on Main Street. This is an extraordinary piece of luck. As well as letting us off the hook, it provides Gad and his hotheads with an acceptable outlet for their frustration. It also diverts attention away from civilians to armed militia. I can live with that! At last we can get on with the job we've been trained to do.

Our troop-carriers – called in by Gad – arrive at that very moment. The corporal blinks, unable to believe his eyes.

"How did you know...."

He stutters to a halt.

"This unit doesn't have a reputation for hanging around when our services are urgently required, corporal!"

I suppress laughter at the expression on the man's face. Gad arrives panting. I explain our new orders. His relief is clear. Even he is pleased to be avoiding Shalom's wrath in the wake of contravening orders.

"Let's get going then; it's a twenty-minute drive from here." He turns to the messenger. "Have the tanks breached the walls of this – what you call it – Arizona building?"

"Yessir. But the major wants to secure it without destroying everything inside."

"How many of our soldiers have been killed so far?"

I intervene, wanting to know what we're up against.

"None, as far as I'm know, sir."

"Has there been any return fire from the insurgents?"

"I haven't heard any shots – only the tanks, sir."

Certainly a strange lack of response from desperate men charged with preventing the capture of vital information. But, I suppose, firing at tanks with rifles would be no better than using pop guns against a charging rhino. It could very well be that they're saving their efforts for the inevitable hand-to-hand clash inside the building. For the first time, I feel we might be able to do something useful if we are able to secure the material intact.

Gad, meantime, is champing at the bit.

"Get back to Shalom, er, Major Shalom, and tell him that we're on our way. Make sure we don't get there before you." Again, the macho challenge. Predictably, the corporal is only too eager to take it up and charges off towards his vehicle. The last of our men exit the building and clamber into the lorries – their mates dragging them inside. We roar off at breakneck speed, this time at least partially justified by the urgency of our mission. Gad is, of course, desperate to show how efficient and professional we are.

The sun is now slanting over the low buildings creating a patchwork of bright light and shadow. The curfew is still in operation and the streets are deserted. Any Arab showing his or her face out of doors is liable to be shot without warning. The four bulldozers and the digger I spotted earlier are now fully awake and engaged in pulverising a row of shops. Already, the entire frontage has been razed, and a choking pall of dust shrouds what remains of the block. Maybe the demolition is the result of sniper activity, or it could be army command have ordered that the road be widened for the passage of tanks and transport vehicles.

Our racing Jeep bounces into a shell hole almost tipping us out onto the road. The troop carrier on our tail swerves just avoiding a collision. Gad is totally unfazed by the near miss. His desire to get back into the thick of things overrides any safety considerations. I pray that I have not overdone my appeal to his fighting spirit.

On this occasion, there can be no mad rush up Main Street. The road is an obstacle course, crammed with tanks and supply vehicles, making it necessary to pick our way slowly to the rendezvous point close to the Arizona building itself. It appears to have been one of the finest in Ramallah. Even after its terrible pounding, the appeal of the rounded walls, fine roof line and expansive windows has not been totally effaced. A few hours ago, it must have been a pleasant place to work or shop in. I remember the map showing stores on the ground floor with offices above. It's hard to imagine terrorists hanging out here, but, of course, anything is possible.

The men are ordered to stay put while Gad and I locate the command centre. It doesn't take long. A sentry directs us up a narrow side street where offices have been appropriated and turned into a temporary HQ. I notice the locks have been forced, and office furniture slung out onto the pavement. Inside, Shalom is barking orders into a cell phone. He impatiently motions us into an adjoining room. Gad scowls at such a contemptuous dismissal.

A minute or so later, the major joins us.

"You took your time getting here, didn't you?"

"Oh well, sir, you know how it is! Just when you're in the middle of a tough assignment, the plug gets pulled. I sometimes think HQ doesn't know its arse from its elbow!"

"Watch your mouth, Katz. One of these days it will get you into deep water."

"It's lucky I learned to swim then, sir."

Shalom opens and closes his mouth like a stranded fish. Despite his hard-line reputation, he finds Gad's blunt manner and self-confidence intimidating, and is no doubt sorry he opened his mouth. He quickly moves on.

"Your orders are to storm the Arizona building, neutralise any opposition, and recover sensitive material."

"As regards the opposition, sir." Gad's voice assumes a sarcastic drawl. "How many defenders are there likely to be, and will we be arresting them for interrogation purposes this time round?"

"Around twenty terrorists inside is our best guess. It would be helpful if some prisoners were taken, but the primary objective is to secure the building and remove hard evidence. Is that understood?"

"Understood, sir."

Shalom glances at me.

"Yes, understood, sir."

"Very well. The tanks have done all they can. You'll need to go in through the windows. I'll leave the details to you. How long do you think you'll need?"

"Half an hour at the most, sir."

"Well, good luck then."

The major strides out of the room.

"He'll leave the details to us. That's a joke! There's certainly no chance of him getting his hands dirty."

Impatient to get started, I cut Gad short.

"We'd better get on. There's a lot to organise."

—⁓—

Marksmen across the street cover our entry points. Jagged holes and black gashes in the walls testify to the violence of the recent shelling. A liaison officer informs us that at least two men threw themselves out of the building during the bombardment. One of them is still alive, but in a coma. The same officer tells us that there may be up to thirty armed men holed up inside; ten more than Shalom thought. The operation could be challenging. My stomach churns in anticipation.

We abseil from the roof and hurl ourselves through the windows into the dark interior. Ugly, two nosed aliens, swarm around me. Tear gas canisters have already filled the rooms with a swirling fog. Through the pane of my mask, I catch sight of something clambering over piles of wrecked furniture. It coughs and splutters and scrambles away. Someone releases a spray of bullets and it slumps to the floor. I hear more shots, and someone screaming. An unmasked insurgent leaps up in front of me like a startled rabbit. His face is beetroot red and covered in a film of sweat. I fire off three rounds from my sidearm at point blank range and he collapses in a heap. Ignoring him, I enter a larger room. Here the gas is less thick and I can make out cabinets and desks. I motion the men forward. Files are pulled out and thrown into bags; computer equipment is wrenched away from the walls. We proceed warily to the next room, and the next.

Soon the air clears enough for me to remove my mask. I stare around as light from the outside world filters in. A soldier reports that the building is secure. Screening walls and false ceilings are rubble, adding to the difficulty of the search. One of my men, scrabbling around the floor, holds up a gashed hand and gazes stupidly at the flow of blood.

I return to examine the bodies of the two men gunned down in the first hectic moments of the battle. The corpse of the terrorist I shot is already stiff and cold. Pulling him over, I see the face of a man, probably in his early fifties. His eyes are wide open, and his lips are drawn back in a grimace of agony. The bald head, smashed spectacles and sober attire, suggest a clerk, not a guerrilla. I search his clothes for hidden weapons but find nothing other than a bunch of keys. His comrade, killed seconds earlier by a member of my unit, appears even more innocuous. To my horror, I see he has a prosthetic arm. Again, there is no evidence of a uniform, and his hair and moustache are peppered white. He is carrying nothing which could have been used to kill or even defend himself. The realisation dawns that, once again, I've been party to the murder of helpless civilians. When I finally catch up with Gad, even he seems subdued. The expected fire fight has failed to materialise – the death of yet another middle-aged caretaker hardly the stuff of heroic endeavour.

In the end, a total of five dead, two prisoners, and nothing of any interest found in the FIDA offices, proves even more frustrating than our earlier failure to capture Arafat. The men are baying for blood. I manage to contain my squad with a mixture of threats and cajolements, but with Gad's lot it's an entirely different matter. They're on the prowl, looking for trouble.

─⟋⟍─

An hour later, the top floor of the Arizona building is alight. The fire may have started accidently, but I doubt it. No one tackles the flames. Firefighters and ambulance crews, like all other citizens in Ramallah, are bound by the conditions of the curfew.

I spot a camera team filming the blaze. God knows how they managed to get in here. Are they brave to the point of madness or simply oblivious to the dangers of being so exposed?

Eventually, a section of the roof collapses. It strikes me more forcibly than ever that our attempts to punish the Arabs will not only fail to halt terrorist atrocities, but swell the ranks of those willing to martyr themselves. Operation Defensive Shield is probably the best recruiting sergeant Fatah and Hamas have had in a long time.

We quit the area and settle into temporary barracks on the ground floor of yet another office block. Again, fixtures and fittings have been ripped out and slung into the street. The men lie down exhausted and fall asleep on the dusty floor, waking only to wolf down hot rations served by the mobile kitchens which have finally caught up with us.

Gad's squad arrive just in time for the food. I want to know what they've been up to in the intervening period, and talk to a soldier I know from Kiryat Arba. Two years below me at school, Dov Harel used to come round to our house with his mother from time to time. I remember she was one of the few friends my mother had among the local wives. Sometimes, while they drank tea and chatted, Dov and I would play chess. Our friendship has grown of late and he keeps me informed about the various goings on in Gad's squad. I'm surprised how long he's managed to hold in there. Although an able enough soldier, he lacks the fanatical commitment Gad normally requires of his men. Due to a series of transfers of those who didn't quite fit in, and the opportune recruitment of more 'promising' candidates, his squad has gained a formidable reputation of late.

"We started that fire. Some of the men piled up desks and chairs; then Sergeant Shraggie doused them with petrol, threw his cigarette on top – and whoosh. We all just stood and watched while the fire took hold."

"What happened next?"

"Lieutenant Katz ordered us to search some houses across the street. I went into a flat they were tearing apart: furniture, clothes, carpets, even the wallpaper! There was a whole family lying on the floor in the front room. That bastard Oren was poking one of the young lads with the muzzle of his rifle, trying to force him to say where his father had hidden the guns. Oren kept at it until the boy was sick. I wanted to say something but I knew what would happen if I did."

Michael Oren's reputation for cruelty has followed him like a dark shadow as long as I can remember. At school he was rumoured to capture small creatures and torture them to death. We were all secretly scared of Oren and avoided him if possible. Now Gad seems happy enough to make use of his 'talents'.

"In another flat they were using the kitchen as a latrine, right in front of a mother and three teenage girls. I'm not sure how much more of this I can take, to be honest, sir."

Dov stares at me through unblinking, watery eyes. Normally, our conversations, although friendly, remain formal. The fact that I'm a couple of years older, and an officer, intimidates him a little, I think. I've always felt there was something rather quaint about his shyness, but now the underlying emotion is unmistakable. I struggle to remain calm though I'm boiling inside.

"Just tell me everything that happened, Dov."

I want to reassure him, but I'm desperate to find out more, even though he might break down in the telling.

He opens his mouth and closes it again, hanging his head in shame.

"You can tell me." I glance round to make sure nobody is listening. "I need to know."

He looks like a schoolboy unwilling to be implicated in some particularly nasty business. He swallows hard three or four times before continuing.

"They took some of the residents out onto the street. Lieutenant Katz was there. He had them stripped and forced to their knees. The men took turns kicking and punching them. It was as if they were militia or even terrorists, not civilians. I know they say all Arabs are terrorists but you can tell the difference. Then he – Lieutenant Katz – took out his pistol and held it against one man's head. The guy shat himself. The lieutenant laughed then kicked him senseless. I'm not sure if he was alive or dead at the end of it."

"Did your mates actually shoot any of the prisoners?"

"No, they just beat them up bad. I thought they might kill them all. I think they wanted to but couldn't quite bring themselves to actually do it in the end."

Maybe the last vestiges of a degraded humanity. I wonder how long it will be before even these props are kicked away. I say nothing to Dov – he's clearly too upset to take anything else on board. Like me, he's beginning to realise that years of indoctrination are not helping him cope with the harsh realities on the ground.

"There's more, sir."

I feel a vast emptiness opening beneath my feet. I'm not sure I want to hear what he's about to tell me. I want to cut short the conversation and leave this miserable country forever.

"They dragged two women down into a courtyard between two blocks of flats. I pretended I had to go and relieve myself and hid behind some trash cans. I saw the guys pull off the women's clothes and beat them with leather belts. Others brought over some female dummies from a clothes shop and started to, to… ." He's unable to speak the words but I know what he's trying to say. "Afterwards they slapped the women around some more. I couldn't believe what I was seeing." He stops, gulps and breathes hard. Tears are spilling down his cheeks. "Is there any way I can transfer into your squad, sir?"

For the first time I properly grasp the meaning of subhuman and find myself unable to reply. After years of suppressing their sexual urges, some of the men have clearly lost control. I think about the accusation that Jeff Schiff distributed pornographic magazines to fellow *Yeshiva* students – an act condemned by Rabbi Goldberg at the time as shameless and depraved. What could possibly be more shameful and depraved than the brutality Dov has just described? At that moment, Gad enters the room and I stare as if seeing him for the first time. It's as if his skin has been peeled back to reveal a hideous thing curled up inside. I turn back to Dov – a man as confused and needy as myself.

"I'll see what I can do, Dov. In the meantime, keep quiet about all of this."

"That won't be hard. I didn't even want to tell you. It was just that… . "

"I know. I'm glad you did, but let's keep it between the two of us for now. I'll talk to Major Shalom about your transfer. I'll think up some reason or other."

"Thank you, sir. I'd really appreciate it."

Dov wipes his face and moves reluctantly back towards his mates. Gad spots me and strolls over.

"What have you been up to, Sam? You should have been with us. Your lads would have enjoyed letting off a bit of steam."

It's as though he knows that I know what he's been up to, and is trying to provoke a reaction. If so, he's disappointed. I find it impossible to confront him with the facts of his crimes. His great talent has always been to champion the popular view, and from that standpoint, subdue dissent. I struggle to keep my tone civil.

"They were so exhausted after everything that's happened today I thought we should stay put until the commissariat caught up with us."

Gad nods as though reassured by my rather feeble excuse.

"Oh, by the way, did you hear that the FIDA offices were burned down? What a piece of luck, eh? The Arabs won't be laughing so much now. Arafat may have flown the coop, but at least there's one less place he and his chickens can hang out."

Again, I feel as if my resolve is being tested.

"Maybe, but there could have been vital evidence lost in the blaze. The place really needed to be gone over with a fine tooth comb."

He stares at me for a moment.

"I never believed for a second we'd find anything of value in that dump. The Arabs may be scum but they're cunning as jackals. Why would they be stockpiling intelligence in a place just waiting to be raided?"

"So, you never actually believed that... ."

"Of course not, and neither did Shalom. All that was just an excuse. We're here to crush their crazy dream of an independent state. Surely you know that! Any fool who thought there might be some sort rapprochement had better think again."

"But there has to be compromise. We can't kill them all!"

"Now you're talking like a conciliator, Sam. Be careful. Anyone who didn't know you better might misinterpret your words."

The implicit threat – the probing challenge – is more to the fore. I feel a powerful urge to have it out with him here and now. I shouldn't allow him to dominate me the way he does everyone else around him. He continues before I can open my mouth.

"Don't you see that any sort of accommodation means an end to everything we believe in? We must be prepared to fight for every inch of ground. Have you forgotten why we are here in Judea and Samaria?" He means, of course, reclaiming the entire extent of ancient Judea. I wonder if there really is a chance that one day we will occupy Lebanon, Syria, Jordan, Iraq and other Middle Eastern countries to win back this land?

"Anyone who resists will have a war on his hands – that includes the Arabs and those godless traitors who call themselves Jews."

"But Sharon… ."

"Sharon knows where his bread is buttered. He doesn't want to concede anything to the Arabs, and he knows we need living space. Why do you think he's always supported the settlement programme? And, of course, the last thing he wants is a civil war. This is just the beginning. We've got to wreck all these fucking refugee camps. That's where the real terrorists are hanging out. You'll see a lot more action soon, mark my words. Weren't you listening to Sharburgh and Rubenstein back at college?" He stares quizzically at me for a moment then smiles. "I need something to eat. Let's talk about this later. It's going to be like old times, I promise. We just need to focus on our job and everything will be fine."

I stand dumbfounded as he walks off and starts bantering with his men. He's seen right through me. All the time he's been assessing my fall from grace. But, if this is true, why is he still willing to humour me? Maybe, in his own egotistical way, he believes he can talk me round – persuade me, not by intimidation but by the force of argument and the power of faith. There is no doubt that his attitude to me has always been at odds with the intolerance he's shown others who have dared cross him.

—⁓—

Gad was right about one thing at least. Our next target is the refugee camps. Shalom has already briefed us on the details of our mission to help end the terrorist menace in Jenin. According to the major, we are likely to be attacked by a citizenry entirely given over to the extermination of Jews. The inhabitants of camps like Jenin, living in dire poverty and forgotten by the world for so many years, have certainly not got much to lose; but can they stand up to the onslaught of helicopters, tanks, bulldozers and crack units on the ground? I doubt it.

It turns out that Arafat was hiding in the *Muqata* compound all the time, but managed to evade capture. God knows how. We really turned the place over. The US have convinced Sharon to leave him be – for the time being at least. Over the past few days images of the beleaguered president, alongside other senior Palestinian politicians, have been beamed around the world. Arabs throughout the Middle East condemn Israel and swear solidarity with their struggling brethren but, as usual, sit on their hands. So much propaganda, so little action, but I suppose they've been crushed too often in the past. I still think that Arafat's expulsion from the region would be a good thing for everyone concerned, and I've no idea why the Americans are so keen to have him stay.

What Gad was saying about civil war in Israel is probably not too far from the truth. If any political party tries to dismantle the settlements, the main ones that is, in Jerusalem and the Territories, there are many in the army who would mutiny. Although the *Haredi* refuse to serve, the most ruthless fighting units are manned by orthodox Jews. Our own battalion recruits exclusively from the Kiryat Arba and Hebron districts. I've never served alongside secular troops, and it's the same for the rest of my squad. If they want extreme measures visited on the enemy, we're the ones they send in.

We're moving out tomorrow. Although I still feel responsible for ensuring the safety and welfare of my men, the old sureties have been swept away. I have no idea what will happen next.

CHAPTER EIGHT

Warsaw: May 1943.

The ghetto is burning. The acrid stench of death hangs heavy in the air.

A savage battle has been raging for over three weeks, and the Germans, unable to prevail by conventional means, are using the weapon of fire to drive the remaining fighters from their underground lairs. To Leo, moving between bunkers in the sulphurous half light, it seems as though everything is being consumed by the flames, leaving behind the bitter ashes of a once pristine world.

He has been assigned the task of evacuating operatives from the ghetto ruins before the Nazi jaws clamp shut. His thoughts are in turmoil as he approaches Mila 18 – ZOB's command bunker. Managing a safe passage out of the ravaged city seems to him an impossible task. And even if they do escape, what then? An alliance with the Polish Free Army partisans roaming the countryside around Warsaw? The prospect worries Leo. However much they may hate the occupier, Polish High Command is, at best, half-hearted in responding to urgent requests from their Jewish brothers-in-arms.

Promises have been made in the past with little to show for any of them.

Stumbling along behind his guide through derelict buildings and piles of rubble, he wonders if anyone will survive the Nazi onslaught. Rumour has it that the enemy is close to locating and destroying Mila 18 – their task made easier by informants prepared to trade their souls. Leo cannot begin to fathom what it would take to tempt a man to betray those few heroes willing to challenge the might of the German military machine. Surely no Jew still believes his life will be spared.

Concern for his sister, who, like the majority of survivors, is hidden in one of the remaining bunkers, overrides all doubts about leading the escape bid. However dubious the outcome might be, Lola must be at his side. That will be his one condition for accepting the mission. He pictures her patiently waiting for him amid the squalor of Nalewki 37 – home since their flat burned to the ground at the beginning of the uprising. Each night, in his dreams, he relives their desperate struggle to escape the fire and smoke – the screams of trapped residents ringing in his ears as he starts out of bed.

He spots a sentry, poised like a ghost in the ghastly light. Leo recognises in him, as with most of his brothers locked in this bitter struggle, a steely determination to resist to the end. No one ever expected to win the battle – survival into a third week proof of the indomitable will of the defenders. When the guns finally fall silent and the flames die back, the world will know that the ghetto Jews refused to die like cattle. As they enter one of the two

concealed tunnels into Mila 18, he feels intensely proud
to be one of the key players in the deadly end game.

Inside, the air is almost impossible to breathe. Although
used to the stench of his home bunker, Leo gags as the
fetid wave breaks over him. People driven from their
former hiding places lie stretched out on the concrete
floor like corpses in a congested morgue. He is quickly
ushered into a side room where three men are bent over
a battered old table. Breathing is a little easier in here,
he guesses because the chamber has its own ventilation
pipe. A torn and discoloured map covers the table's
surface. Freidman is present, having set up the meeting,
and Axel, the sardonic operative who recruited him into
the organisation almost two years ago. The third man
must be the ZOB commander who, despite his youth and
disheveled appearance, makes Leo feel like a boy in the
presence of a worldly-wise parent.

The commander smiles warmly through his fatigue.

"So, you must be Rudolf, the policeman we've all
heard so much about. Welcome, my friend, to our modest
accommodation."

"Thank you, sir. I was surprised when Freidman said
you wanted me to lead the evacuation. I'm not sure what
I have to offer such a mission."

"You underestimate your talents. You have acquired
a reputation for seeing things through to the end, which
is exactly what we need right now. I'll be honest with
you, our job here is almost done, and I am persuaded
that we can create more trouble for the Nazis fighting
alongside our Polish brethren beyond the ghetto. Please
be good enough to cast your eyes over this plan of the

ghetto's sewer system. Unfortunately, it is the only viable escape route available since the Germans redoubled their guard around the perimeter wall. Axel is absolutely certain of this." The latter nods, clearly unwilling to go over old ground. "So, here we are – reduced to wading through the filth our Nazi friends would happily drown us in if they could."

"We've given the bastards good reason to wish us dead."

Freidman's contribution produces one of his chief's rare but brilliant smiles.

"The idea of an agreeable posting to Warsaw has certainly become somewhat tarnished of late."

Leo notices that his friend's despair – so apparent in the pre-uprising days – has been replaced by something akin to elation. The battle for the ghetto has clearly revived his spirits.

"But back to business, gentlemen. Time is short."

The commander runs his right index finger along a line on the map, marking an offshoot from one of the main sewage pipes.

"This auxiliary duct will take you a good distance into the *Aryan side*. We are hoping that the Nazis will have overlooked it, or believe it too small for people to use. It will be a tight squeeze!" He casts a long, calculating glance at Leo. "We have moved people through sewage tunnels before, of course, but this time it will be more difficult. Not only the limited space, and the fumes, but the distance involved – over a kilometre, if the scale of the map is correct."

There is a lengthier silence as everyone contemplates such a terrible journey. Leo wonders if he will be able to withstand the choking claustrophobia of the pipe. Not only will he be expected to subdue his own fears, but be able to coax his reluctant companions through the ordeal. The nuts and bolts of such a mission may keep him focused, but nothing is certain.

"I'm not ordering you to do this, Rudolf "I ask you to take charge only because I think you are the best man for the job."

He finds himself replying automatically, his voice sounding detached and strained as if issuing from the throat of some poor fool agreeing to his own suicide.

"I'm honoured that you think I'm up to the task, sir."

"We know you will not let us down."

The commander's total confidence allows him to believe, for the first time, that he might actually possess the qualities to see such a mission through to its end.

—⁓—

"So grandfather, did you get the people out? Did the Germans find the bunker? Did Mordecai and the rest manage to escape in time?"

"Hold on, hold on! One question at a time, Sam. Give an old man a chance!"

While aware that many of his countrymen are hooked on the idea of beating the odds – of snatching victory from the jaws of defeat – Leo yearns to spare his grandson the cruel disdain arising from such hubris. Unlike many of his generation, charred by the Shoah crucible, he has retained a surprising degree of equanimity. Revealing the worst so that sanity might prevail in the future, has been a guiding principle throughout his life. He is determined that Sam will one day be able to separate fact from fiction – pity from pride. Surely mankind cannot be doomed to repeat all of its mistakes forever. If history is to be of any use at all, it must allow people to make headway instead of blundering back along false trails.

—⁓—

The sewer is worse than anything Leo could have imagined. The rank fumes alone threaten to end the mission before it has properly begun. He strives to focus on a positive end to the drag through toxic darkness. Trucks have been promised to carry them out of Warsaw, but he finds it hard to believe that the transport will actually make it to the rendezvous point. If he and his comrades are not quickly plucked from the perilous streets on the *Aryan side*, capture, torture and death will swiftly follow.

He suppresses whatever personal doubts he has and encourages his people on. More should have been here but an ambush sprung by the Nazis on Mila 18, a mere twenty-four hours after his nocturnal visit, ended in the death of most of those remaining in the command bunker, including the ZOB commander and his most trusted lieutenants. A coup for the German commander, Jurgen Stroop, fearful of censure from his masters in Berlin, a disaster for the fighters reliant on their chief's courage and brilliant tactical skills. Among the dead, Axel, suffocated by gas inserted through holes drilled into the bunker's roof; and Freidman, gunned down while defending one of the two entrances. How the commander died, Leo has no idea, but his passing signals the end of meaningful resistance in the ghetto. Maybe he never had any real intention of escaping. Meanwhile, the Germans mop up, the ghetto smoulders, and a few survivors flee to fight another day.

It's not only the Nazis they have to worry about when they surface. Many Poles would betray them in a heartbeat. How can he ever forget or forgive the crowds cheering wildly on the *Aryan side* as Jews leapt to their deaths from burning buildings on the edge of the ghetto? Or, in final desperation, threw their children out of top-floor windows. How could people have stooped to this – more debased than any Coliseum crowd? And teams of professional blackmailers hunting Jewish escapees, happy to fleece wretched families before betraying them to the Nazis. He struggles to hold onto the conviction that most Poles are innocent of such depravity and are equal victims of Nazi brutality.

Leo is suddenly jolted out of his reverie. Behind him, someone has slipped and fallen. Frantic yells and splashing ensue. They are passing below a manhole cover, and Leo is only too aware that the racket may be audible at street level. He turns and hisses a warning. Everyone freezes and the furore instantly stops. Only the sound of laboured breathing betrays the presence of any living being.

The sounds of another world filter down into hell: the excited bark of a dog, and the high-pitched yelling of children as a game threatens to get out of hand. A shaft of sunlight snuffs out and relights as a pedestrian strolls by. The trappings of an existence all but forgotten by the huddled Jews. Will they ever know such bliss again? Leo, for one, has pledged that if by some miracle he is returned to that impossible dimension of laughter and light, he will never again take anything for granted – not the smallest aspect of living or the most insignificant detail of routine. He wonders if his sister, standing motionless behind him, is turning over the same thoughts in her mind. Contemplating her passive misery brings tears to his red-rimmed eyes.

He motions his flock forward. The fumes seem to intensify, as if gathering for a final assault. He has no doubt everyone is reaching exhaustion point – especially the two weakened survivors from Mila 18. It is impossible to predict how much longer they can hold out. At that very moment, someone launches into a terrible fit of coughing, cut short as if by a knife slash to the throat. Muttered words, passed up the line, confirm that for one of their number the struggle is over. Leo reluctantly orders the body to be left where it is. The preservation of the living is his only priority.

An hour later, after what seems like an eternity of wading through the stifling darkness, the survivors arrive at the rendezvous point. He calculates it must be late afternoon with the trucks unlikely to appear before nightfall, and prays that his comrade, Simcha – liaison officer between ZOB and the Polish Free Army – has managed to make the necessary arrangements. If not, all their efforts will have been in vain. Even if rescue does arrive, the long wait is not going to improve the situation. In his heart of hearts, he believes they are unlikely to make it, and has already devised a plan to save Lola. Cupping both hands round her ear, he rapidly explains what he has in mind. She tears herself away and turns to face him, her expression angry and contemptuous. Grabbing his head, she pulls it down to her level, her hissing breath searing his eardrum.

"Do you really believe that I'd leave without the others? And you! You should be ashamed of yourself! You are responsible for everyone here, not just me. Either we all get out together, or we all perish here together."

Lola's fierce rejection shocks him, but, of course, she is right. It can never be every man for himself in a situation like this. The commander trusted him to see things through to the end, whatever that end might be. What could he have been thinking? He thanks God for his sister's good sense.

Simcha! Everything now depends on him. The afternoon and evening seem to stretch out to infinity as the fugitives crouch, praying for the moment they can crawl forth from this putrid hole. At least while moving, the enormous effort of placing one foot in front of another blotted out less immediate concerns. But now the chill, the stench and a terrible thirst, threaten to overwhelm their waning resources. It has not been possible to carry many supplies and the flasks of clean water are nearly empty. Leo realises, too late, that he should have insisted on stricter rationing from the outset.

The concourse of the world above continues unabated as the pleasant May evening brings locals out onto the streets. This time, the mutter of conversation and the clinking of glasses suggests they are close to a café. The torture of food, and particularly drink, so near and yet so far away, gnaws at them hour after weary hour. Leo fights to control the crazy urge to throw open the manhole cover and snatch what they need at gunpoint. His fingers stray again and again to his holster strap. He calms himself by imagining German soldiers patrolling the streets, or even sitting at the café's tables. One pistol against sub-machine guns and grenades is not good odds. Instead, he tries to focus on contingency plans in case the trucks do not arrive. If there is no word from Simcha by midnight, they will emerge and try to quit the city by foot. Their chances are poor, he knows, but anything is better than perishing in the sewer. If he waits too long, most of his companions will be too sick to walk.

As the evening deepens into night, they hear the tables dragged inside, and raised voices and laughter as customers take their leave and head home. Eventually, the street is silent. Strain as he might, he can hear nothing to help him work out what's going on above ground, and considers taking a look for himself.

Suddenly, a tapping on the cover and an urgent voice.

"It's Simcha. Is anyone there?"

A sense of relief floods over him; at least they are not alone.

"Thank God! It's Rudolf. Are the trucks here yet?"

"They're on their way, but with so many checkpoints, I can't say for certain when they will arrive. You'll have to stay put for the time being. German patrols are everywhere. I had to bluff my way through the curfew a few minutes ago."

"We've got to get out of here – soon!"

"I know, but you'll never make it without the trucks. I'd better go before somebody spots me talking to this manhole cover."

The sharp tap of Simcha's shoes on the cobbles grows fainter until the sound disappears. Leo longs to leap out and join him, but remembers Lola's censure. His fate is bound up with that of his comrades. He knows that if anyone can get them out it will be Simcha. His blond good looks and bluff manner have served ZOB well on the *Aryan side*. For years he's fooled Germans and Poles alike, hence the commander's decision to permanently base him over the wall. In his time, he's passed as a Nazi officer, a Polish policeman and a professional blackmailer. It's not only his appearance and personality, but his amazing acting skills that have seen him through. If he really has persuaded the Polish Free Army to provide transport to save a few miserable Jewish hides, then his talents are as important to the cause as ever.

Leo passes on the message of hope. Help is on its way; only a few minutes longer to wait. He prays that the news will buoy them all up for a last stand against growing enervation and despair.

Lola is fighting to remain upright. For the past hour, she has lost all feeling below her knees, and the desire to sink into oblivion is overwhelming. Even the prospect of sitting in sewage up to her neck seems more appealing than standing bent over for one more second. Three others have already succumbed to fatigue, and are being propped up by those still strong enough to take the strain.

The sudden roar of approaching engines changes everything. The prospect of imminent escape galvanises the survivors into action. They push frantically towards the manhole cover. Leo thrusts people back, knowing that panic could wreck everything on the cusp of success. While desperate to believe that the lorries revving in the street above are their passport to freedom, he cannot ignore the fact that they could just as easily be German troop carriers. Everyone is crowded together and a well-placed grenade would catch them all in its lethal spray. He experiences the familiar tug of helplessness that has threatened to topple his resolve for so long now.

The sound of Simcha's voice barking out orders releases a dam of stress. The relief is orgasmic.

The reverberating clank of the heavy metal disc, torn from the ground and crashing onto the cobbles, is music to Leo's ears. Stars shimmer overhead, and the cool breeze on his cheek is sublime after the acridity of the duct.

Simcha peers down.

"We must move quickly. The drivers will wait for a few minutes only."

He sounds on the edge of panic; the prospect of careering through streets, filled with Nazis, must be unnerving him.

With the last of his strength, Leo pushes everyone up through the aperture. Finally, Simcha grasps his arm and hauls him out. On the street, people flap around like stranded fish as they try to stand up on their numb legs. The Polish Free Army rescue squad, initially reluctant to touch the stinking survivors, quickly overcome their squeamishness and bundle them into the back of the waiting trucks. Leo feels hard, round objects slamming onto his back as someone upends sacks of mouldy potatoes over them. The weight gradually forces him down until he can barely breathe. The lorry lurches forward and they are on the move. He prays that the soldiers manning the checkpoints will be reluctant to search the reeking freight. Someone shifts restlessly beside him. If anyone is left alive at the end of this dreadful journey, it will be nothing short of a miracle.

All of a sudden they come to a shuddering halt. Maybe the dreaded roadblock. Once again, Leo grasps the butt of his trusty pistol. With a full chamber, he can do considerable damage. He imagines himself erupting out of the vegetable blanket, gun blazing. Almost immediately they are on the move again. Either they've been waved through without the usual search, or the stop was nothing to do with the Germans.

Minutes later, they stop for a second time. This time the engine is switched off. Escaping the city was never going to be so easy. Leo hears the driver insist that both vehicles are carrying a consignment of vegetables urgently needed in Plock – a suburb only a few miles beyond the city boundaries. The tailgate is unbolted and drops with a loud clang as someone climbs on board. The point of a bayonet suddenly scrapes along the floor, mere centimetres from his neck. It is all he can do to remain still. Two hands grasp a batch of potatoes near his arm, and a German voice curses as the fingers crush the rotting pulp. A few more harsh words, and the tailgate slams shut. He wonders if Lola is in this vehicle or the other. Are both lorries being searched? It's impossible to tell.

The engine roars back into life, and the lurching, swaying journey continues. Finally, they slow down. Excited voices and laughter reassure him they are close to their destination and safety. The lorry clunks through its gears, and slowly reverses before stopping. The full effect of mental and physical exhaustion suddenly hits him, and he is barely able to crawl out of the truck. Glancing around, he sees they are inside a large, gloomy warehouse. He can make out four other vehicles, and packed shelves reaching up to the ceiling.

His companions, now huddled together near the entrance, are too tired to be afraid, or even curious. Like Leo, they are covered in two layers of grime: the saturated sewer filth and fragments of rotten potato adhering to their sodden garments. He spots Lola sitting on the floor, head bowed and hands splayed over her face. He staggers over and slumps down beside her. She looks up, the ghost of a smile playing over her bitten lips.

"Well, we actually made it. You got us out, Leo."

He smiles in turn.

"I didn't do so very much. Everyone just kept going."

"Take some credit, brother! We would never have made it without your encouragement."

"Do you think they'll give us something to drink?"

"Simcha's trying to negotiate food and water for us. I heard him talking to the Polish driver. I think they're a decent bunch. Not like the others we've encountered." Lola stops, unwilling to continue. When she resumes, it's as if she's struggling to believe what has happened. "Do you know, I actually fell asleep during the drive here. Even when we were being searched, I couldn't have moved even if I'd wanted to."

"I nearly got stabbed. A bayonet just missed my throat."

"They'll not get you as easily as that! God has other plans for you, I think."

"I'm not sure where God fits into any of this."

At that moment, Simcha reappears. His face has lost its strained look and is wreathed in smiles. He grasps Leo's hand.

"I'm glad you're okay. It was touch and go at that checkpoint. Covering you all with potatoes was a great idea. You've got the Polish CO to thank for that. He reckoned the Nazis wouldn't want to get their hands dirty."

Lola smiles wearily.

"Maybe they were also concerned about what's going on in the ghetto."

"You're right. Their officer kept glancing up at the red glow in the sky. He seemed pretty tense. We've certainly given them something to think about." Simcha pauses for a moment. "A few more hours and we might have rescued the commander and his staff. A squad of volunteers was on its way through the sewers when word arrived that the Nazis had... ."

"There's no point in thinking about that now," Leo hastily intervenes. "He wanted as many out as possible. That's why we're here. He said himself, we should continue the fight after he was gone. He probably never had any intention of leaving his post."

Simcha frowns and sighs.

"I don't suppose we'll ever really know." He smiles again, his handsome face lit up as though the Germans had just offered him their unconditional surrender. "You're going to get some rations and new clothes.

The major says he can use everyone to fight the Nazis. He told me it's only a matter of time before the Poles raise hell in Warsaw. We may get the opportunity to die like heroes before the end."

Leo nods.

"That's all we can ask. If Poles and Jews are able to fight alongside each other for the common good then something positive may come out of all this yet."

—ɯ—

Aware of the effort involved in unearthing such painful memories, Sam wonders, not for the first time, why his grandfather is so determined to keep going. Although eager to miss nothing, he knows his questions often irritate, so he tries hard to sit still and listen. He's not sure what he's supposed to take from it all. If not the heroism of the ghetto fighters, then what? Father has often told him that Leo is a ghetto hero – his struggle against the Nazis an example for everyone to follow – yet he finds it hard to remain civil in the old man's presence. Grandfather, for his part, clams up when Benny comes anywhere near. On religion there is certainly no meeting of minds. Knowing how bitterly critical his father is of all things secular, this might account for their mutual dislike.

Leo's amused voice returns him instantly to the present.

"Where were you, Sam? I hope I'm not boring you too much!"

"No, no. I was just thinking about how lucky you and Auntie Lola were to escape from the ghetto."

Leo nods appreciatively, knowing that his grandson's lie is motivated by good intentions, even if the real reason for his lapse in concentration is something else entirely.

He decides not to pursue the matter. If the boy is troubled, the reason will surface soon enough.

"Fortune certainly smiled on us that day, and continued to favour us during the following months. Simcha was right. The Poles led us deep into the forest – fed and armed us. The weather was good and camping out was wonderful: fresh air, clean water and sleeping under the stars. We were expected to kill Germans, of course, and I knew it could only be a matter of time before we were captured and shot ourselves, but it seemed worth it to all of us. We heard that the Nazis had razed the entire ghetto, rounded up the few remaining survivors and shipped them to Treblinka. That, of course, only made us more determined to die fighting." Leo shifts restlessly against his pillows before continuing. "Simcha was killed a few days after our escape. He was shot by a group of partisans who claimed he was a Nazi spy. We knew it was a damned lie, but there was nothing we could do about it. What did one man's death matter anyway, especially another Jew's?" Sam is struck by the bitterness in his grandfather's voice. He also notices the familiar wince of pain before the story resumes. "I became an elite sniper. Our Polish hosts taught us all how to handle our rifles, but I apparently showed particular aptitude. I was taken deep into the forest to try out with proper sights, and I hit everything I aimed at."

Leo smiles bleakly, allowing his memory to stalk the forest glades where he hunted the enemy during the long, hot summer months following the ghetto's destruction.

—※—

Leo is lying so still a hind emerges into open ground and starts to nibble on a tussock of sweet grass. Sunlight bathes the meadow, brightening even the thick stands of encircling spruce.

The scene is deceptively tranquil. A squad of German soldiers is rapidly approaching the glade where the partisan snipers lie concealed. Soldiers might pass as close to him as the deer, oblivious to their mortal danger. Even his rifle's stock and long barrel are wrapped with strips of green cloth. The camouflage is perfect. The deer suddenly lifts her head and is gone. In response, his right index finger gently caresses the trigger.

He detects furtive movement. The Germans know the glade ahead spells danger – their fear undiminished by the medley of birdsong and sunlight. A series of terse hand signals, and four men – two at each end of the extended line – sink onto their stomachs and elbow crawl over the layer of dry pine needles. With a clear view of the open ground, they settle down to provide covering fire for their comrades. The others, crouching low, move to the very edge of the forest then spread out – twenty feet between each man. Slowly, tentatively, they abandon the safety of the trees and begin their slow sweep.

A shot suddenly rings out, followed by four more. Five men are dead even before they hit the ground. Those meant to be covering the squad have no idea where the shots have come from, and return fire in an entirely haphazard fashion. The survivors crash back into the safety of the forest, gather themselves together, and beat a hasty retreat. The squad leader is one of the casualties, and, deprived of his leadership, the men have no stomach for further fighting. Liquidating partisans is proving increasingly costly. Gone are the days when they were simply required to round up terrified civilians, shoot them through the head, and shovel their corpses into shallow graves. Five Germans are stiffening in the glade without the capture or execution of a single 'bandit'.

Minutes later, a low whistle brings five patches of ground to life. The snipers shake off remnants of grass and moss, swing their rifles over their shoulders and vanish back into the trees.

CHAPTER NINE

Jenin: April 2002

"Operation Defensive Shield" has been raging in Jenin
for over a week. The Arabs are fiercely resisting our
attempts to subdue their ramshackle refugee camp.
Reservist units of more than a thousand infantrymen,
supported by squadrons of Merkava tanks and Cobra
helicopters, were expected to mop up within a few
days, but nothing has gone according to plan. So far,
twenty-three of our soldiers have died – thirteen lured
into a well-organised ambush late last night. Word has it
that specialised bulldozing equipment has been ordered
in to flatten the town centre.

Most of the men remain convinced that if we can crack
this nut, mission will have been accomplished. It's
pretty clear to me, however, that we cannot win by
conventional means. Not until the Arabs are removed
or eliminated will the situation ever be resolved. But
surely only psychopaths or zealots would be willing to
consider such ethnic cleansing. Unfortunately, messianic
pioneers from Judea and Samaria, fired up by their
hatred of Arabs and armed with an absolute certainty
in the imminence of *Redemption*, fall into both of these

camps. I find it hard to believe that, until recently, I counted myself a member of this master race of God's chosen.

Trying to keep the company log up-to-date, I find myself increasingly distracted by Corporal Ben-Hagai's aggravating monologue next door. With only a flimsy canvas wall separating my quarters from the NCO's mess, I cannot help but hear every word. I remember very well the day he first spoke up at military college; the day of my humiliation and redemption. Unlike poor Jeff Schiff, he fitted right in, quickly becoming one of Gad's most brutal henchmen.

"At last we've got a man at the helm who gets the job done. My father was with Sharon in Beirut. What happened in the Sabra and Shatilla camps was... ."

A voice I don't recognise interrupts him. The tone is dry and acerbic.

"What happened in Beirut was a disaster! Sharon handed our enemies a stick to beat us with."

"So what if he did! It hasn't done them much good. The important thing is that he showed these fucking *towel heads* we meant business. They won't forget him in a hurry, that's for sure."

I sigh and lay my pen down, waiting for yet another diatribe – the sort of *Kach Party* special so beloved in Kiryat Arba.

"Whether they forget or don't forget him is irrelevant. I haven't seen any terrorist down on his hands and knees recently pleading to be saved from Ariel Sharon. He's so fucking fat, he can't see what he's pissing out of anymore!"

A subdued ripple of laughter suggests that even if the men are amused by such irreverence, they are hoping the company rabbi isn't lurking nearby. Use of such profane language would certainly engender a savage rebuke. Ben-Hagai ignores the taunt and ploughs on, apparently indifferent to the prospect of rabbinical disapproval.

"Send in the air force and bomb them all to fuck, that's what I say."

"Great idea!" The newcomer again. "Then the world would bust us wide open. If it was just a matter of killing Arabs then fine, but it isn't. We need to keep our allies sweet."

Just when I thought I had discovered a moderate in the ranks, the carpet is pulled from under me. This man is clearly a lot smarter than Ben-Hagai, who, like so many others in the unit, finds it impossible to conceal his hatred of *Goys* beneath a cloak of reason. As for Sharon – of all the leaders we've been cursed with over the past ten years, he is by far the worst. The man who might have achieved a diplomatic solution is long since dead and buried. As if peering into someone else's warped memories, I recall my delight when news of Rabin's assassination hit the press. The celebratory mood persisted in Kiryat Arba and Hebron for weeks afterwards.

The corporal is unwilling to concede the point. He's just too stupid and stubborn to back down.

"Our so-called allies won't save us from suicide bombers. Fuck America, and the rest of them! And fuck public relations!"

His adversary starts to laugh, his scathing tone now replaced by outright derision.

"What the hell are you talking about, man? Bush is so worked up by his war on terror, he's happy to support us in most of the things we're doing – or at least turn a blind eye, which amounts to the same thing in the end. That allows us to get on with the job of killing terrorists, and piling on the propaganda. Reminding the world about Sabra and Shatilla isn't going to help anybody."

Ben-Hagai grunts and slumps into silence. Pounding fists, not mental acuity, are the corporal's speciality.

I must find out who the unknown speaker is. He sounds so much more plausible than the usual run of barrack-room lawyers. As luck has it, I emerge from my quarters at exactly the same moment Rabbi Kimmerling enters the mess. We nod, but I can see suspicion glinting in his pale blue eyes. I'm sure he senses my unspoken heresy. I wonder again what the hell I'm doing here. The answer is clear, if I'm being brutally honest with myself. My moral cowardice is perhaps the worst part of the whole, depressing business.

Kimmerling's appearance ends the debate, and the mess tent empties in anticipation of afternoon prayers. I watch as the men pass by. Only one soldier, sporting sergeant's stripes, is unknown to me. He must be the mystery speaker – a recent addition to Gad's squad, by the sounds of it. He'll fit in very nicely.

I return to quarters and slump behind my desk. What the hell am I going to do? Things can't go on like this. I wonder what scares me the most: continuing along the same, old road, working cheek by jowl with fanatics like Gad, or returning home to face disgrace and shame. As if conjured by my thoughts, Gad sticks his head round the tent flap. Since our conversation a week ago, we've hardly spoken. On the surface little appears to have changed, but I'm sure he's on to me and watching for signs of weakness or indecision.

"Hi Sam. Taking it easy I see. Remember what they used to say back at school about the devil finding work for idle hands." He laughs, but the barb strikes home. "Are your father and mother well?"

The ostensibly polite enquiry is probably a veiled reference to the means by which I distracted him from torturing civilians back in Ramallah. He's most likely figured out by now what lay behind my impassioned appeal to his fighting spirit. I decide to act the innocent and see where it takes me.

"They're fine. Father and Mr Dayane drove up to Jerusalem for a meeting last weekend. It only took them half an hour on the new highway."

Even at this dangerous juncture, I can't help thinking about the roadblocks and delays experienced by most Arabs in the Territories. Barred from the newly constructed trunk road linking the bulk of settlements with Jerusalem, their journey can take several hours – sometimes half the day if there has been an 'incident' or the roads are busy. And then to be further impeded by arrogant young men pushing guns in their faces. It's extraordinary how these sorts of things have been preying on my mind lately when most of my countrymen couldn't give a damn.

"Good, good." Gad responds in a flat voice. He abruptly changes tack. "Tonight is our last chance to get things right. The operation so far has been a bloody shambles."

He's as slippery as an eel. Just when you think you've managed to head him off, he's probing for fresh weaknesses. I struggle to keep my cool.

"It has dragged on a bit, but there's still time to... ."

"Mark my words, it's now or never. We should have flattened the place days ago. Talk about lions led by donkeys!"

He's definitely probing to see if our head-to-head last week has shored up my crumbling will. I decide to sidestep the challenge and enquire about his new NCO.

"You mean, Sergeant Tiran? He used to be in a special ops unit, trained in targeted assassinations. A man of action with a brain in his skull. When his transfer application came through, I jumped at the chance of getting him. Why do you ask?"

I explain the altercation between Tiran and Ben-Hagai. Gad looks thoughtful for a moment. "Ben-Hagai's a fool. A good man in a fight, for sure, but a fool, nonetheless. I'll talk to him. You never know who might have been listening in." He smiles his feral smile and glances at his watch. "I'd better go. There's still a lot to do before the off."

I heave a sigh of relief when he's gone. Every encounter with him these days makes me uneasy. His reaction to Ben-Hagai was interesting though. I'm reminded how insightful he can be.

—⁂—

A moonless night, pitch dark on the outskirts of town. Not a solitary light flickering among the piles of jagged breeze block. The sector has taken a terrific pounding over the past few days, and the defenders are gone – either dead or withdrawn to new positions. But tonight, Jenin's beating heart is the target; refugee citizens and militia alike, as yet unaware of their approaching nemesis.

In the east, a distant, deep vibration begins, muted at first, but growing in intensity. Within seconds the night sky is alive with unseen, whirring blades. Nothing moves on the ground as if every living thing is frozen in anticipation of imminent ruin. Rapid, continuous explosions rend the curtain of the night to shreds. A helicopter, suddenly illuminated in the lurid glare, swings violently away and is lost in a plume of black smoke. The volume of destruction rises to a crackling crescendo. Gad's prediction is close to the mark – tonight's onslaught clearly intended to end the protracted assault.

Soon the beat of the helicopters is replaced by the snarl of bulldozers, and the high-pitched whine of megaphones as civilians are ordered out of their homes in the path of advancing units.

We proceed cautiously into a warren of narrow alleyways on high alert for concealed booby traps. The fanaticism of our enemies is demonstrated by the fact that these same crude weapons are as likely to kill or maim their own people. Again, I marvel at the hatred we've stirred up in the hearts of local people, clearly willing to take their chances in the hope that as many of our soldiers as possible will be blown to pieces.

Up ahead, an armoured D9 is engaged in obliterating a row of houses. The driver's orders must be to clear a way for tanks and soldiers. A solitary, white-clad figure suddenly leaps into the path of the advancing bulldozer and begins a furious, arm-thrashing dance. The din of the engine and falling rubble masks the yells of this grotesque puppet, making it impossible to hear whether he's raining down curses on the aggressor or pleading for the lives of his family, perhaps cowering inside the last breeze block house left standing. At the climax of his wild extravaganza, the Arab freezes as though gripped by a sudden, terrible realisation. He drops slowly to his knees and bows his head. I wonder for a moment if he's praying, then, in the glare of bright headlamps, a crimson flower unfurls on the back of his robe. The vision is abruptly terminated as the vehicle veers away, its massive blade slicing through the gable wall. We sprint back up the alley to avoid the choking pall of dust.

Clear of the demolition, Gad stops, unfolds a grubby map and waves me forward. He no doubt wishes to consult over our current position. Our mission, to locate and destroy a terrorist bunker, believed to be manufacturing APDs, may fail if we lose more valuable time. The last thing we need right now is to stray off course in the bewildering maze of alleyways criss-crossing the centre of the refugee camp. We agree on a route which will hopefully avoid bulldozers and trigger-happy snipers. The shabby buildings, crowding close around us, shudder as shells explode up ahead. Survival depends on total concentration and rapid response. Try as I might, however, my unease persists. Everything is fuzzy and out of kilter. The longer I work alongside madmen like Gad and Shalom, the more apprehensive I feel.

Grandfather's sad face suddenly materialises out of the darkness. These unpredictable visitations have become more frequent of late. I stumble and almost fall. A soldier, walking close behind, grasps my arm; the grip of his powerful fingers feels more like a warning than a support.

The alley widens out a little and a fetid stench fills the air. There is obviously no garbage disposal or drainage of any kind in this quarter with untreated sewage swilling around our feet. The place reeks of misery and despair. Stereotypes of Arab animals rolling in their own filth, peddled so readily by my colleagues, owe their existence to places like this. Most of the refugees, stripped off their rights and property, have been rotting here for forty years or more.

Screaming up ahead heralds yet another crisis. A group of civilians has been dragged out onto the street. What the hell is going on? Has Gad finally taken leave of his senses? I can scarcely believe that he has so recklessly thrown caution to the wind. Three men, undressed down to their discoloured underwear, are being paraded in front of the scoffing soldiers. A huddle of female relatives avert their eyes, anxious to spare their menfolk further shame. One old woman shrieks as though she's being forced to dance on hot coals. My first test has come more quickly than I bargained for. Gad turns to greet me, his eyes shining with dangerous excitement. He shouts to make himself heard over the din.

"We can make use of these scum as shields. Maybe their snipers will think twice before shooting at us. What do you think?"

I know what I think, but what can I say? At a briefing, earlier in the day, Shalom authorised the use of human shields. Despite the glaring inappropriateness of employing them under present circumstances, Gad just can't resist the urge to persecute any Arab unfortunate enough to stumble across his path. Why has it taken me so long to appreciate the toxicity of the brew distilled in the Territories? Whatever the reason, the antidote is now coursing through my veins. I know without any shadow of a doubt, however, that any hint of criticism at this highly charged moment will only serve to confirm Gad's suspicion that I've lost my way. It's possible that even in this most dangerous of situations, he's testing my resolve. Sick at heart, I feel the moral high ground slipping away from under my feet.

"Maybe we should let these men put their clothes back on. We don't want to antagonise enemy snipers more than we have to."

The sop, suggested to make me feel a little better, is surprisingly accepted.

"You're right! I only made them strip to give that old bitch something to really howl about." He turns to the three prisoners shivering nearby. "Get your rags back on. You're coming with us. And, sergeant, bring that young ruffian along as well. By the looks of him, he's already graduated from suicide bombing school."

Tiran wrenches a lad of around seven away from his frantic mother. Wriggling free, he races off with the sergeant in hot pursuit. I suddenly spot what looks like a brown toolbox jammed inside a doorway and yell a warning. Too late – the wire is tripped and a shattering explosion tosses both bodies into the middle of the street. We stand, Arab and Jew alike, stunned by the swift brutality of death.

Gad, first to recover, draws his pistol and aims it at the knot of cowering Arabs. What's he going to do now? The question remains unanswered. A tiny cloud of dust spurts from the wall behind his head, followed by the crack of the rifle shot. We hit the ground. The enemy sniper is probably positioned behind the dome of a dilapidated mosque, a hundred metres or so ahead of us. Only good luck and remarkably poor marksmanship have saved Gad's life. Bullets whine and ricochet as several more enemy militia target our position. We provide covering fire for our machine gun crew as they rush to access the nearest stairway. Our orders to move quickly and quietly through the town, concentrating on the task at hand, have struck the rocks of racial fanaticism.

Renewed gunfire crackles over our heads. An Arab leaps from the roof and is shot several times as he attempts to rise. Seconds later, our machine gun, now positioned on the roof, opens up, concentrating its considerable fire power on the mosque; crumbling parapets and balustrades disintegrate under the lethal hail.

As the fusillade subsides, we struggle to get back on track. The Arab militiamen are either dead or fled. Four soldiers are ordered to return Sergeant Tiran's corpse to base. Everyone is subdued by the tragic turn of events, but I know how quickly this mood could convert to rage. Fortunately, the hostages have escaped in the chaos of the firefight, and there's no talk of replacing them. Progress is even slower in anticipation of another ambush. I inwardly curse Gad's blind foolishness.

A few hundred metres further on we arrive at an unmarked junction. Jenin is defeating all our attempts to chart its bewildering intricacies. We check our position and continue in the most promising direction.

Just when I think things can't get any worse, we come upon a tank completely blocking our new route. How the thing managed to force its way up such a narrow street, God alone knows. As it lurches forward, the armoured flanks scream in protest as they gouge the walls on either side. There seems little chance that the people living in this sector will have had time to evacuate their homes. The reservists appear to have completely withdrawn, leaving mechanised units to root out 'the bad guys'. Every commander in the task force must have been instructed to keep casualties to a minimum because of the negative effect the high death toll has been having on public support for the operation.

As the tank fights clear of the street, a door ahead of us opens and an elderly man in a wheelchair is pushed out. He's wrapped in a white sheet – probably hauled off someone's bed. At first I find it hard to believe the evidence of my own eyes. It's as if some feeble emissary has been dispatched to the very doors of hell itself to plead for the eternally damned. Perhaps his relatives believe that the sight of a helpless old cripple may wring any remaining drops of compassion from the stony hearts of the occupier. If so, their optimism is ill-founded. Through the general din, I hear the desperation in the old man's voice as he beseeches us to spare the homes of his family and neighbours. He is speaking in fluent Hebrew, perhaps another reason for his selection as spokesman. His clasped hands, held out in supplication, complete the vision of hopeless valour struggling to gain mastery over fear. The situation is further complicated when yet another bulldozer crashes through the wall of an intersecting block. In a bizarre twist, a flag, hanging from its dusty cabin, sports the crest of the Beitar Jerusalem football team. Does the driver actually perceive some link between the success of his team and the destruction of the refugee camp?

The tank is returning, or another is arriving – it's impossible to tell. Again, I wince at the scream of tortured metal as it roars towards us. Before I realise what I'm doing, I leap into its path, screaming at the top of my voice and waving my hands in the air. The old man, silent now, stares at me blankly – his eyes purged of emotion. His tattered head towel has fallen away and is straggling down his left shoulder. At the last second, I decide to throw myself at the wheelchair in the hope of knocking it out of the way. Strong arms suddenly wrap themselves round my chest, holding me rigid. Struggling to break free, I fall backwards through an open door, landing heavily on whoever is attempting to save my life. From a horizontal position, I see the chair and its occupant hauled under the tank's left track and torn along its entire length. Shaking off my rescuer, I rush out onto the street. The tank has come face to face with the bulldozer. The commander is out on the turret shouting something to the driver. Gad raises his arms and turns both his thumbs upwards in a triumphant gesture. He applauds, exhorting the men to do the same. The hellish scene imprints itself forever on my mind: Gad's grinning face, bright yellow in the blaze of headlamps, the cheering, clapping soldiers, the menacing bulk of the stationary vehicles, and, finally, the wheelchair ironed flat as if lifted from some children's cartoon. The old cripple, who dared confront the madness sweeping through his home town, must still be wedged beneath the tank.

There's surely no going back now! Gad has witnessed my futile attempt at rescue and will know what motivated it. For my part, I experience intense hatred for those who have poisoned our lives to the extent that we accept what has happened here as heroic. In a moment of blinding epiphany, I see father for what he is – a coward, concealing his fear behind a smokescreen of righteous bluster; and Gad's father, using his faith as justification for numerous acts of violence against the weak and innocent. We boys are the product of years of relentless brainwashing. Questions boil over in my mind. How could I ever have accepted such a vile cocktail of lies? Why did mother agree to move to Kiryat Arba after her father's death? How can love possibly be so blind? I promise myself that if I get out of here alive, I will expose religious fascism for what it is. Nothing can ever justify this slaughter!

Gad is approaching. I ready myself for the inevitable showdown, even though I know that this is neither the time nor place for such a thing. The concern in his voice takes me completely by surprise.

"Are you all right, Sam? Someone said you'd tripped and almost fallen in front of the tank."

"I... ."

"Lucky Dov Harel was there to catch you."

In a flash, I understand two things. Firstly, Gad appears not to have witnessed what happened – those who did, apparently disinclined to expose my folly. And secondly, although everything revealed to me moments earlier remains true, I feel vastly relieved to be let off the hook. Perhaps moral cowardice runs in the male side of my family. The fact that Dov saved my life slowly percolates through the mental turmoil.

"I didn't realise it was Dov who pulled me clear."

"He's a good man in a tight spot."

"I must thank him. Where is he?"

"Save it for later. We've got to organise our withdrawal from this sector."

"What do you mean?"

"Shalom radioed through. Apparently, our target sustained a direct hit. Like everything else these rats build, their so-called impregnable bunker collapsed on their heads. No survivors, he said. Pity really, but it looks like the bloody reservists are going to get all the glory." He suddenly laughs out loud. "That D9 driver was something else though! Maybe we should request a transfer to his unit. What do you think?"

Again, the feral smile and the covert challenge. Despite everything just said, I feel like a marked man.

It's all over. The city centre – an area of about three and a half thousand square metres – has been virtually levelled. There must be dozens of Arabs buried, dead or alive, beneath the debris of their own homes. Journalists, first aid organisations, and the UN, all so far denied access, are clamouring to get a look. The number of civilian casualties fluctuates wildly according to who you listen to.

I hear a light footfall outside my quarters, followed by a discreet cough. Dov has arrived at last. I was expecting him well over an hour ago. It was he who wanted to meet after our return from the aborted mission. I call out somewhat impatiently for him to enter. The flap is pushed back; I gasp in astonishment. His face is swollen and heavily bruised – his left eye a slit sunk in a dark blue cushion.

"What the hell!"

"Don't ask, sir. I'm sorry I'm late, but I had to sort out a few things before I could get here."

"Who did that to you? You need to see a doctor. We can talk later when… ."

"No, sir. I'm fine, honestly. It looks worse than it is."

"Have a seat, man. What's so urgent it can't wait?"

Dov wastes no time in getting to the point.

"Lieutenant Katz has it in for you. I thought you should know. The men have been muttering about what happened yesterday."

He suddenly chokes, tears shining in his one good eye. I find myself unable to reply for a few moments. When the words come, they sound flat and inadequate.

"I haven't thanked you for saving my life. I could have got us both killed."

Dov tries to smile through his distorted features. The effort causes him to wince in pain.

"It was the least I could do, sir. I wanted to save the old man as well, but it was too late for him. I didn't want to see you go the same way – that would have suited these bastards only too well." He pauses for a moment as emotion returns in a surge. "I don't know what he's planning to do – Lieutenant Katz I mean – but you'll need to be careful."

"Did he do this to you?"

"No, sir. I walked into a door." Despite the pain, the absurdity of the statement forces another smile.

"For God's sake, Dov, what happened?"

"It doesn't matter, sir. What matters is that you survive to tell the tale. Not just about the lieutenant, but about what's going on, here in Jenin and in the rest of the region. People need to know the truth before this madness can end. I've tried to believe otherwise but it's impossible to deny it now. I said something in the mess this morning; I just couldn't help myself. Ben Hagai took exception. That's why... ." His hand gestures towards his injured face for a moment.

Dov is striving to articulate what's been uppermost in my thoughts for a while now, but the dangers involved in expressing such views are painfully obvious. 'Soft touches' have mostly been forced out, and it looks like both of us are high on the removal list."

"He may try to discredit you," Dov seems obsessed with my situation, despite his own peril. Perhaps he feels my background and rank make me particularly vulnerable. "Or get rid of you altogether. Maybe arrange some sort of accident. It's happened before. I'm not saying he would, but... ." Again, the nervous hand gesture. "I might be out of order, sir. I know you and the lieutenant were friends, but I've seen what he's capable of."

"No. You're probably close enough to the mark. I guessed that he must have worked out what really happened with the tank, though he pretended not to for some reason. I was glad enough to believe him at the time."

"I think he was angry I'd intervened. There was something in his tone of voice when he spoke to me afterwards. He smiled and congratulated me, but I could tell it wasn't exactly heartfelt."

I nod slowly. Gad has always found it hard to hide his true feelings, even when circumstances or some ulterior motive have made evasion necessary. A snapshot of that disturbing smile flashes threateningly across my mind's eye.

"There's more, sir."

"About Lieutenant Katz?"

"No. About the things that happened in Jenin."

"Oh, I think I know enough to... ."

"I heard the men talking. Maybe you'll get the opportunity to explain what really went on in there."

"So will you."

"Yes, but if something were to happen people need to know. So few are willing to speak out. There are going to be two official versions: Sharon and Arafat's propaganda lies, and then a stack of conflicting reports by foreign journalists trying to get at the truth. Normally, most decent folk wouldn't listen to a murderer like Sharon, but with things the way they are at the moment, he's become a rock for them to cling on to."

It's strange how much I've underestimated Dov. I always considered him a decent, down-to-earth guy with little interest in politics or politicians. His appraisal of the current situation reveals a keenly intelligent mind.

"They've been shooting civilians and leaving them to die on the streets, then shifting the bodies out of the town under cover of darkness to undisclosed locations.

Someone squealed, so a petition was presented to the High Court to try and stop it."

"Was it successful?"

"It's too early to be certain, but last night they were still wrapping up corpses in plastic bags and loading them onto lorries."

"How do you know this?"

"From a driver delivering supplies yesterday afternoon. He told me that he was involved in the operation. Usual practice is to hand the dead over to their families, but nobody was claiming them. Hardly surprising, I suppose, given what's been happening. Then special orders arrived and that was that. The thing was that a lot of the corpses were unarmed civilians."

"So you think they were shot on the streets by our snipers?"

"It seems that way. That and being buried under the rubble caused by the bombardment and these blasted bulldozers."

I recall the man on the street, targeted by a sniper while pleading for his home and his family; and, of course, the old man, crushed by the tank. Could such deaths have been sanctioned as a means of terrorising the population? The government talks so much these days about the evils of terrorism, but behaves in a way indistinguishable from what it condemns. Again, the moral high ground seems as unattainable as ever – more like a moral cesspit into which we are all sinking without trace. I realise Dov is repeating the sorts of stories normally dismissed as terrorist propaganda. The driver would be unlikely to contact the press with such information for fear of retribution.

"The driver also told me that he personally witnessed two Red Crescent nurses shot dead by our snipers." Again, my world lurches as though about to crash down around me. "It was after an artillery unit shelled a block of flats where militiamen were supposed to be holed up. The nurses appeared through the rubble trying to provide first aid to the injured people inside. The street was totally lit up so there was no way anyone could have made a mistake. They were given no warning before they were shot. Later, he saw two boys machine-gunned by a tank. He thought they were just trying to get home."

"How old were they?"

"Around eleven or twelve."

"What is it with these tank crews?"

"Most of them are in elite units like ours, sir. Did you see Lieutenant Katz chatting away to that tank commander? He's one of these pre-military academy guys."

"I didn't notice. I thought they were all reservists."

"That particular crew was drafted in to do the dirty work. I heard him telling Lieutenant Katz that he was from a small settlement outpost near Ariel."

The pre-military institutes were set up to answer critics of the *Yeshivat Hesder* programme's religious exclusivity, open, as they are, to orthodox and secular soldiers. But, in practice, the gap between the recruits is too wide to allow for much integration.

"Is there anything else, Dov?"

"No, sir."

I doubt whether either of us will survive the next few months of service. Dov's beating is only the beginning. The warning, probably dispensed as much for my benefit as his, cannot be taken lightly. Knowing Gad as I do, he's unlikely to be satisfied with my disgrace and expulsion from the unit. Dov's theory of an unfortunate 'accident' will be his preferred choice. I realise the necessity of keeping us both focused and choose my words carefully.

"We've got to think things through, Dov. There has to be something we can do." Even as I speak, I feel the rising panic of the trapped beast. The walls surrounding us are just too sheer and slippery for escape. I struggle to submerge these fears for Dov's sake. "If we work together we have a chance. In the meantime, go and see the doctor about these injuries. That's an order, okay?"

"Yes, sir. Thanks for everything, sir."

Dov salutes and leaves the tent. I sit back and rack my brains. Where do we go from here?

—◊◊◊—

Next morning, word reaches me that Dov has hanged himself. No foul play here. A suicide note, begging his mother's forgiveness for bringing such shame upon the family, is found pinned to his tunic. The whole thing will be hushed up, if I allow it to be.

I can't think or function properly. Dov must have known exactly what he was going to do before meeting with me. And I was arrogant enough to believe that I had calmed his fears and strengthened his resolve to fight back! The truth is I've failed in this as I've failed in almost everything else in my life. Too late, I remember the suppressed horror and disbelief working beneath the surface of his narrative. Gad will be delighted, of course. The thought of such smug satisfaction at the death of a good man makes my stomach heave. Anger and resentment are turning into something much more intense – my earlier trepidation supplanted by a desire to strike back.

That afternoon, we are summoned to a briefing session. Before providing details of our impending withdrawal from the sector, Shalom passes on the congratulations of our superiors. Operation Defensive Shield has been dubbed an unqualified success by Prime Minister Sharon and his cabinet; the terrorists, according to Sharon, will now find it much more difficult to manufacture bombs, train operatives, and smuggle weapons into Israel. Shalom's heavy-jowled face breaks into an uncharacteristic grin. Even though our mission in Jenin was called off at the last moment, he has obviously been marked out for special praise. Perhaps promotion is just around the corner. His elevation onto the General Staff would be viewed as a victory by the rabbinical supporters of *Gush Emunim*, who are working so hard to gain influence in the IDF. That is, after all, why the *Yeshivat Hesder* initiative was conceived in the first place – infiltration and control of elite units regarded as necessary first steps in stiffening the resolve of a nation grown flabby and degenerate.

Gad, standing just behind Shalom, avoids my eye. Our mutual contempt is now common knowledge; there is no point in pretending otherwise. Dov's death has finally and irrevocably blown every bridge linking our paths in life. In a very real sense, the knives are out. Unfortunately, the advantage lies with my enemy. A blade thrust or sniper's bullet could come at any moment from any direction. Even the men under my command are potential executioners. As far as I am aware, no one, now that Dov is gone, shares my antipathy for what has happened here. There is little I can do to even the odds and give myself a fighting chance.

The impossibility of grandfather's situation and his extraordinary survival, is my only hope now. His brave decision to take his fate into his own hands and confront the forces of evil has become a beacon of light in a dark place for me. I wonder if I will be able to muster similar courage when the time comes.

CHAPTER TEN

Eastern Germany: January 1945

Leo squeezes his eyes shut and waits for oblivion. He expects there to be no pain, only darkness as if a light has been switched off.

Kneeling at the edge of a trench, his bent body appears to have no flesh – a skeleton, held together by a tunic so faded and filthy that the original striped pattern is barely discernable. He knew, as he hacked at the hard-packed soil a few hours earlier, that he was most likely digging his own grave, but experienced no fear at the prospect. For many months, Leo has felt nothing at all. Even news of the Red Army's rapid, westward advance failed to elicit any response. His burning passion to survive, has long since turned to cold ashes.

The executioner is moving rapidly along the line of passive prisoners – each gunshot terminating another miserable life. The Kommandant has decided that there is no more useful work to be wrung out of the emaciated scarecrows at his disposal, and he can see no point in transporting them deeper into the Fatherland ahead of the approaching Russians. The gun barks loudly in Leo's left ear. He barely flinches as one of his old friends and former comrade-in-arms from the Polish Free Army partisan unit, topples head first into the trench.

In what he believes will be the last seconds of his life, Leo strives to recall his mother, father and sister, as they were in the happy days before the world changed. A faint smile plays over his lips as the Nazi officer walks up behind him. His only real regret is not knowing what happened to Lola. Since his capture, no news has scaled the high perimeter walls of this halfway house of the dead.

The barrel of the Luger presses against his nape. The scorching metal blisters his skin. He hears a loud click, followed by another, then another – each more urgent than the last. Cursing, the German slams his boot into Leo's back. The latter falls in the same limp fashion as the others, even though the rear of his skull, and the brain inside, remain intact. Landing face first in the soft earth, he feels no pain. Harsh voices register hazily as if in a fading dream.

"Fill in the trench. We've wasted too much time already. If we don't get out tonight, we're done for."

"But the Kommandant says if we're caught, we'll be treated as prisoners of war."

"And you believe him, you goat's arse? He's telling us that shit to stop us running away. Just don't get taken alive, that's all!"

Leo is vaguely aware of rubble pounding on his back. He finally lets go and sinks beyond further hurt.

—◦◦◦—

Strong hands are pulling him to his feet, and someone is wiping dirt away from his face. He wants to resist but hasn't the strength. Instead, he tries to protest, but his mouth is dry and clogged. Why can't the devils just leave him be? Haven't they done enough already?

He finds himself staring into a pair of bleary eyes, brimming over with tears. The man is wearing an unfamiliar uniform, his narrow, pock-marked face ploughed by a livid scar. The grubby, peaked hat, with its red star, means nothing to Leo. Even stranger than the uniform, however, is the sight of someone so overwhelmed by grief. He barely remembers that such an emotion is possible.

It is almost twenty-four hours since he was left for dead – his survival due to a failure by the increasingly apprehensive German guards to properly back-fill the trench. The Russians are amazed to find anyone still alive. Even those who have witnessed their fair share of horrors, are deeply moved by Leo's resurrection. He is gently washed, checked over by the battalion doctor and fed small portions of rich broth prepared by the company cook. There seems nothing the liberators won't do to coax him back to life.

Next morning, he is moved to a well-stocked field hospital, close to the border with Germany. Here, resistance has crumbled to the extent that Soviet divisions are pouring unopposed into Silesia and Sudetenland. The hospital is being run by its original German staff – from the chief medical officer down to the most humble orderly. The Soviet commander has decided that the highly experienced medical team is best qualified to care for his wounded men, and has striven to protect them from arrest and harassment. Although so far ignoring strongly worded protests by the NKVD officer on his staff, he knows it can only be a matter of time before he is overruled by political diktat and forced to replace the German team with inferior Russian medics. The real power lies with Stalin's guardians of ideological purity, and the fact that he has put the welfare of the injured before self interest is evidence of rare moral courage.

Leo's recovery is boosted by this fortuitous arrangement. As days pass into weeks, then months, he gradually reinhabits his shattered body, accompanied on the long journey by the nurse assigned to his case. Inge Shmitte is wholly dedicated to her calling. As well as aiding his physical recuperation, she spends hours at his bedside encouraging him to remember details about his life before the war. Intimacy grows, and their relationship subtly changes. Inge's gentle, inspiring words slowly revive his will to live, while, for her part, a powerful shift of emotions transforms her professional concern into something much more profound and personal.

In the slow course of his rehabilitation, Leo moves beyond hatred and the desire for revenge. He finds himself able to open up to Inge in ways he would not previously have believed possible. In this new, receptive state of mind, the fact that she is German seems the most natural working out of a complex process.

One morning Inge comes to Leo who is now up and about. With the help of a protein-rich diet, light exercise and extensive physiotherapy, he has put on weight and his muscles are recovering their former strength. His skeleton has slipped out of the limelight back into its customary role of supporting act. Lately, he has thought of little else than the fate of Lola and the rest of his family. Somehow he must get to Krasnow and discover what has become of them. He knows that if his sister is still alive she will most likely have returned there. Recent news of Hitler's death and the fall of Berlin merely increases his desire to make the move. He and Inge have agreed to leave the hospital together but have no idea how it might be done. The medical staff, despite being treated fairly by their Russian guards, are prisoners all the same. This morning she is uncharacteristically agitated.

"It's all over for us, Leo. Our CO has been removed. I think the Russians intend to staff the hospital with their own people and move us all over the border. They say German prisoners are being marched to death camps in Siberia."

Her anxiety is well founded. Once their immunity has been stripped away, the nurses, in particular, will be vulnerable. Removal from the relative safety of the hospital, where the staff's dedication has inspired the respect of guards and patients alike, will be tantamount to a death sentence. Leo's brain lurches into a new gear. He must think of a way out. A mass exodus of staff is impossible, of course. Each individual will have to take his or her own chance. The guards, who have been here since the beginning, are their only hope now, and a slim one at that. A few may escape but most will not. In any event, he will get Inge out or die in the attempt; there is no question of them being parted.

"I don't know if I can persuade the guards to help us; they're probably more scared than we are. We might manage something together, but we can't get anyone else out."

"I won't leave my friends behind."

Her anguished tone almost overturns his need to convince her. He loves her so much, but cannot afford to jeopardise their chance of escape.

"You must! There is no choice in the matter."

"Surely we can take Eva along! One more won't make any difference! She's really close to one of the guards. He'll do anything for her."

Leo is deeply moved that, despite her mortal danger, Inge is begging for the life of her friend.

"He may have to. If we're caught, it will be all up for us."

"There are always risks."

He smiles. She's getting the idea. He feels his old confidence returning. After all, he escaped from the ghetto where the odds were so much worse. The infatuated guard could be the key to success.

—ɯ—

His grandson is staring at him in amazement. Risk everything to save two German nurses! Leo reads a complete lack of understanding or empathy in the boy's eyes. All his talk of being coaxed back to life – of Inge's gentle compassion – have failed to dent Sam's antipathy. The response is disappointing, though entirely predictable. He struggles against the fatigue and pain weighing more heavily on him than ever. He wonders how to get back on track.

"Yes, Sam, I was willing to risk everything. Of course I was! Inge saved my life. She brought me back from the dead. I know this is difficult for you to understand, but please try."

He is coming to the toughest part of his story where he must attempt to draw the strands together, and encourage the boy to see beyond everything that has gone before.

"But these people were Germans, grandfather!"

"Yes, that is true. But healers such as Inge and Eva cannot be blamed for the sins of the Nazis. They saved lives. All through the war they worked with the injured and dying. In me, Inge didn't see a Jew, or a disease-ridden rat, but a fellow-human being in distress. Someone in great need. That is one reason why we became so close."

"How do you know she always saved lives? Maybe she worked in a camp like the one you were in. Maybe by helping you she was looking for a way to escape. Father says that by the end of the war the Germans would do anything to save their own skins."

This was true, of course. After the war many Nazis assumed new identities and fled abroad. Some of the real monsters cooperated with the Allies against the perceived Communist threat, thus gaining for themselves immunity from prosecution. Others simply melted into the massive international relief operation playing out over war torn Europe – not because they felt burdened with guilt, but for wholly selfish reasons. On the other hand, there were those who woke up to what they had done and tried to make amends. But how can he convince the boy that Inge did not fall into any one of these camps?

"Sam, you will have to take my word for it! Believe me when I tell you that this woman gave me back my life.

She taught me the meaning of love. Nothing I tell you about her is invented or exaggerated."

The gravity of the statement, and the intensity of his grandfather's appeal temporarily subdue Sam. Leo is only too well aware, however, that he must soon get to the point or everything he has worked for with the boy will have been for nothing.

—⚬—

Leo, Inge, Eva and the two Russian guards hurry through the dark corridors. Will they be able to prise the NKVD pincers apart, and even if they do, how far can they hope to get? Outside, the humidity of the night wraps itself around them like a thick blanket. Leo's efforts to remain calm and focused are threatened by a rising tide of panic. How can his plan ever hope to work? How can he be so reckless with the life of the person he loves most in the world? The answer is clear – he has no other option. Events are poised to overtake them.

The hospital is cordoned off from the nearby village, so no one can get in or out without the express permission of the military apparatchiks. As they approach the security checkpoint, a young officer steps out of the shadows and motions them to halt. Two soldiers, grasping automatic weapons, take up positions on either side of the barrier. Glancing at the officer's shoulder strap insignia, Leo correctly identifies him as an NKVD lieutenant. His sharp, supercilious eyes give the impression of sleepless vigilance. If anything, the Soviet political agents are more paranoid than their Nazi counterparts.

One of the guards hurriedly explains that they are under orders to transfer the prisoners to NKVD headquarters for questioning. Leo makes out the word conspiracy, devised to convince skeptical patrols that the captives were part of a foiled attempt to rescue the German CO, confined to quarters inside the hospital. The hope is that by tapping into legitimate security concerns, their story will sound genuine. The officer listens impassively and then demands all their papers. Everything is in order – authorisations meticulously forged, right down to the regional commander's neat signature at the foot of the transfer warrant. After what seems like an age, they are waved through. They proceed, trying not to hurry too much. Leo prays the officer will not phone ahead to verify the authenticity of the written orders. Although he knows this is unlikely, his love for Inge multiplies all threats to the escape bid.

They soon join the main road into town. Just beyond the junction, hidden from passing traffic by a thick stand of conifers, a small truck is waiting for them. The driver normally conveys supplies of food and medicine to the hospital, and the lorry looks like any other Red Army ordinance vehicle. Leo hopes they can slip out of the area unnoticed before the alarm is raised.

Although fully aware what will happen if they are caught, the driver and the two guards have decided to desert to the west. They have no illusions about their fate if they fail to act. Anyone tainted by contact with fascist aliens, whatever their background and former record, is now in grave danger. Helping Leo and the others escape will at least provide some meaning to their increasingly futile lives. Leo feels sorry that the three men must leave their country behind them, and never look back. They had no choice when originally ordered to guard the facility. There seems to him little difference between the means employed by Nazi and Soviet authorities to tighten their grip on power – both regimes content to sacrifice natural justice and innumerable lives for what they claim to be the 'greater good'. The idea of the means justified by an increasingly shadowy end, conceals the ultimate betrayal of ordinary people. The horrors of the past ten years have flowed like a black river from this source.

They clamber through the flaps into the back of the truck and bury themselves under lengths of musty tarpaulin. As the vehicle splutters into life, Leo ponders the luxury of a trip under tarpaulin instead of rotten vegetables. He can't help smiling a little at the thought. Will there ever be a time when he can pick up the pieces of his life and return to a normal existence? Will he and Inge one day be married with any measure of peace and security? As they lurch on through the night, he tries, with little success, to get a fix on these unbearably distant days in Krasnow before he was separated from everything and everyone he knew and loved. The old life seems like a tantalising dream, dangled just beyond his reach. Inge's hand, clasped in his own, provides his only hope for the future.

—⁂—

Hours later, they approach the city of Kraków on the banks of the same river that, hundreds of kilometres to the north, runs through his home town. This is as far as the lorry can go and as good a departure point as any.

They have not been stopped once on the way here, but waved through every checkpoint. Security on the open road still appears to be in the hands of military personnel, clearly less zealous than the NKVD units who will soon replace them. Leo's calculated risk has paid off. Poland is still in turmoil and they should be able to merge into the mass of refugees flooding in and out of the stricken country. He pities these displaced people, separated from everything they once held dear. In this sombre mood, he even finds himself contemplating the fate of the officer who allowed them through the cordon surrounding the hospital. No excuse, however watertight, will save him from the wrath of his superiors. He may well be shot as an example to others.

"So, we said our goodbyes and parted ways. Eva went with the Russians. As it turned out, she was very much in love with the younger of the two guards. I suppose that was why they agreed to risk so much for us. I don't know what happened to them. But if they got out of Poland before the communists sealed it off, they might have had a chance."

"What did you do?"

Leo is aware that his grandson is making no mention of Inge, perhaps having convinced himself that she left with the others. That must not be allowed to continue. The boy is going to have to face the fact that his grandmother – his own mother's mother – was a German woman. The taboo shrouding the subject since his unwise decision to enlighten his son-in-law must now be broken. Beyond the torrent of questions, induced by the hope that he may have misunderstood the confession,

Benny made no further reference to the subject, not even – as far as Leo knows – to his own wife. He doubtless remains terrified that if the truth ever leaked out, it would destroy his standing within the Orthodox community. For the thousandth time, he curses his foolishness in ever believing Benny capable of comprehending such a union. This, even in light of the fact that Inge threw in her lot with the creation of the Jewish state, and laboured to make it a reality before her tragic death in 1961. If the father couldn't face up to the truth then the son must be encouraged to break the mould and reject the racist creed spreading its runners into all corners of Israeli society.

He resumes, for once not knowing where the story will take him.

"Inge and I had already decided to return to Krasnow to find my family and see if we could rebuild our lives in the old community. I had little hope that this would be possible, of course, but we were both determined to find out one way or the other. I believed that Lola might also have tried to get back if she could. I had heard nothing of her since I was taken."

He pauses in order to give Sam time to reply, finding himself holding his breath in anticipation of the likely response. He notices that the lad is paler than usual, breathing harder and unwilling to meet his eyes. The silence between them becomes ever more oppressive as the seconds tick by. Finally, Sam asks the question that has been growing in his mind since his grandfather first mentioned his connection with Inge.

"Why would Inge return with you to Krasnow?"

"Because," he speaks slowly with deliberate emphasis, "Inge and I were in love. She wanted to meet my family, to know where I came from. Do you not understand, Sam? Inge became my wife. She was your grandmother!"

Leo feels a great weight lift from his mind. At last he has spoken the words. In the hushed silence that follows, Sam's eyes go blank as if his brain has switched itself off. He rises to his feet.

"I have to go. Mother will want me to wash up the breakfast dishes."

He speaks without emotion, like an automaton. The shallowness of the excuse, given that wild horses wouldn't normally drag him out of the room before the story was finished, alarms Leo almost as much as the boy's tone of voice.

"Sam, did you hear what I said?"

"I'll see you later, grandfather."

"But, Sam... ."

The door slams shut, and Leo is left trying to work out what has just happened. Perhaps the boy simply needs time alone to come to terms with the new, alarming facts of his existence. On the heels of this overly optimistic assessment comes the stark realisation that Sam might never be able to make the adjustment, and, by blurting things out in such a crude way, he, Leo, might have done more harm than good. He knows from past experience how adept people are at suppressing thoughts that create fear or undermine the sense of who they believe themselves to be. On the other hand, this may have been the one opportunity to reveal the truth before matters are taken out of his hands. He eases back against his pillows, piecing together the bleak memories of his return to Krasnow on that fateful Autumn day in 1945. For once there is no eager audience hanging on his every word.

—⚏—

Leo and Inge return on a day of wind and rain. The Vistula is running high – its waters brown and fast flowing. They have trudged the final ten kilometres into Krasnow, and are tired and soaked to the skin. Their journey to Warsaw was uncomfortable, crammed in a six-berth compartment with a dozen other travellers. The train often stopped for no apparent reason – once sitting for three endless hours before getting underway. On two separate occasions the carriages were emptied, and the passengers forced to stand at the side of the tracks in the pouring rain while their papers were checked by a squad of sullen policemen.

Approaching the town, they see lights twinkling in the gathering darkness. They pass Squire Kreitser's old mansion house. Even at a distance, it's clear that the building is derelict: the windows, black gashes in the wall, and beams gaping through the steep roof like ribs stripped of flesh. God only knows what has happened to the squire and his family. They were certainly in residence when the invaders arrived. Like Leo's father, Kreitser had good things to say about the previous German occupation, choosing to ignore the ugly rumours that had been blowing over the border for years. All the old shtetl houses, close to the river, are gone, and he experiences a growing sense of foreboding as they push deeper into the town. What condition will the family home be in? Will they be able to shelter there for the night?

The square and the surrounding streets are intact. Apart from the synagogue, burned down before he and Lola fled, little appears to have changed. Psychologically, of course, everything has changed. Leo's mental landscape has been razed and rebuilt so many times, virtually nothing remains of its original structure. Although the neighbourhood is familiar to him in every physical detail, it lacks the warmth and intimacy of former association. Now that the journey is almost at an end, he is strangely reluctant to take the final few steps.

All too soon they find themselves gazing up at the first floor windows of the old family flat. Everything seems exactly as he left it. A light is burning in the sitting room and Leo wonders who is home. He still retains a vestigial hope that it might be Lola, returned from her long exile. The prospect of finding his parents in residence never even occurs to him. Although only six years have elapsed, it feels to him like an entire lifetime since he turned his back on his old life and struck out into dangerous waters.

A tentative hand touches his shoulder and he springs round, fists raised. He finds himself staring into the face of the girl whose parents owned the flat above their own. Although instantly recognisable, everything about her has changed: her eyes are wary and reluctant to meet his own; her face is too pale and lined for someone little older than twenty-one. All a far cry from the rosy cheeked, guileless teenager who hung around with Lola.

"My God, it is you, Leo!" She looks as though she's seen a ghost. "I thought it was when I saw you coming up the street, but I couldn't believe it. Is Lola with you?" She gazes blankly at Inge for a second. The tiny spark of hope that Leo has been tending for so long is instantly snuffed out. Lola has clearly never been back here.

"It's good to see you, Nina. How are your mother and father?" Leo resorts to customary politeness in an effort to contain his turbulent emotions.

"Father died last year. He never properly recovered from a beating he received for forgetting to bow to an SS captain." The words pour out dispassionately as if she's reporting a series of events unrelated to herself. "Mother is well, though she hardly ever leaves the flat these days. I don't think she really believes that the Germans have gone. It's the same for a lot of people around here. Hela Linsky's mother was raped by a squad of German policemen who broke into her house. Hela was lucky to escape. She ran out the back door when they... .

"Do you know what happened to my parents?"

Leo's interruption is as much about staunching Nina's relentless flow as his need to know what has happened to his own family.

She falls silent, clearly unwilling to answer such a direct question. Leo holds his breath in dreadful anticipation of hearing his worst fears confirmed. When she resumes, her detachment has gone and she sounds like a bewildered child.

"I'm not certain. A month or two after you left, the Germans came here. I remember we were woken at three in the morning by them pounding on the outside door. They eventually broke it down and got into the stair. We thought they had come for all of us. Mother was so scared she… ." Nina stops, aware that this is not what Leo wants to hear. "They were on your landing. I think your father must have opened the door because there was no more noise. We didn't see them taken away. We… ." Again, she pauses, perhaps reluctant or unsure how to proceed. "We heard afterwards that every Jew in Krasnow had been arrested that night. Next day, there was a lot of gunfire in the woods. People said that the Germans soldiers had… ."

"Has anybody been out there to find out what happened?"

"I don't know. It was forbidden."

Certain that Nina is not going to tell him everything she knows about the Nazi round ups, he abruptly changes tack.

"Who is living in our home now?"

She looks as though she is about to bite into a cyanide capsule.

"A Polish family. The council decided that since it was unlikely that any Jews would ever return, those citizens in most need would be allowed to move into the empty houses."

Leo fills up with sadness and rage. He cannot believe that the Poles in his home town have taken such cynical advantage of the Nazi slaughter. To occupy houses with no knowledge of what has happened to their owners is an appalling act of theft, surely as illegal as it is morally reprehensible. The authorities wouldn't have a leg to stand on if he insisted that the property be returned to him. He knows, however, with absolute certainty, that nothing remains for him in Krasnow. The sense of dislocation, building up since his arrival, rushes in like water through the hull of a torpedoed ship.

Nina continues, like an exhausted runner struggling to reach the finishing line. Maybe she feels the need to justify the unjustifiable on behalf of her community.

"I'm sorry things turned out the way they have, but no other Jews have come back. The rehoused families were in such a desperate state, it seemed like the right thing to do after what happened. The war has been hard on… ."

"I think I understand what has happened here, Nina." Leo's flinty tone cuts her short. "We must be on our way. If Lola comes back please tell her we are leaving Poland. Tell her we intend to emigrate to Palestine as soon as the arrangements can be made."

"I will, but you must stay the night before you go. You both look so wet and done in." Her invitation sounds half-hearted at best.

"No, no thank you. We're fine. Please pass on my best wishes to your mother. I hope things work out for you both. And, I'm sorry to hear about your father."

Despite his bitterness, he feels pity for an old man all but beaten to death by the same people who exterminated his parents. He must try not to forget that many Poles have suffered greatly during the occupation, including, no doubt, the people now living in his flat. He hopes Inge will understand his need to get away from this place and never look back.

As they quit Krasnow, the wind drops and the rain clouds are replaced by a bright half-moon set against a myriad of sparkling stars. The air grows steadily cooler, and Inge shivers, not just from the cold press of wet clothes against her skin, but at the thought of what her people have done to innocent families the length and breadth of Europe. She squeezes Leo's hand.

"I feel ashamed of what has happened here. How can you ever forgive us?"

Leo's reply is swift and unequivocal.

"What has happened here, and in Poland, has nothing to do with you! People must take responsibility for their own actions, not the actions of others. The young man who lived in Krasnow is dead long since! What I am today, I owe to you."

She moves in closer, pressing herself against him. He feels reassuringly solid in the gathering darkness.

"Do you really think we can get out of Poland?"

"Yes, if we don't waste any more time. The situation is chaotic enough to allow for almost anything at the moment, but once the Russians gain full control, as they soon will, the borders will be sealed tight."

"What about the Allies?"

"The Allies will do nothing for Poland. Stalin has everything sewn up here."

Leo stops in his tracks and turns to face Inge.

"You know, I do feel sorry for those Poles who put their lives on the line to help my people, but I can't forget the men, women and children butchered in the woods while their neighbours stood by and did nothing." Thoughts of his own parents buried in a mass grave, alongside hundreds of other helpless victims, suddenly overwhelm him and he is unable to continue. He stops in his tracks, tears coursing down his cheeks. When he resumes, his voice trembles with emotion.

"That is why we've got to get out of here while we still can."

As the town lights fade behind them, Inge forgets the misery of her aching legs for a while as she contemplates the quality of the man she has come to love so deeply.

—⁂—

November 1945

Leo and Inge lean over the deck rail watching the ponderous dip and heave of the black waves. It has been a long, unrelenting voyage – the old cargo boat struggling to make headway in the storms which have plagued them since leaving Spain.

Leo has been granted much time to reflect on why his family, and other Polish Jews, did not emigrate to Palestine, or even the United States, years before the Shoah shattered their lives. He recalls the smashed windows and acts of intimidation in Krasnow long before the war began. Anti-Semitic violence in Poland's larger towns and cities must have been a great deal worse. In order to escape the depressing realities of these times, he immersed himself in the plethora of exotic stories filtering back from the Holy Land: of *kibbutzim* flowering in the desert sun; of heroic pioneers struggling to create a new homeland in the midst of desolation; of thrilling encounters with Bedouin Arabs mounted on camels. The same images again fill his thoughts – images he hardly dared entertain during the years of death and destruction.

His dream is shared by many others. The ship bound for Cyprus – the final staging point in the journey to Palestine – is full of the displaced and traumatised Jews daring to contemplate a future free of persecution. This doesn't explain why his wife of less than five weeks is willing to join him on such a voyage. She is here because of her love for him, and the fact that there is nothing left for her in Germany. Her father, an outspoken and persistent critic of the fascist regime, died years ago in Dachau, while her older brother, deeply ashamed of his father's stance and robust in his support of the Führer, succumbed to wounds received at Stalingrad. She scarcely remembers her mother who ran off when she was five years old. The only thing Inge ever received from her was a postcard of the Statue of Liberty, arriving the same year as war enveloped Europe.

Three days after their marriage, word reached them of Lola's death in the Warsaw uprising. Leo had contacted the Displaced Persons Bureau searching for information, and, as it turned out, he didn't have long to wait. She was identified as a fighter killed in the last ditch attempt to defend the city against advancing SS units. At least Leo knows that his sister died resisting the enemy, and was not gassed or worked to death in some anonymous camp. The news of her empowerment provided some measure of consolation. On the other hand, it only increased his determination to quit Poland and rid himself of the burden of association.

He desperately desires that something unsoiled and wholesome will emerge from the ashes of the countless dead; that their sacrifice will not have been in vain.

Until then, he refuses to mourn his lost family. There will be a time for such healing when the future has been secured.

Inge pulls him closer and kisses him. She senses his pain, and struggle to keep on track. He, in turn, feels her empathy glowing like warm coals in the darkness. The contrast of her cold hands reminds him that they should return to their quarters. The thought of the fetid heat and lack of privacy encourages them to linger a little longer, however, and they pace the deck trying to generate some much needed warmth. Leo prays that the weather will ease, and the time hasten towards the end of the voyage. With any luck, they will be in Cyprus within three days – their journey to Palestine all but over. They have been told that local fishing boats will ferry them to the shores of the Holy Land. The prospect of journey's end sustains him as they finally return below decks.

—※—

"You sail tomorrow, just before midnight. Do you remember what I said would happen at the other side?"

"Yes, Chaim." Leo smiles, struggling to conceal his frustration at being treated like a child by the younger man. "We will disembark from the fishing boat and be rowed ashore where your brother will be waiting. He will check our documents and make sure we get the right papers to show to anyone who asks."

"That is correct. Do not forget the password, and the agreed response. You will be taken to a kibbutz, near Jaffa, where you will work until the mandate is ended and we are granted statehood. After that, it is up to you."

"Do you think that will happen sooner rather than later?"

"A year at the most. The Americans will convince the British to give way. There is a lot of pressure being applied through the United Nations. Their government will quickly understand that they have little choice in the matter."

"The United Nations?"

"Yes, my friend. The UN has replaced its dismally weak predecessor. We all hope it proves more effective in the long run."

"I trust our Arab brothers feel they are being properly represented there. We must get off on the right foot."

Chaim stares uncomprehendingly at him for a moment.

"What are you talking about? These 'brothers' you speak off are the enemies of our blood, and avid Jew-killers. Do you not know what has been happening in Palestine for the past thirty years? The Arabs have resisted us since our pioneers first arrived on these shores. They do not wish to work with us! They wish to break us and throw us back into the sea!"

"Then we must convince them that what we offer is of benefit to everyone living in the region. If they understand our good intentions, the old enmities will be resolved, I'm sure."

Chaim shakes his head.

"Never trust an Arab! In time you will feel exactly as I do."

Leo ponders their fortuitous meeting three days earlier. Approaching the couple as they disembarked, Chaim was clearly aware who they were and why they were here.

He told them later that he and his associates are on hand to meet every boat arriving in Limassol – their mission to ease the passage of thousands of émigrés into Palestine. Although Chaim's prejudices worry him, he decides to focus on more pressing matters for the time being. Once they are established in their new home, he will work, like all reasonable people, to improve the relationship between the newcomers and the local population. He prays that the curse of Jewish segregation can finally be put to rest in the Holy Land. The need to establish a new order in the world has never been greater; and his persecuted people must be at the forefront of such a movement.

—⁓—

The night is perfect with neither moon nor wind to complicate the beach landing. The long sail out of Limassol has gone without incident. The soft splash of the dinghy's oars creates a lulling effect, and Leo's eyes begin to close. Inge prods him awake and stares at him curiously.

"How can you fall asleep at a time like this? If we are caught now, the British will pack us back off to Poland!"

The beach, only a few hundred metres distant, is plainly visible – the white sand gathering the faint glimmer of starlight. Minutes later, the fisherman wades into shallow water and pulls the boat up onto the sand. They leap ashore and stand for a moment, savouring their arrival in the land of their dreams. There is little time for celebration, however. A dark figure approaches, bows in greeting and addresses them in *Yiddish*.

"It may rain before dawn."

Leo offers the agreed response.

"Yes, but the new day offers hope."

The man smiles and shakes both their hands in turn.

"We are glad you are here. My name is Isaac. My brother will have explained what is required. Have you brought the necessary documents?"

"Yes." Leo hands over the tattered brown envelope he has been so carefully guarding for months. "I hope everything is in order."

He experiences a twist of anxiety. Papers have been such a vital part of his life for the past five years, it seems strange to be handing them over to a total stranger. Without a second glance, Isaac thrusts them into his coat pocket.

"Now, you must change out of these clothes into something more appropriate for Jewish pioneers." He leads them to a heap of what looks to Leo like old rags discarded on the sand. "We must hurry. Do you have any questions before we go?"

Inge looks uncertainly at her new clothes but says nothing. Leo, apprehensive about their illegal status, is unable to restrain himself.

"Are we likely to encounter any police or customs officials?"

Isaac replies as Leo and Inge hurriedly dress.

"No! The British understand well enough what is going on here. They tend to leave us alone, so there should be no trouble. But you never know, which is why we have to be cautious. Hundreds of immigrants are arriving every day. After independence, every resident will receive citizenship, and more will quickly follow."

Isaac echoes his brother's confidence regarding the imminent creation of a Jewish homeland. Leo hopes that it is not the result of wishful thinking. He has heard much talk on the subject before. He recalls the feverish excitement in the ghetto whenever the topic was raised. Eager to learn more, he returns to the subject first raised with Chaim.

"Why are the British so easy going? Are they keen on granting us our independence?"

"Not really. Our people in America are doing their bit, of course, but the British know what will happen if they continue to stand in our way. We have given them good reason to fear us. You must understand that we are taking matters into our own hands now. Come, we must go."

Though worried, Leo decides to ask no more questions. He will find out soon enough why fear has become such an important factor.

The burial of their old clothes in the dunes behind the beach and the donning of new apparel, although uncomfortable and ill-fitting, is full of symbolic meaning for Leo. As the sky lightens in the east, he feels that he is emerging from the dark prison of his previous life.

—⚶—

September 1949

Leo slumps down at the communal eating table, pours himself a glass of water from an earthenware beaker and takes a long, cool drink. The weather has been unseasonably hot, and cropping dozens of young trees in the orange groves has proved more demanding than usual. Men and women start to arrive. The aroma of cooking food entices the nostrils of the hungry workers as they trade the day's gossip, and discuss the encouraging rise in the price of oranges.

Listening to the lively chat, and occasionally contributing his own observations, Leo experiences an enormous sense of well-being. Not a day goes by without him proffering a quiet prayer to God for his change of fortunes. He loves the *kibbutz* with its camaraderie and bounty in equal measure; and the right of its members to participate fully in all decision-making.

Haskel Cohen sits down on the bench beside him. Haskel arrived last year, having decided, like so many American Jews, to leave his old life behind and help build the new state of Israel. And like most of those who had no part in the Shoah, he is enormously idealistic – his certainty fuelled by the simple, unshakeable belief that Jews are here to reclaim what is rightfully theirs. At the other end of the scale, there are people living in the *kibbutz* who are victims of the worst atrocities – whose hatred of *Goys* has been fired into such a hard, crystalline element that change is virtually impossible.

Despite his naivety, Haskel is so infectiously enthusiastic that Leo can't help liking him. He leaps into argument in the same exuberant fashion as a dolphin leaps into the waves.

"Well, Leo, another hard day at the orange trees? Is the fruit ready for picking yet?"

"I wouldn't know, Haskel. I'm working with the fledging trees; mostly planting out on the reclaimed land, and pruning for future growth."

"You make it sound like what's happening all over the country. We are seizing back the land so that we might repopulate it and make it fruitful once more."

Leo smiles wryly. Trust Haskel to make such an absurd analogy. Against his better judgement, he decides to play along.

"Maybe, but there doesn't seem to be much pruning going on. Encouraging extravagant growth has no long-term advantages. We must crop back foolish ambition or live with the consequences."

He feels sorry the moment the words have left his mouth. The problem is that he just can't help himself, especially when Haskel spews out the sort of chauvinistic nonsense that has become so prevalent since independence. Although in the past he has dismissed many bad policies as the inevitable consequence of fear and uncertainty, likely to evaporate as his people gain more confidence in themselves, he is not so sure anymore. Events over the last few months have been impinging on his new-found contentment, creating unease in his mind.

Despite the warning note in Leo's voice, Haskel is not put off.

"Surely you see the need to defend ourselves. If we don't seize more land, we're done for! The Arabs will push us back into the sea. It's obvious to anyone with eyes in their head that the original chartered allocation of territory by the UN was woefully inadequate."

Other people are listening in. Lewis Leftkowitz – an Auschwitz survivor – suddenly pipes up.

"We must show the Arabs no mercy. Believe me, they will happily murder us all in our beds. It is kill or be killed. I have not returned from hell to the Promised Land to be persecuted all over again."

Leo knows that if it hadn't been for Inge, he could so easily have turned out like Lewis. It is ironic, and a source of considerable anguish, that he cannot declare his wife's true nationality to his *kibbutzin* comrades. She works harder than anyone else to make the dream of Israel a reality, but there is no way that people like Lewis would ever accept her if the truth came out. It is this knowledge that fuels his anger and spurs a powerful response.

"You're wrong, Lewis. If there is to be a future for our people, we must encourage tolerance. Only then can we move forward, and inspire others. We've both been to hell and back, but we need to dig deep now. I am one of the few people here who can say that to you, and you need to listen."

Lewis recoils as if lashed by a whip. The recent, carefree chatter of the refectory has been replaced by a tense silence; even the clink of plates and cutlery has died away. Leo's exasperation is quickly replaced by profound sadness, and tears spill down his cheeks.

"For God's sake, Lewis, let it go before you destroy what you have most cause to love!"

Without a word, Lewis rises to his feet and stalks out of the room. Unsurprisingly, Leo's appeal has fallen on stony ground. He slowly turns to face Haskel, who is staring fixedly at the floor as though he hopes it might open and swallow him up. The exchange has left him in turmoil. Leo knows well enough that, despite his bravado, the American is in awe of the Shoah survivors. Lewis might be beyond his reach, but Haskel can still be influenced.

Leo suddenly notices Inge standing close to the refectory doors. She must have witnessed the exchange along with everyone else. He knows what she is feeling. She has pleaded with him to avoid such confrontations. He studies her sad eyes and ashen face, noticing the way she involuntarily clasps her bulging abdomen where their baby is growing by the day. He continues nevertheless, determined beyond love for his wife to let everyone in the room know how he feels about the recent war with the Arabs.

"We cannot continue to treat the people who are our neighbours in such a way. How can we behave like this after all we've been through? You must try to understand the terrible things that are happening – that have already happened. Destroying villages, throwing people out of their homes, prohibiting their return – all of these things were done to us by the Nazis. Do we really wish to turn into the very thing we have most cause to hate? We cannot continue to annex Arab property or shoot so-called 'infiltrators' who return in desperation to claim what is theirs. We cannot continue to lie to the world in order to cover up our crimes. Why do so many of you refuse to accept that?"

No one dares interrupt him. Despite being known as a quiet, humorous and hard-working member of the community, Leo's past associations are well known – especially with Mordecai Anielewicz and the ghetto freedom fighters. His words carry great weight here.

"I came to Israel with my wife to make a fresh start. I did not come to revive old nightmares, or oppress the people already living here. If we fail to pull things together, or discard our humanity, this beautiful land will die the death of a thousand cuts!" The flames blazing up inside him suddenly fizzle out. He stares round as if newly aware of the hiatus he has created. "I don't know about the rest of you, but I am hopeful that food will soon appear on the table. For God's sake, let us eat and be thankful for what we have!"

CHAPTER ELEVEN

Kiryat Arba – January 2003

"We, reserve combat officers and soldiers of the Israeli Defence Forces, who were raised upon the principles of Zionism, sacrifice and giving to the people of Israel and to the State of Israel, who have always served in the front lines, and who were the first to carry out any mission, light or heavy, in order to protect the State of Israel and strengthen it.

We combat officers and soldiers who have served the State of Israel for long weeks every year, in spite of the dear cost to our personal lives, have been on reserve duty all over the Occupied Territories, and were issued commands and directives that had nothing to do with the security of our country, and that had the sole purpose of perpetuating our control over Palestinian people. We, whose eyes have seen the bloody toll this Occupation exacts from both sides.

We who sensed how the commands issued to us in the Territories, destroy all the values we have absorbed while growing up in this country.

We, who understand now that the price of Occupation is the loss of IDF's human character and the corruption of the entire Israeli society.

We, who know that the Territories are not Israel, and that all settlements are bound to be evacuated in the end.

We hereby declare that we shall not continue to fight this War of Settlements.

We shall not continue to fight beyond the 1967 borders in order to dominate, expel, starve and humiliate an entire people.

We hereby declare that we shall continue serving in the Israel Defense Forces in any mission that serves Israel's defence.

The missions of occupation and oppression do not serve this purpose – and we shall take no further part in them."

Sam reads through the Combat Reserve letter again. Today is the first anniversary of the letter's publication in January 2002, and it's back in the headlines as more soldiers sign up. He recalls the stir when it first hit the press, and his own doubts about the motives of the signatories. Since then, everything has changed. He now regards the declaration an act of outstanding courage on the part of the five hundred soldiers who were prepared to accept the hostility of army chiefs, politicians, journalists, as well as the vast bulk of their peers.

He folds the newspaper and leans back in his chair. His mother has laid out breakfast, but food is the last thing on his mind right now.

He has been engaged in much soul-searching of late. The headline-hitting letter endorsed by so many hardened veterans – some of whom are members of elite commando units and, a few, like him, the sons of orthodox settlers – has finally convinced him that he must act according to his conscience. Neither the *Redemption* of the sacred land of Israel, nor the interpreted authority of the *Mishna*, nor, indeed, the alleged will of God Himself, can weaken his resolve to publicly oppose the occupation – to add his voice to the rising chorus of disapproval.

—⁂—

Miriam returns home to find her son slumped in the chair, his head in his hands as if burdened by an inconsolable grief. When she left the paper propped up on the breakfast table she had expected a very different reaction, but, knowing how he's been of late, she says nothing, electing instead to busy herself around the kitchen. Eventually, he rallies, even attempting a smile, but the strain is visible.

Since Benny left, things have deteriorated to the extent that she is planning to move out of Kiryat Arba as soon as she possibly can. There is nothing she will miss here. The hard stares and angry mutterings, following her around any public place she enters, are a hard burden to bear. Close on the heels of marrying Benny, agreeing to settle in the Territories was the worst choice she ever made. She is aware that regrets of this nature are pointless. She can't change what has happened, but can, perhaps, put the past behind her and move on.

While just about able to cope with her own pariah status, Miriam finds it harder to endure the hostility directed at her son. She often wonders what life might be like in Westernised cities like Tel Aviv or Haifa. Condemned by orthodox zealots as dens of iniquity, she imagines such places as havens of freedom and tolerance. Casting about for something to say that might cheer him up, she returns to the open letter.

"So, are you surprised there are so many soldiers who think the way you do? The papers say that hundreds more have signed up to the Combat Reserve Declaration since last year."

Sam sighs and slowly shakes his head.

"No, not really. Look at Dov, a decent guy who suddenly woke up to the reality of what he was doing, and knew he couldn't do it anymore. There must be plenty more like him."

"Yes, but to sign a document like that!"

"These are the brave ones! There are thousands of others who hate the occupation but are too scared to speak up, especially if they come from places like this."

"There are a few from the settlements who've signed. The paper printed a list of soldiers from Gaza and the West Bank."

"Yes, I saw that." Sam gets up and pours water into the kettle. "They put the rest of us to shame!"

"What you have done is just as hard to live with."

"Not quite. I offered a few criticisms of the way our unit conducted itself in Ramallah and Jenin, and they suspended me pending an enquiry. Of course, that's only because they knew I would end up with a knife in my back if I stayed, and they wanted to avoid another stink in the press. If I shut up, I'll be transferred out of the unit and everything will be covered up. They'll probably even make sure I don't have to serve in the Territories again."

"So, what are you going to do?"

"God knows! If I do nothing, or cooperate with the bastards, then I dishonour myself and disgrace Dov's memory. If I go public, even father will have to pack up and get out of here."

These last words are uttered with a hint of sadness. Surprisingly, the prospect of his father being forced out of his spiritual homeland troubles Sam.

"Oh, he'll get over it. Mark Katz is right behind him. They'll most likely blame me for filling your head with shameful ideas."

Sam suddenly frowns.

"That's another thing. How are you going to manage if I… ?"

"Don't worry about me, Sam. I'm getting out of here as soon as arrangements can be made. It's over with your father. To be honest, I can't bear to be in the same room as him anymore." Sam says nothing as he pours boiling water into the stained teapot that's been sitting in the kitchen as long as he can remember. "I'm amazed we lasted this long – especially when I saw what was going on. I still can't believe I let it happen. What your grandfather would have made of me agreeing to move to this awful place, I shudder to think."

Tears spill down her face. Sam moves quickly to comfort her.

"Grandfather would have understood."

"I doubt it."

On a sudden impulse, he decides to ask her a question that has troubled him for many years.

"Why did they get on so badly? I mean father and grandfather. Why could they never stand to be in each other's company?"

"It didn't start that way. They used to be great friends. Your father wasn't so set in his ways when we first married. He was intrigued by dad's experiences in Poland. He often told me back then that Jews like dad represented the only good thing to have come out of the Shoah."

Sam is struck by the bitterness in his mother's voice.

"So, father looked up to him?"

"Hero-worshipped him would probably be a better way of putting it."

"What changed?"

Miriam stares at her son for a few moments. Does he really know nothing about his grandmother? She had assumed that Benny or her father would have told him, thus conveniently releasing her from the responsibility of broaching the issue. Probably more to do with her reluctance to hand Benny an advantage in the struggle for the boy's allegiance, if she's being perfectly honest. Feeling guilty, she swallows hard and tries to answer the question as honestly as she can.

"One day we were talking after supper. It must have been during *Yom Kippur*. You were just a baby. I remember you were sitting on my knee and I was trying to get you to finish off your food. Dad and Benny were discussing the war, and Benny asked how he and my mother had first met. I thought it was a strange question because

I assumed that he must have heard the story before; perhaps he had, of course, but dad would most likely have glossed over the details, leaving him curious."

Something stirs sluggishly in Sam's subconscious; something repressed and threatening. With a jolt of surprise, he finds that he is having to force himself to listen to his mother. He restrains an impulse to make some ridiculous excuse to leave the room.

"Dad had had quite a lot to drink that evening and was probably off his guard, but he wasn't one for feeling ashamed of anything he'd done in good faith. You remember how he was?" Sam shrugs, feeling increasingly uncomfortable. "Everything came tumbling out: the concentration camp, the liberation, my mother nursing him back to health, their marriage in Poland before they emigrated to Palestine. The fact that dad had married a German woman shocked your father to the core. He didn't utter another word. After that, he avoided dad, and things were never the same between us either."

Sam bends forward in his seat, covering his head with his hands.

"Sam, what's wrong? Are you okay?"

He doesn't reply. Memories are resurfacing, not slowly and reassuringly, but with the force of molten rock thrust up by irresistible pressures. His grandfather's despairing cry rings as loudly in his ears as it did the day he fled the old man's bedroom. How easy to deny who you are and become the very thing you most loathe; how easy to banish love and compassion from your life. He struggles to comprehend his grandfather's years of suffering, of resisting and killing in order to endure; his years of astonishing survival, rounded off by the miracle of redemption at the hands of the woman he loved. Sam grasps what it must have felt like to be rejected at the end of such a life by your only grandchild.

He takes his mother's hand and presses it against his cheek. She is staggered by the intensity of his reaction and feels more guilty than ever. When he eventually speaks, he sounds stunned as if groping for meaning.

"He told me, you know, but... ." He stumbles to a halt as a measure of insight emerges. "After he died, I convinced myself that he and grandmother had met and married in Palestine. When anyone asked, I trotted out the lie until I believed it myself."

Miriam holds him tightly as he weeps for the depth of his betrayal and a wrong he can never put right.

—⚉—

From nowhere a stone strikes Sam on the side of his head. Others smash against the wall of the house he is passing, leaving angry welts on the gleaming whitewash. The pain in his left temple is excruciating and blood trickles down his cheek. He hears shrill cries and pounding feet as his child attackers make good their escape. He experiences no anger, or inclination to pursue them. What would be the point?

Gad is back in town and a showdown cannot be far away. Sam's support – recently channelled through local websites and newspapers – for the band of soldier *refuseniks*, has undermined any chance of reconciliation with the *Yeshiva* authorities. At a public meeting his father made it known he no longer had a son, or a wife. The declaration means that he has been effectively stripped of dispensation from the wrath of righteous Jews who might wish to act against him. Sam knows more than most how the minds of his adversaries work, and he has no illusions about the seriousness of the threat to himself and his mother.

He pulls out a tissue and dabs the scratch. The blood is already crusting, but next time… .

Arriving home, he finds the lounge window smashed, the front door splintered and splattered with excrement. The street is as quiet as the grave. There are no anxious neighbours gathered around, though the violence must have occurred within the past hour. They might have been in sympathy with the attackers, but most likely were too scared to get involved. Despite his anger, Sam can't find it in himself to blame them.

It suddenly occurs to him that his mother must have been at home during the attack. Panic surges, and his heart skips a beat. He rushes inside, praying that she might have been out visiting one of her few friends. His hope is in vain. She crawls out from under the kitchen table and smiles ruefully up at him.

"When I heard the door opening, I thought they might have come back for a second round, so I hid again." Sam merely shakes his head, staring around the damaged room as if unable to believe the evidence of his own eyes. "Don't look so surprised, Sam. Something of the sort was bound to happen sooner or later." Her exasperated tone jolts him out of his trance. "It wasn't that bad really. When I heard the crowd coming up the street I was terrified, but when they started yelling and hammering on the door, I got angry and called them some bad things. Then a brick came through the window. If I'd kept my big mouth shut, they might have left without causing any damage. At least I know how the Arab families living in Hebron must feel."

Noticing the cut on Sam's head, her self-mocking tone instantly changes to concern.

"What happened to you? We'd better get you down to the clinic right away."

"I'm fine. It looks worse than it is. Anyway, I doubt that any doctor at the clinic is going to treat me." He kicks at the shattered fragments of glass littering the floor. "Did you happen to see if Gad was among the people who did this?"

The question has to be asked, though he doubts that his former friend, and comrade-in-arms would have been part of such a mob assault. It's not his style. Violence, yes, but up close and personal. He may, however, have had a hand in stoking the passions leading to the attack. At one time the prospect of confronting Gad would have intimidated him, but a deep-rooted anger has replaced his former trepidation, and he feels a fierce desire to strike back. Before he leaves they will meet. He owes it to himself, Dov, and most compellingly of all, to his grandfather.

"I'm not sure. I didn't see any of them. When things got really ugly, I locked myself in the bathroom. Does that make me a closet hero?"

Now it's Sam's turn to smile.

"You did just fine, but this can't go on. You must leave here now."

"I'm not going anywhere without you, Sam! Don't try that women-and-children-first thing with me, because it won't work!" Her determination is genuine and he wisely decides to drop the matter, at least for now. She is, after all, her father's daughter. "And, as for Gad, you need to stay away from him. I know what you're thinking. But this isn't the time for heroics. He's not worth it. You must realize that!"

"I have to speak to father."

"A lot of people are gunning for you right now. The only thing to do is lie low and take the arguments to those who might pay some attention. Nobody's listening around here. Your father has made his position very clear. I don't want you going anywhere near that house."

"I hear what you say, but father and I will talk, and if Gad is around, so be it!"

"You know what will happen if he is. Where's the sense in walking into the lion's den?"

Ignoring her, Sam turns away, picks up a brush and starts to sweep the shards of glass into a jagged pile. She stares at him for a few moments, shakes her head and walks into the pantry to fetch the black shovel she considered using as a weapon a mere half an hour ago. Would she have wielded it in earnest? Her son is right about one thing at least. Their departure cannot be delayed much longer.

—⁂—

"Well, well, look what the cat's dragged in. Why don't you fuck off out of here and move in with your towel-head chums?"

Gad's hallmark smile is fixed in place and his eyes are cold. Sam knows that his former friend is spoiling for a fight.

"Just ask my father to step outside for a few minutes."

"You're not listening are you? There's nobody in this house who wants to speak to you. You've made your bed, so go lie on it!"

Gad is enjoying himself. The situation could hardly suit him better. His words, he knows, are hitting their mark. If Sam can be goaded into turning on his tormentor, so much the better.

"I'll go when I've spoken to my father, not before."

"You'll go now – the easy way or the hard way – it's your choice!"

A small crowd of neighbours has gathered, and the tension barometer is rising. Aware of his audience, Gad is playing to the gallery. The drama is heightened by Mr Katz's sudden appearance on the street. Seeing Sam, his features twist into a snarl of fury. He backs away, his voice strangely high-pitched – verging on hysterical.

"What are you doing here? Get out now before I call the police."

Sam can almost smell the fear fuelling this unexpected outburst. The former firebrand bigot appears to have lost his nerve. He notices that Gad has turned pale – his smile now transformed into an anxious frown. He suddenly feels the stress of the past few days slough away. His mother is right – none of this is actually worth it. Turning up, ostensibly to speak to his father, was an excuse to confront Gad. To withdraw now, without any kind of macho display, would mark a rare moral victory. If his grandfather was able to liberate himself from prejudice and hatred then surely he can summon up a fraction of the same resolve. It occurs to him, not for the first time, that the old man's stories were part of a process intended to ameliorate such moments of crisis.

His father appears at an upstairs window and their eyes lock. Everything around Sam fades, and in that heightened moment of empathy, he senses his father's remorse for all that has come between them. He slowly turns and walks away. He will talk to his father at a time and place of his own choosing. Gad, furious that his strategy has failed, unleashes a verbal tirade, but to no avail. Everything has changed. Sam will take from here a new-found confidence, as well as greater insight into the motives of those he must soon challenge. It might even be possible to lay his own demons to rest at last.

—⚊—

"Did you know your father has left Kiryat Arba?"

Sam stares blankly at Dov's mother for a moment. Having arrived on her doorstep to pay his respects, the last thing he expected was to be greeted with this disturbing snippet of news. Unprompted, she continues to fill him in.

"He told Mrs Katz that he was just going out for a short walk to clear his head. She said he left everything behind, apart from his wallet and his jacket."

She pauses as the realisation suddenly dawns that Sam might not have come to chat about his father's disappearance.

I'm so sorry, Sam. Please come in. I've quite forgotten my manners."

She ushers her guest into the front room and seats him in a comfortable armchair.

"I hope your mother is well."

"She's fine, everything considered."

"Yes. I heard what happened at your house. If it's any comfort, a lot of people have told me how sorry they are.

He smiles wryly.

"Unfortunately, nothing will change until the same people are prepared to do more than express their sorrow in private."

Mrs Harel is reluctant to meet his eyes.

"You're right, of course. After everything that's happened, I should know that better than most, shouldn't I?"

Too late, he appreciates how such words were bound to be interpreted by the grieving mother.

"I'm sorry. I didn't mean to... ."

She smiles through her tears.

"I can hardly begin to guess what Dov went through. It's hard to, to... ."

"Yes, of course."

There is an awkward silence as he wonders what to say next.

"Did my mother tell you that we're going to stay with her friend in Haifa until we can make more permanent arrangements?"

"I'm pleased you're getting out. Your mother is lucky to have such a good boy."

Sam feels more guilty than ever. Mrs Harel has no one left in her life – her husband having died while Dov was still at school. The circumstances surrounding her son's suicide are common knowledge, and while some will privately sympathise, as they did when his mother was attacked, such feelings remain largely unspoken. How can she escape the wreckage of her life? There is no option for her but to sit tight and make the best of things.

"When will you be leaving?"

"Not for a few weeks. There's still a lot to be arranged."

She abruptly changes tack. "Did you hear what happened in Hebron last night?"

Even when faced with her own insoluble problems, Mrs Harel cannot contain the urge to gossip. Maybe it's this side of her character that helps her to keep going.

"No."

"An Arab shop was set on fire. The papers are saying that three young children living upstairs were killed, and the mob wouldn't even let the fire engines through. They all got arrested, including Gad Katz."

After their recent confrontation, Gad, no doubt the ringleader, would have been on the prowl, eager to find an outlet for his frustration; and where better than Hebron's Arab quarter? But three children burned to death in a district already teetering on the brink! Ironically, his resolution to tread the path of peace may have resulted in this atrocity. If Gad is imprisoned some good might come of it, but he doubts whether the arrest will be anything more than a palliative to reduce local tension. As with most violence directed against Arabs in the Territories, this incident, despite its seriousness, is unlikely to be pursued with any real intent to see justice done.

"Was Gad's father involved?"

"I don't think so. He gave up the chairmanship of the Committee for Safety on the Roads last year. They say he hasn't been too well and was asked to step down."

Sam can only assume, she is referring to Mr Katz's mental health. This would certainly explain his strange behaviour a few days ago, and might be another reason for his son's unrestrained violence in Hebron.

"Can I get you a cup of tea or something a bit stronger?"

"Thanks, but I probably should be getting home. Mother doesn't like to be left on her own after what happened."

"Yes, of course. Give her my best, won't you?"

"I'll come back and see you soon."

"You're always very welcome, Sam. Thanks for everything you did for... ."

She falters as the reality of her son's death hits her afresh. Embracing Sam, she seems unwilling to let go. To her he feels like a rock firmly anchored in dangerous seas."

Walking home, he is assailed by guilt. For Dov's sake he should do more to help. But what? There is no quick fix. However much he might want to, he can't lead the town's traumatised victims out of the Promised Land.

CHAPTER TWELVE

Tel Aviv: Summer 2005

Sam is writing yet another press release. The futility of the task suddenly hits him and he swings back in his chair, so violently he almost tips over.

It's just over two years since he left Kiryat Arba, and added his signature to the original Combatants letter of January 2002. Since then he has studied politics and human rights at college, and spent a short spell in prison as a result of his refusal to serve in an IDF reservist unit. He now works for the peace group, *Courage to Refuse,* which is committed to establishing stronger links between Jews and Arabs, and bringing the occupation of the Territories to an end.

Amazingly enough, he was recently reunited with Jeff Schiff, the student so brutally expelled from the *Yeshivat Hesder* where they both trained as orthodox army recruits. When Sam met Jeff at a peace conference in Tel Aviv, he could hardly believe his eyes. The charismatic young man, now an activist with *Peace Now,* seemed unchanged. Instantly recognising Sam, he strode across the room and the pair embraced in front of a hall full of delegates. As of old, Sam experienced a lifting of the heart and a burst of renewed confidence. No wonder Gad had plotted to get rid of Jeff.

"I never believed we'd meet again, especially here. I thought Gad had you in his thrall."

"He did. But things changed. I just couldn't keep jumping through the same old hoops, especially after Jenin."

"Of course. That must have been awful. I could see, even back then, that you had your doubts. Maybe if we had got to know each other a bit better, but time, as they say, was against us." He smiled wryly. Sam recalled the last time he saw Jeff – frog-marched out of the college assembly hall after his public denunciation. Jeff's apprehensive but defiant mien remained with him for years afterwards.

"Gad was cunning beyond his years. He figured me out, set me up and plotted my expulsion before I rightly knew what was happening."

Unable to help himself, Sam asked the question that had been plaguing him for so long.

"Was there any truth in what Tsvi Shach accused you of?"

Jeff grinned without a hint of irony.

"No, not a word of it, more's the pity! I wasn't and never had been in that part of Hebron. To tell you the truth, I didn't rightly know what a prostitute was until Rabbi Goldberg explained the nature of my heinous crime. Did you?"

"Not really."

"We led pretty sheltered lives back then. I'm not sure why Goldberg felt he had to make an example of anyone over sexual impropriety. Maybe a facet of his own guilty conscience, who knows. And, as for the magazines, they didn't belong to me. I've no doubt Gad and his goons planted them in my room. These guys probably got a lot of pleasure out of them before stacking them under my bed. The worst of it was that I didn't even get a chance to read them myself!"

Sam laughed, but Jeff's tone quickly changed.

"I was beaten to a pulp after they got me clear of the college precincts. I spent two months in hospital recovering from internal injuries – three broken ribs and a punctured lung. My father took it up with the Yeshiva authorities but they denied any knowledge of the violence, simply repeating their policy of expelling recruits who acted contrary to core religious principles. When he went to our *Knesset* representative, the coward didn't want to know. That's how it is in Israel – heads in the sand, lies and cover-ups."

"It works for the most part. The US Congress in particular really wants to believe that Israel is a bastion of democracy in a region overrun by oppressive regimes. Truth is, our human rights record doesn't bear scrutiny."

"You army guys were so courageous in speaking out. I don't know if I could have done that."

"It took a long time to pluck up the courage. Anyway, what did you do after you got out of hospital?"

"I went to college and mastered in law. Since then I've been working to expose the Hesder IDF infiltration plans. Without much success I might add."

"These things move at a snail's pace. It's really great to see you again, Jeff. Maybe we'll get a chance to work together in the future."

"I've no doubt about it. Us young guys must stick together."

Sam was struck, as he was the first day they met, by Jeff's powerful aura. He felt more optimistic and cheerful after their chat than he had done in a long time.

Now, however, he is buried beneath an avalanche of doubts. As the scourge of international terrorism grows and the situation in the country rapidly deteriorates, he feels that everything he is working towards will surely fail. Just when he thinks *Courage to Refuse* and other Israeli peace organisations might be making headway, the government receives yet another boost to its propaganda campaign. All the while, a sustainable future for both Jews and Palestinians is slipping away.

As Sam suspected, Prime Minister Sharon's decision to withdraw from the Gaza Strip is buying him time while he cunningly exploits the steady build-up of international hostility towards Arabs, and Muslims in particular. As far as the international community is concerned, Sharon has apparently ditched his hardline past and assumed the new role of international statesman and man of peace.

Once more, he picks over the huge setback to the cause of freedom in Israel following the New York terrorist attack in 2001, and the more recent European bombings. What a coup for *Kadima*! It can surely only be a matter of time before another Hamas extremist offers Sharon the perfect excuse to ditch the road map altogether and transform Gaza, with its three million inhabitants, into the largest concentration camp the world has ever known. And, who knows, get the relentless settlement of the West Bank back up to speed. When he considers the citizens of Gaza, packed into a tiny strip of land, denied basic amenities and even food supplies by their hostile neighbours in Egypt and Israel, he is reminded of his grandfather's harrowing descriptions of the Warsaw Ghetto in 1942.

He is also deeply dismayed by the rifts in the peace movement itself! Only yesterday he was subjected to a blistering attack from a peace activist who accused him and "his kind" of wrecking democracy in the region. Why he believed this necessary, Sam has no idea. Maybe he felt that *Courage to Refuse* was somehow impinging on his space, or eclipsing his own group's message. Apart from the foolishness of rebuking a fellow traveller in the struggle for peace and enlightenment, his belief that democracy has any legitimacy in Israel outside the Jewish community is absurd in itself.

On days like this he wants to pack up and leave Israel forever, but his destiny lies here and he knows he must persist in the endless search for compromise. He is aware, however, that as he struggles to heal divisions, others are pulling in exactly the opposite direction. There are few days he doesn't think about Gad, recently released from an farcically short prison term following his conviction for fire raising and manslaughter. Since then his former friend has been prominent in the settler protest movement. Sam saw him on TV recently, leading a solidarity protest against the pullout from Gaza.

On impulse, he pushes back the pile of papers awaiting his attention, opens a drawer in his desk and pulls out a file containing a bunch of newspaper cuttings he has been collecting for the past few months. It holds powerful reminders of how much is at stake in the battle for Israel's soul. The first cutting contains an appeal from Amnesty International to the Israeli Ministry of Defence. The eloquent condemnation of the army he was once a part of seems more apposite than ever.

"Members of the IDF who commit grave human rights violations and war crimes, such as killing children and other unarmed citizens, recklessly shooting and shelling densely populated residential areas or blowing up houses on top of people and leaving them to die in the rubble are not brought to justice and held accountable for their acts."

His eyes are suddenly blinded by tears as the terrible images that have plagued him since Jenin and Ramallah return with extraordinary force. He relives the seconds it took for an old crippled Arab man to be crushed to death under the tracks of a tank in Jenin's squalid refugee camp; and is forced, once again, to endure Dov's anguished account of the atrocities committed by Gad and his men on the streets of Ramallah. With difficulty, he finishes reading the plea.

"At the same time conscripts and reservists who refuse to serve, precisely to avoid participating in such acts, are sent to jail for months. What kind of message is such a policy sending to Israeli society?"

The next cutting is a letter from Yigal Bronner – a *refusnik* – to an unnamed Israeli general.

"Dear General,

In your letter to me, you wrote that given the ongoing war in Judea, Samaria and the Gaza Strip, and in view of the military needs, I am called upon to "participate in army operations."

I am writing to tell you that I do not intend to heed your call.

During the 1980s, Ariel Sharon erected dozens of settler colonies in the heart of the occupied Territories, a strategy whose ultimate goal was the subjugation of the Palestinian people and the expropriation of their land. Today, these colonies control nearly half of these territories and are strangling Palestinian cities and villages as well as obstructing – if not altogether prohibiting – the movement of their residents. Sharon is now Prime Minister, and in the past year he has been advancing towards the definitive stage of the initiative he began twenty years ago.

I am an artilleryman. I am the small screw in the perfect war machine. I am the last and smallest link in the chain of command. I am supposed to simply follow orders – to reduce my existence down to stimulus and reaction, to hear the sound of "fire" and pull the trigger, to bring the overall plan to completion. And I am supposed to do all this with the simplicity and naturalness of a robot, who – most – feels the shaking tremor of the tank as a missile is launched towards the target.

But as Bertolt Brecht wrote:
General, your tank is a powerful vehicle
It smashes down forests and crushes a hundred men.
But it has one defect:
It needs a driver.
General, man is very useful.
He can fly and he can kill.
But he has one defect:
He can think.

And, indeed, General, I can think. Perhaps I am not capable of much more than that, but I can see where you are leading me. I understand that we will destroy, get hurt and die, and that there is no end in sight. I know that the "ongoing war" of which you speak will go on and on. I can see that if "military needs" lead us to lay siege to, hunt down, and starve a whole people, then something about these "needs" is terribly wrong. I am therefore forced to disobey your call. I will not pull the trigger. So, General, before you shoo me away, perhaps you too should begin to think."

Sam imagines what his grandfather would have made of such sentiments. He would no doubt have interpreted Yigal's refusal to further participate in the war of occupation as an act of extraordinary courage. Could such a letter have been written by a German soldier sick to the heart of Nazi butchery? Of course!

Seeking other causes for optimism, he recalls the brief letter he recently received from his father to say he was well and living in Jerusalem, and expressing a strong desire to meet. Despite being urged to caution by his mother, now remarried and living in Jaffa, he has linked reconciliation with his father to the wider peace he hopes the country will achieve.

Remembering Jeff Schiff and heartened by the positive direction his thoughts have taken, he returns with renewed vigour to the press release supporting the latest European directive that Israel's new wall is in breach of international law.

—⁓—

Sam and Jeff watch as a bulldozer rips apart a grove of productive olive trees in preparation for the next section of the separating wall. Less than half a kilometre away, a massive crane swings a concrete block into place as the barrier continues to thrust its way across open country. Several Arab men and women watch as their homes and livelihood are torn apart. Sam feels their frustration and despair.

They have been sent here on a bipartisan fact-finding mission to expose the government's flouting of legal procedure and human rights in the Territories. Having kept in touch since their fortuitous meeting at the peace conference, they sounded out their respective parties about working together to monitor the recent wall-building activities. Given their past connections and experience, the offer was quickly agreed by both organisations.

Sam views the wall as a potent symbol of the fear disabling all hope of reconciliation. As the *Intifada* bites deeper so the desire for permanent security becomes ever more attractive to his people. In the long run, he knows that it provides no answer to the country's problems. Israel cannot simply shut the world out, however tempting that might seem. There are weaknesses in the most impregnable fortress. Is it already too late to break the deadlock and grant the Palestinian people a viable state? He knows that the only chance of such an outcome is if the hated bulldozers turn their attentions to flattening the illegal Jewish settlements springing up across the West Bank, and politicians begin the formidable task of building bridges between the two communities.

He turns away from the depressing sight and meets his friend's troubled eyes. Jeff looks as sombre as he feels, his ready smile for once shut away behind pursed lips and knitted eyebrows.

"And they talk about a road map! That's what they're pinning their hopes on in America! When I was over there, it was all they ever wanted to talk about. A wall map would be more appropriate, god knows! I wish they could see what's really happening on the ground – whole communities divided, friends and family cut off from each other."

"Until the settlements go, there's no chance of any real progress. How can the Palestinians ever have a viable state when all their towns are separated and bisected by highways they're not even allowed to drive on?" Sam smiles bleakly. "There are always going to be good reasons to beef up security in the region. The suicide-bombing cult was a god-send for Sharon. Look how often government spokesmen use the word 'terrorist' these days? And the Americans swallow it whole! Face it, Jeff, the Gaza pullout was a smoke screen to obscure what's really happening around here."

Sam can't resist revisiting a topic they discussed during the taxi trip from Jerusalem. Jeff shakes his head.

"As I said, Sharon may have bitten off more than he can chew there. We both know only too well the significance of land. The withdrawal from Gaza could bring matters to a head quicker than any of us thought."

"It could, but while they're still expanding settlements in the West Bank, Gaza is a distraction."

"I never realised what a pessimist you are, Sam."

He feels unusually despondent for a moment, finding it hard to argue with his friend. Jeff's ready optimism is something he is only too eager to grasp hold of these days.

"I'm just trying to be realistic. We'll never achieve anything by clutching at straws, or concentrating our efforts on a sideshow. People need to know what's really going on here."

"The wall will deter suicide bombers, I'm sure, but it's only constructive dialogue that will bring about a lasting peace."

"You mean a two state solution?"

"Yes, I suppose I do."

They are interrupted by the high keening of an elderly Arab woman. As the last, ancient olive tree in the grove is assaulted by the bulldozer, she kneels down, clasps her arms round her chest and begins rocking back and forth as if mourning the death of a beloved family member. The agonised crack as the trunk succumbs to inexorable steel makes Sam wince. When they resume, their conversation is muted

"I still think Gaza will backfire on them."

"I hope you're right, but I believe the protests will diminish in time. The diehards know the government won't dare touch the settlements that really matter, particularly the ones in East Jerusalem. Maybe we should try to interview some of the villagers, though I'm not sure they'll want to talk to us!"

Jeff is more sanguine.

"They might. They know well enough that their only chance is if we can sway public opinion against this insanity. Let's see if we can get some shots of the smashed trees, and that bloody bulldozer as well."

—⁂—

Sam hits the ground as hard as he ever did in combat training. A bullet thumps into a stunted olive tree, a few metres to his right. Jeff and his team dive for cover in a drainage ditch at the far end of the grove.

The man on the hill, who no one believed would use his rifle in deadly earnest, hails them.

"I warned you not to trespass on our land. Next time I won't miss."

Although only too well aware of the danger, Sam can't help smiling at the irony of the situation. They are more than two kilometres from the nearest settlement, being shot at by a Jew accusing the Palestinian farmer and his family of trespassing on their own land. It could only happen in the Territories!

Sam hears Jeff shouting into his mobile phone, presumably exhorting some police official to send help. He knows from experience that his friend's efforts will probably fall on deaf ears. The police and local army militia are understandably reluctant to take on the settlers. He's seen it all before in Kiryat Arba and Hebron. That's why he and Jeff are here today.

Life has become busy and increasingly challenging over the past few days. Only yesterday, they were held at gunpoint while army regulars ransacked a food lorry, acting on a tip-off that there was bomb-making equipment hidden on board. The pair had been attempting to ensure the safe passage of the vehicle carrying essential supplies into a hard-pressed Palestinian township. Although nothing incriminating was found, the cargo was impounded and the Arab driver arrested.

And the day before that, they had spent the entire morning at an army checkpoint trying to ease tensions after the shooting of a local taxi driver who attempted to ram the barriers. The soldiers had insisted that the man was a terrorist but could provide no evidence to validate their claim. Sam later found out that the driver had been detained at the checkpoint every day for the past fortnight without explanation. Maybe he was being punished for looking at a soldier the wrong way, or had failed to display enough humility when originally challenged. His final act was likely due to intense frustration more than anything more sinister.

And now here they are, being shot at while trying to protect a farmer and his family from serious intimidation. Unfortunately, the very fact that there are Jews present seems to have made matters worse, bringing the settlers wrath to boiling point.

A few minutes later, the roar of an approaching vehicle and the slamming of doors alert Sam to the fact that the police have arrived. He has underestimated Jeff's powers of persuasion. He rises to his feet. Four armed officers stroll towards him. One of them asks if he has a pass permitting the group to be in a "restricted area". He beckons to Jeff, who has all the necessary paperwork. From experience, they know such permissions are vital. The man makes a great fuss of checking the papers – only handing them back after a prolonged radio conversation with some superior back at the station. He stares with distaste at the workforce of Jews and Arabs, smiling and chattering nearby.

"This is a very sensitive area. You must understand that tensions are running high."

Jeff feigns innocence.

"And why would that be? Surely the farmer has a right to harvest his own crop from his own trees on his own land. We're just here to help him out, not to upset anyone or cause trouble."

"The fact that you are here at all is only making matters worse for the Arabs. Why don't you leave them to get on with their work."

Jeff's response is immediate.

"We will leave if you guarantee them the protection they have a right to."

The officer studiously ignores the plea.

"If you stay, we cannot guarantee your safety."

"Maybe if you confiscated the settlers' guns our chances would improve." Sam, although aware that his sarcasm is wasted, just can't help himself. "Then we could leave, knowing the farmer was safe to pick his olives." He also appreciates that even if the settlers were deprived of their guns, they would quickly resort to cruder weapons, but at least their main advantage over the unarmed Palestinian civilians would be lost.

"You know as well as I do that they are armed because of terrorist insurgents roaming the area!"

As usual, the old 'terrorist' potato is pulled out of the fire. Sam and Jeff have heard it a thousand times before. The 'terror' threat justifies every injustice and atrocity perpetrated in the Territories. No Israeli spokesman has ever acknowledged that terror works both ways, or that the Israeli state was founded on the back of notorious terrorist groups

Jeff smiles sweetly.

"Oh well, we'll be sticking around for a while then."

The stony-faced officer turns away and waves his men to follow. But the police will have to be careful. It will not be so easy to cover up any nasty incidents given the presence of a determined coterie of Jewish activists, equipped with the correct paperwork. With any luck, the settlers will be told to steer clear, at least until Sam and his volunteers have departed. Unfortunately, this is the main problem. They are spread too thinly on the ground, and can only be in any given locality for short periods of time.

Sam musters the small but motivated workforce. At least the present level of cooperation between Jews and Arabs shows what can be achieved; the farmer clearly appreciates their presence here, cracking jokes with Sam and Jeff as they all get back to work. The grove will be cleared by the end of the day if they are left to it. A vain hope as it turns out. By lunchtime their antagonists are back, this time minus their guns. The cruder weapons, Sam envisaged earlier, have replaced the bullets. Stones, as well as a continuous barrage of insults, fly from the nearby hill.

A little while later, three settlers enter the grove. Sam lays down his basket as the men approach. Whatever transpires, he must remain calm and focused. One of them immediately berates him.

"How can you – a Jew – bear to work alongside these animals? Have you no pride or conscience?"

Forcing back the response that springs to mind, he attempts conciliation.

"We're only here to help gather in their harvest. All we ask is that you leave us alone."

Jeff quickly arrives on the scene and to Sam's relief takes over.

"We don't want any trouble, nor does the farmer. Nothing will be achieved by violence. These people only want to earn a crust working their land."

"Their land! What are you talking about? This is not their land! Do you not know that all this land was granted to us by God? We are here to redeem the land from these interlopers. These," he gestures towards the bowed backs of the Arabs working nearby with a derisive sweep of his hand, "these are the agents of Satan."

The man's Midwest Yankee twang increases Sam's irritation. The arrogant presumption of yet another 'Johnny-come-lately' threatens to topple his self-control. Unlike many other peace activists, Sam has sung from the same warped songbook as these people, and is more emotionally involved in this sort of stand-off.

Jeff, sensing his friend's difficulty, maintains his upbeat, friendly manner.

"Yes, but surely they have some rights! If we can only learn to live side-by-side in peace, the violence, which benefits no one in the long run, will end."

Another, much younger man, shakes his head in disgust. His dark features and thicker lips suggest African origins. Sam can't help wondering how he gets along with his fellow settlers. The Arab - Jew divide is, of course, only one layer of the bitter prejudices dividing Israeli citizens. In Kiryat Arba, the tiny minority of *Sephardim*, from north Africa, were viewed as little better than *Goyim*. Maybe these differences have been put to one side because this settlement is so much smaller, and surrounded by an overwhelmingly indigenous population. It also occurs to him that the man could easily pass for one of the Arabs he is so clearly determined to persecute.

"The violence will only cease when the Arabs are banished from our land forever. If you were a Jew, worthy of the name, you would know that. It is you, and those like you, who delay the fulfilment of God's promise to his people."

Sam is only too well aware that this argument can never be won. Compromise with fundamentalists has always been out of the question. The flames of his anger are quickly doused by a cold dash of futility. He bends down and scoops up a handful of olives into his half-filled basket to signify that the debate is at an end. Jeff merely shrugs as the three men stalk back up the hill. After a few more minutes they are all gone, probably aware that nothing further can be done without the threat of their firearms. But they will be back once the spotlight has passed over. Sam feels hugely sorry for the people who have to endure such abuse day after day. His life, although unpredictable and dangerous at times, is relatively straightforward by comparison.

By late afternoon, the trees have been stripped of their fruit and the farmer, eager to extend traditional Arab hospitality, invites the visitors back for supper before they return to their tents. Tomorrow, work will continue on another farm, this time less than a kilometre from another, larger Jewish settlement.

After the meal, which Sam knows is far heartier than the family would normally consume, they all settle down to drink the strong, sweet tea served by the farmer's wife and daughters. He is keen to find out if his host could ever envisage living alongside those who have persecuted his people for so long.

He smiles when Sam poses the question. His face, although scarred and pitted like the olive trees he has worked all his life, retains a quiet dignity. Despite everything, he appears to hold no permanent grudge.

"If they would leave us alone, and give us a chance to sell on the open market, I, for one, would be happy for them to live nearby. All we want is fair treatment. But they refuse to recognise that we have any rights at all, and would shoot us like vermin if they thought they could get away with it. And sometimes they do! It was only because you were with us today that the police allowed us to continue working. It's not our attitude to peace you should be worried about." His tone, although surprisingly mild, is tinged with regret. "Things could be much worse for us, of course. We, at least, live on our own land. Those who exist in the refugee camps will not see things the way I do. Too many youngsters have never known anything other than squalor and abuse at the hands of the occupiers. They hate Israel even more than their parents and grandparents – the same as were driven from their homes and denied the right of return."

Sam recalls a book he once read at college written by a former CBS news producer, Joan Peters. She argued the Palestinians could no longer sustain the myth that they were the original inhabitants of the region now known as Israel. According to her, the so-called indigenous population were recent immigrants themselves with no more right to the land than the Jewish settlers. Although the work was peppered with contradictions, and based on dubious scholarship, it had been well received by those desperate to accept its thesis. Numerous endorsements from many prominent American Jews of the day endowed it with a kudos wholly undeserved.

From information gleaned earlier in the day, he knows that his host's family have lived here for over two hundred years. This means little or nothing, of course, to the settlers, especially first-generation Americans who have been around for less than ten. Against all reason, these people view themselves as the true inheritors of huge swathes of land across the Middle East. Sam wonders if peace can ever be achieved when so little compromise is possible. The only ray of hope, despite his earlier scepticism, lies in recent events in Gaza where it has been demonstrated that Jews can be successfully evicted from stolen land. In the long run, this may work against the settlers' darker agenda.

His host's laugh returns him to the present with a jolt.

"I hope I haven't depressed you too much, young man! You look as though the burdens of the world have settled on your shoulders. While there is life there is hope – a truth we make much of these days. The fact that you are here now and we break bread together shows what is possible, does it not? Take some heart from that, I tell you!"

—w—

February – 2006

"So, Sharon is out of the equation, but what has changed? The Jihad factions give the government all the excuse it needs to speed up the settlement programme, and persecute the Arabs. Without *Hamas* lobbing their homemade rockets over the border and denying Israel's right to exist, our leaders would be at a loss. Talk about handing your enemies a stick to beat you with!"

As Sam hurries through the Jerusalem streets, he recalls Jeff's words, spoken before they parted ways. The dogs of war, unleashed against the 'enemies of Israel' are still snapping at the heels of hope. He ponders the recent 'retaliatory' shelling of Gaza, the spate of targeted assassinations, the threat of another incursion into Lebanon, and air raids inside Iran. Mulling over such a pot of bad news is an effective way to avoid having to think about his imminent meeting with his father. How much he has changed, if he has changed at all, or what he has been doing for the past four years, is unknown to Sam and his mother.

—◊◊◊—

The flat has three pokey rooms, the largest acting as both lounge and kitchen. It is unkempt and smells musty. Father has lost weight since I saw him last, and his face is lined and weary. During the initial small talk, he tells me that he has been working as a filing assistant in an accountant's office. The job, he says, is tedious and poorly paid, but it is all he can get.

The atmosphere is very formal. We continue to exchange pleasantries, like two people who once knew each other in a somewhat superficial way, lost touch and met by chance a few years later. He offers me tea and I sip warily wondering where all this might be leading. Feelings of sadness and regret at our long estrangement are tempered by resentment for the long years it has taken me to shake off his perverse influence.

At first, he is unwilling to meet my eyes and gazes down at the grimy, patterned rug. The silence between us grows increasingly uncomfortable. Just when I think I can't stand much more, he speaks.

"I know you're wondering why I contacted you after all this time. And I can guess what you're thinking." He pauses for a moment, perhaps expecting some response. "You're thinking what a sad bastard my father is, and what does he want from me now."

His words spur me on.

"I always hoped that you would get in touch, but I thought you were most likely too ashamed of what I did ever to want to speak to me again."

My anger and frustration are suddenly eclipsed by regret. Things could have been so different if there had been more respect and honesty in our relationship. I get the feeling that he's thinking much the same thing but can't quite summon up the courage to express his remorse. When he replies, I can tell by the strain in his voice and the frequent pauses that he's working up to something.

"I've been reading your articles in the *Courage to Refuse* newsletters. I didn't realise how difficult things were for you in the army. What you say about Operation Defensive Shield and Dov Harel was… ." He falters and for the first time looks me straight in the eye. I feel the moment of truth has arrived. "I, I just wanted to apologise for how I acted towards you and your mother. Too little too late, of course, but I know now how wrong I've been about everything. Your grandfather was a brave man. Maybe it was knowing how much less of a man I was that I couldn't take. I've done some terrible things – ignored so many chances to… ." His voice finally chokes as he loses the fight to master his emotions. I'm astounded. If anything, I expected a lecture on the wrath of God crashing down on the heads of self-hating Jews, or, at the very least, an appeal to return to the fold before it was too late. I can't help wondering if he's serious or executing some new ploy to throw me off my guard? What has happened to all his primal religious beliefs?

After a moment or two, he manages to speak through his tears.

"You seem a bit confused, Sam! It's hardly surprising, I suppose, after everything that's happened between us. I've had years in this hole to consider my moral cowardice, and my ability to undermine everything and everyone I love. Alongside Mark Katz, I was one of the worst bigots and thugs, but, hard as it might be for you to believe, I could never really think like him. I hated what I'd become though I covered it up well enough, even from myself. All these things are clear to me now. Even my faith turned out to be skin-deep in the end!" He looks at me with desolate, haunted eyes. "You probably remember my uncanny knack of making myself scarce when things got hot. You probably thought I was scared, and it was true in a sense – not so much of being injured or killed, but of being forced to confront what I'd become."

I can think of nothing to say as his confession flows on. It's hard to believe that the man sitting in front of me is the father I thought I knew and understood so well.

"I was in awe of your grandfather." I remember what mother told me and incline my head. Seeing my reaction, he smiles faintly and moistens his dry lips with his tongue. "I see you know something about how things used to be between us. Truth is, I worshipped the ground he walked on. In those days we talked and talked. He told me about his experiences during the war, just like he did with you, I guess. It pained him to talk about it, but he was desperate to convince me that the path of forgiveness and reconciliation was the only way forward for Israel. He didn't spare me the horror. He knew I professed strong beliefs, but I suppose he believed that religion was ultimately about teasing out what is good in all of us. If only that were true! Your grandfather was naïve in the best possible sense. He still believed that our people could find a way to overcome their fear."

I feel I must be dreaming as revelation follows revelation. Although mother did tell me how different their relationship was before I was born, I grasp for the first time the extent of grandfather's struggle to enlighten both father and son. Somehow, hearing it from my father's own lips, makes the whole thing more real – more extraordinary.

"When I found out that he'd married a German woman, despite everything he'd told me, I viewed it as a shocking betrayal – certainly not the act of someone intent on laying the past to rest and re-engaging with life. All I could think of at the time was what my friends and colleagues would say if they ever found out I was married to the daughter of a German woman. Everything turned sour. I started looking for excuses to deny him; to drag him down to my own mediocre level."

Father is clearly so desperate to get things out in the open, to make amends, that the suspicion he might be lying is laid to rest. In his efforts to remember, to understand, he's almost forgotten I'm in the room.

"It was around then that I started giving your mother so much grief. She loved me, I think, and thought that I loved her, so it was hard for her to understand why I was behaving so badly. The truth is, I did love her, but everything got so confused in my mind I lost sight of what was most important in my life. That she put up with my arrogance and abuse for so long, beggars belief." He catches my eye and smiles grimly. "Your love and loyalty was the prize I desired above all things."

"Why did you stick it out with mother if you thought she was so bad?"

"Oh, the sanctity of marriage, and the disgrace of admitting that I had married, not only a *Goy*, but a German *Goy*. I believed that everything would come out in the aftermath of a messy divorce, and that you and I would be ostracised by the people I most wanted to impress." He sounds bitter and desperate at the same time. "You know how important racial purity is to true believers, especially on the mother's side. All sorts of rules exist to keep the bloodline pure. I didn't have the courage to face up to anything in those days. I even falsified and destroyed documents linking you and your mother to your German heritage. I don't think Miriam knew anything about that."

"But you believed in a God who sees everything and would know how you really felt and what you had done!"

"That's true, and it shows what a sham my religious beliefs were! The hypocrisy of it all – the mendacity – has undermined everything I once believed holy. Far more important to me at the time was what my fellow-believers thought. It was their acceptance – their approval, if you will, that I craved most of all."

His wish to atone is so heartfelt that I am greatly moved. The feeling that I must offer something in return becomes irresistible.

"You're not the only one who made mistakes. I knew well enough what was going on, but I wasn't brave enough to do anything about it. Even at school, I hated Gad and his father, but tried to pretend otherwise. That just made things worse, I guess."

"Yes, but you were young and didn't know any better. Besides, I was filling your head with all the wrong ideas, and fighting your mother for your affections. The whole business was an obsession; winning you over became more important than your welfare. What a thing to admit!"

His voice catches. He is clearly still being confronted with new insights. I push on, determined to expose my own weaknesses.

"I did things as a soldier I'm not proud of. You can't guess how often I looked the other way when I knew something awful was happening. It took me years to act on my better judgement." He stares at his teacup, unwilling to catch my eye. I suddenly realise that I must reveal my own guilt in the matter which plagues me most of all. "You weren't the only one to reject grandfather. Even when he was trying to help me understand, I pushed him away. I couldn't accept that my grandmother was German either. We all make mistakes. The main thing is that we admit them and move on. I'm still trying to find my way."

"I hope you do, Sam. Maybe one day you'll be able to find it in your heart to forgive me."

This time he breaks down completely. I put my arm round his shoulders. It's hard to believe that my prayers have finally been answered in such a way. Grandfather's unwavering belief that people can redeem themselves has been vindicated today. I only wish he could have witnessed the reconciliation of father and son. With courage and perseverance perhaps anything is possible.

The end.....

Epilogue: A glimpse into two possible futures

1

Tel Aviv – November 2014

It seems hardly possible that I once harboured hope that things might be turning round in Israel. The peace movement was gaining ground and I believed there was a real chance of reconciliation between Arabs and Jews. It looked as though the withdrawal from Gaza, and the likely adoption of the "two state solution", were going to be the beginning of something really significant. Sharon, that wily old leopard who never changed, and never had any intention of changing his spots, was hailed as visionary and peacemaker.

When the leopard keeled over in January 2006, the Israeli people honoured his memory by returning *Kadima* as the largest party in the *Knesset*, but denying it the majority required to run the country alone. The usual motley crew of fundamentalist factions were enlisted as coalition partners and, as always in Israel, provided with political clout way out of proportion to the number of voters they represented.

Stubborn optimists proclaimed Ehud Olmert the new Moses, ready to lead his people into the Promised Land. Unfortunately, the promise of better times was illusory. While calling for renewed negotiations, Olmert, like most other politicians, was busy undermining the viability of a Palestinian state with plans to consolidate and expand existing settlement blocks in East Jerusalem and the Territories. Meanwhile, *Hamas'* election as ruling party in Gaza and its failure to recognise Israel's right to exist, set alongside Fatah's endless dithering and infighting, played further into his hands, providing him with the excuse that there was no viable Palestinian partner with whom to negotiate.

Continuing assassinations and kidnappings raised tensions which finally exploded into war with Lebanon in 2006. As usual, America and Europe sat on their hands while the IDF pursued unfinished business with *Hezbollah* and *Hamas*. These were the worst of times, as we once again smashed the lives and property of innocent people, wrecking the infrastructure of one of the few Arab nations struggling towards democracy. Anti-Semitic hatred rose to unprecedented levels in the Middle East, culminating in Iran's mendacious President, Mahmoud Ahmadinejad, hosting an international Holocaust deniers' conference in Tehran. Manna from heaven, of course, for Binyamin Netanyahu and Avigdor Leiberman, skulking in the wings. Everything the peace movement had worked towards was starting to unravel.

When the army finally withdrew in disarray from Lebanon, they left behind a strengthened *Hezbollah* and increased hatred for our people in the region.

The invasion of Gaza in the winter of 2008 added to rising tensions. Ostensibly waged against rocket-firing *Hamas* terrorists, this war quickly became an assault on helpless civilians already living in abject fear and misery. After ten days of blasting homes and schools, and killing hundreds of innocent people, the army pulled out. A tide of international criticism came crashing down on our heads, but, as usual, the truth was concealed beneath a tissue of lies and propaganda. The military's response to the handful of crude, home-made rockets fired into our southern territory had, as usual, proved wildly disproportionate.

I didn't think things could get any worse but I was wrong. In February 2009, Likud was elected and Netanyahu formed a coalition grouping of right-wing parties, including Lieberman's odious, *Yisrael Beiteinu* party. Now we had a government more extreme than *Kadima*, and even less likely to engage with *Fatah* moderates. Predictably, despite half-hearted US pro-testations, all efforts to initiate talks broke down as a short-term freeze on settlements was lifted. The con-struction of East Jerusalem settlements resumed and more Arabs were forced to quit the city.

And so it continued for the next three years. While the *Knesset* dissembled, and the Palestinian people tottered on the brink of civil war, most of us sat on our hands content to watch *Fatah* and *Hamas* slog it out on the streets of Gaza and in the West Bank refugee towns. Even their half-hearted attempts to bury the hatchet changed little, apart from providing Netanyahu with yet another excuse to avoid talks. As attacks upon Israeli citizens began to steadily increase, inside and outside the country, people stubbornly refused to grasp the severity of the situation.

In the spring of 2012, father was blown up on his way to a meeting organised by Jews and Palestinians living in the poorer suburbs of Jerusalem. Both groups were seeking ways to encourage greater cooperation, as well as attempting to address security issues on the streets of their city. No one survived the bomb blast which reduced the service bus he was travelling on to a heap of tangled wreckage. The joint initiative foundered in the aftermath of the atrocity. I had been enormously proud when father joined the peace movement, not long after our personal reconciliation; and even prouder that he had chosen to work so closely with those he'd once regarded as blood enemies. My personal loss encapsulated the tragedy unfolding throughout the Middle East. But this was only the beginning!

A little over a year after father's death, the worst possible catastrophe occurred. Although predicted for many years, and following a number of failed attempts in the past, the bombing of *Al-Aqsa* on the Temple Mount came like a bolt from the blue. The mosque was badly damaged and dozens of worshippers were killed when three devices exploded during morning prayers. News that right wing, orthodox elements in collusion with a shadowy grouping of American Christian *Zionists* were behind the attack, added to the ferocity of the reaction in the following days. Spontaneous riots broke out in Jerusalem, across the Territories and throughout the Middle East, as Moslems attacked any Jews and Westerners they could lay their hands on. Many innocent people died on the streets, and embassy buildings were besieged and burned. The rioters appeared impervious to the losses inflicted on them by the IDF. Too late, we realised how tenuous peace had really been, and how precious *Al-Aqsa* was to millions of Moslems throughout the world; too late we grasped the explosive power of the powder keg concealed beneath us.

Instead of using diplomacy as a means of resolving the conflict, our government decided, in its infinite wisdom, to spray petroleum on the blaze. The IDF occupied Gaza and the major Palestinian cities on the West Bank. Not content with this sure way of pulling the few remaining uncommitted Arabs into the fray, plans were drawn up to remove Palestinian residents from Jerusalem. This impossible measure was to be implemented in order to "reduce tension" in the city but, predictably, the proposal alone unleashed the most vicious and prolonged riots of all.

In the autumn of 2013, a majority of the UN Security Council voted that a unilateral force be dispatched immediately to restore order in Jerusalem. This emergency measure, the last chance to achieve peace in the region, was vetoed by the United States government still under the thrall of the powerful pro-Jewish lobbying organisation, AIPAC. Instead, the rioters, now dubbed terrorists, were assaulted by a combined US and Israeli force. There was nothing any of us could do. Palestinian civilians now regarded all Jews and their Western allies as the enemy, and who could blame them?

Real terrorist operations rapidly expanded behind the *Green Line,* into the heartland of Israel itself. The army called me up for the second time; I refused and a warrant for my arrest was issued. I knew it was unlikely to be acted upon immediately given the enormous problems facing the country, but, surprisingly enough, I experienced doubts about denying this latest conscription order. After all, Israel was being directly threatened. The fact that our own actions had created the crisis somehow didn't seem enough reason to turn my back on my country. The knowledge that prolonged violence and further bloodshed could only make matters worse won out in the end. Many of my former colleagues took a different view, however, electing to bear arms in defence of Israel.

In the spring of 2014, the crisis deepened and elections were hastily convened. Extreme right-wing candidates were returned in unprecedented numbers, making Netanyahu's beleaguered party even more dependent on the religious minorities. Much needed diplomacy was ditched in favour of a raft of hardline policies. The IDF was granted even greater powers with martial law extended indefinitely. Those of us who understood where such legitimised brutality would lead, waited with a sense of foreboding.

We didn't have long to wait. In May a 'dirty' nuclear device was exploded in Tel Aviv. Grandfather's greatest fear had finally materialised. The country in which our people had invested so much faith and hope was now paying a terrible price for turning its back on reconciliation. Thousands were killed outright in the explosion. The lethal cloud, settling on the city and surrounding area like a death shroud, affected many others. The hospitals were unable to cope. Foreign aid, rushed through in the days following the blast, could do little to alleviate the suffering. My mother and her husband, who had been staying with relatives in Tel Aviv, were among those who died from radiation poisoning. Their burns were so severe, I could only try to make them as comfortable as conditions would allow. Mercifully, short bouts of agony were followed by long periods of unconsciousness. Mother finally slipped into a coma and passed away within a few hours. Having been working a few miles outside of the city, I missed the worst of the fallout, but still felt vaguely ill – constantly tired and lacking appetite. Even though they refused to confirm or deny responsibility for the bomb, all evidence pointed towards al Qaeda in league with the Iranian government.

Retaliation was swift. As the world reeled from news of the Tel Aviv bombing, short-range nuclear missiles were winging their way towards key Iranian targets – both military and civilian. At the same time, the IDF, freed from all constraint, rounded up and executed thousands of Palestinian civilians in the Gaza Strip, the West Bank and in Jerusalem itself. Many others were shot by settlers bent on settling old scores. I can only imagine the jubilation experienced by Gad and his followers in Kiryat Arba as their dream of redeeming sacred land and exterminating the enemies of Israel seemed to be coming to pass. In their minds, *Redemption* had finally arrived. The price for such an outcome was much higher than anything they could ever imagined having to pay.

Incredibly, following strikes against Iran, the government of that stricken country managed to launch a few of their own nuclear missiles. Those who claimed that the *Ayatollahs* had been secretly building a nuclear capability were proved correct. The weapons, inferior and crude in most respects, were shot down long before reaching their targets but created further radiation fallout across Middle Eastern countries.

Despite frantic American efforts, further Israeli missiles were launched against targets in Iran, as well as in Egypt and Syria – both of whom had declared support for the Iranian government, and threatened invasion. It seemed that once the nuclear option had been unleashed, there was no holding back.

As I write, the entire region is in chaos, and war rages unchecked. Oil fields burn; black smoke blots out the sun over vast swathes of desert. Western powers can only gesture futilely from the wings, their military might neutralised as the Middle East descends into hell.

These may well be my last words. For the past few days I have been incapable of keeping food down, and I can't walk far without resting. Others complain of similar symptoms, and worse. The weird thing is that I am able to think more clearly than I ever have before. I've been reflecting on the people who figured so prominently in my past – for good and ill. I also wonder why I ignored, for so long, the urgings of sanity. Again and again, I sensed the evil around me but did nothing about it. On the streets of Jerusalem, I knew well enough that those eulogising Baruch Goldstein were nothing more than the ringleaders of a racist lynch mob, but that did not stop me joining an elite army unit dedicated to attacking Arab civilians when and wherever possible. It was only after things turned really ugly that I woke up to what was happening. Many young Germans must have been similarly influenced before the Second World War, pulled along by Hitler's rhetoric and the pace of events until they lost sight of what was most important in their lives. Grandfather understood the danger and tried to enlighten me. Although he failed in the short term, perhaps without him I would have ended up like Gad. At least the seed he sowed bore fruit in time.

The irresistible tide of events has undermined all such personal victories. The evil that scorched the world seventy years ago has unleashed an all-consuming inferno. The will to resist at all costs, linked to the insidious conviction that we are indeed the Chosen People, has blackened hearts and led to terrible crimes against those whom we should have embraced as brothers. It now appears the only thing we have been chosen to do is end civilisation. The noble concept of nurturing humankind's enduring qualities, envisaged by grandfather during the first heady days of love for his German nurse, quickly fell among weeds and was lost in their rank growth.

Hope for the future grows dim, but hope is the only thing I have left. Perhaps we can finally achieve redemption, but not before we cast off the manacles of fear, and triumph over our own failures.

2

Tel Aviv – November 2014

I spoke to father on the phone this morning. He told me that the East Jerusalem scheme is beginning to bear fruit.

I was so proud when he first told me that he had become part of an initiative, instigated by Jews and Palestinians, to encourage cooperation and launch joint development projects in the poorer suburbs of the city. Over the past two years he has become a new man, far removed from the sad and bewildered individual I encountered in Jerusalem eight years ago.

The success of such schemes, and the resumption of talks between the government and the Palestinian leaders, suggest that things are looking up. I was particularly heartened by the news that *Fatah* and *Hamas* have finally settled their differences and produced a joint negotiating team. With Obama's second-term presidency squarely behind the "two state solution", the prospect of peace is, at last, turning into something more tangible and achievable.

The first seeds of hope began to sprout when Netanyahu's administration fell apart after Avigdor Lieberman and his *Yisrael Beiteinu* thugs walked out of the coalition. The truth was that 'Bibi' had lost his way, unable to appeal to either moderates or extremists in his struggle to be all things to all men.

After emergency elections in the Spring of 2014, *Kadima* was voted the majority party and its leader, Tzipi Livni, appointed Prime Minister. She surprised us all by throwing her weight behind the "two state solution". Despite heavy opposition, even within her own party, she reinstated the settlement freeze in East Jerusalem and began to dismantle the rash of illegal settlements peppering the Territories. At last the stalemate appeared to be breaking, with the Palestinians welcomed as equal partners in negotiations.

There is a long way to go, of course, but such optimism has not been experienced in this part of the world for a very long time. Support for extreme right-wing parties appears to be waning, with *ultra-orthodox* and other radical religious groups increasingly isolated and vilified by the mainstream press. For the first time in decades, the ruling party is not being propped up by tiny, unrepresentative minorities in the *Knesset*. The present coalition is comprised of parties recognized and elected by the majority of voters in the country.

The peace groups are also pulling together in a way I would never have believed possible until recently. The new-found collaboration encourages the government to respect the views of outside agencies such as the UN and the European Court of Human Rights, long committed to helping us establish justice and real democracy in the region. Even parts of the hated wall are being dismantled as many recognise the implausibility of skulking inside a permanent fortress. The concept of achieving security through meaningful dialogue is now becoming a real possibility in people's minds.

A new honesty has broken out in the country. People are less inclined than before to pretend everything is fine; or, by the simple act of turning a blind eye, indulge in the illusion that all our problems will somehow vanish into thin air. The hardline *Zionist* mantra that everyone against the continuing persecution of Palestinians is either anti-Semitic or, if a Jew, self-hating, is being replaced by a genuine desire to find less violent ways to solve the country's ills. The sense of relief is palpable now that people are being more honest with themselves and others. For the first time, I believe that the great disaster poised to engulf the Middle East can be averted. When someone like father, previously so intolerant, is able to break bread with those he once viewed as abhorrent, and the "agents of Satan", there is hope for us all.

On days like this when I am able to contemplate a prosperous and stable future for my people, I believe that grandfather can finally rest in peace.

Glossary

Chapter One:

Canaanite: a pejorative term used by fundamentalist Jews to describe Arabs living in the disputed West Bank Territories. The seven nations of Canaan were the ancient blood enemies of the Jews living in the region during Old Testament times. God was claimed to have ordered their extermination by his chosen people.

Towel Head: a derisory term sometimes used to describe Arab citizens.

Chapter Two:

Shtetl: Yiddish term for a Jewish village, where the population followed a traditional way of life. These communities were largely wiped out by the Nazis during the Second World War.

Volkdeutschen: small communities of German nationalists living in the vicinity of Polish towns and cities before and during the Second World War.

Cheder: a traditional elementary Jewish school.

Yom Kippur: or the Day of Atonement, is the holiest day of the year for the Jewish people, often associated with prayer and fasting.

Kol Nidre: an Aramaic declaration, recited in the synagogue before the evening service of *Yom Kippur.*

Yiddish: a fusion of Hebrew and Aramaic into German dialect. The language developed in the Rhineland during the 10th century, and later spread to central and Eastern Europe.

Chapter Three

Purim: a Jewish holiday commemorating the deliverance of the people from Persian tyranny - usually involving lots of food and drink.

Eretz Israel: or greater Israel (the extent of the promised land according to Genesis) comprising the current state of Israel, the West Bank, tracts of Jordan, Lebanon, Syria, Iraq, Kuwait, Saudi Arabia, the United Arab Emirates, Yemen and territory in southern Turkey.

Halacha: collective body of religious laws for Jews, including biblical law, later Talmudic law and rabbinical law, as well as customs and traditions.

Goyim: collective name for all non-Jews.

NRP: National Religious Party. An extreme right wing party, particularly popular with fundamentalist settlers on the West Bank for its championship of the settlement programme.

Time of Redemption: the period which fundamentalist Jews believe will herald the coming of the Messiah to redeem his chosen people.

Gush Emunim: or Block of the Faithful. A Jewish Messianic party which was committed to establishing Jewish settlements in the West Bank, Gaza and the Golan Heights. The party no longer officially exists but still retains vestiges of its former power and influence.

Haredi: a collective name for ultra-orthodox Jews.

Hassids: a branch of ultra-orthodox Jews who promote spirituality through Jewish mysticism.

Chabad and Satmar Hassids: different branches of Hassidic Jews.

Kach Party: far right party founded by Meir Kahane, committed to expelling all Arabs from Israel and the West Bank.

Knitted Skullcap: a derisory term used by some ultra-orthodox Jews to describe orthodox settlers.

Zionism: a form of nationalism and culture which supports a Jewish state in territory defined as the land of Israel.

Chapter Four:

Juedischer Ordnungsdienst: the Jewish police force which operated inside the Warsaw Ghetto.

Judenrat: council of Jews administering the practical affairs of the Warsaw Ghetto. Often viewed as a corrupt organization set up by the Nazis to do their bidding.

Blueys: nickname used by ghetto Jews for Polish policemen who worked for the Nazis.

Greens: nickname used by Jews for German soldiers assigned to guard the ghetto.

Chapter Five:

Kabbalah: a body of mystical teaching of rabbinical origins based on an esoteric interpretation of Hebrew scriptures.

Kivunim: a Zionist plan proposing the breakdown of all Arab states in the Middle East into small units along ethnic lines under the overall control of Israel.

Lubovitcher Rebbe: a prominent leader of Hasidic rabbis.

Lurianic School: revolutionary branch of Kabbalistic religious belief.

Al Aqsa: Islamic temple built on Jerusalem's Temple Mount. Viewed by Moslems as their second most important holy place.

Yom Kippur War: war fought in 1972 between Israel and Arab states led by Egypt and Syria.

Yeshiva: a Jewish educational institute focusing on the study of traditional religious texts.

Yeshivot Hesder: colleges throughout Israel where Orthodox Jews are able to pursue their religious studies while preparing for active service in the Israeli army.

Tochnit Daleth: Israeli military blueprint for the 1948 war which advocated the expansion of Israel through destruction of Arab communities and the expulsion of the indigenous population.

Judea and Samaria: Jewish name for the occupied West Bank Territories, linked to the idea of regaining territory once ruled by Israel in ancient times.

Chapter Six:

Umschlagolatz: the railway loading-point in the Warsaw Ghetto where Jews were rounded up and deported to Treblinka extermination camp.

Chapter Seven:

Keffiyeh: traditional Arab headgear.

Muqata or Mukataa: the fortress containing the offices of the PLO in Ramallah. The Muqata was built during the British Mandate as one of the many defensive Tegart Forts constructed throughout the region.

Fatah: major Palestinian political party and largest faction of the PLO. Founded by Yasser Arafat in 1959, to promote the military struggle against Israeli aggression, it is now regarded as the more moderate wing of Palestinian politics.

Chapter Eight:

ZOB: (Zydowska Organizagja Bojowa) Jewish fighting organization in the Warsaw Ghetto during the Second World War.

Chapter Ten:

Kibbutzim: a collective community in Israel traditionally based on crop and fruit growing. Often combining socialist and Zionist beliefs.

Chapter Eleven:

Mishnah: the first major written redaction of the Jewish oral tradition sometimes called the oral Torah. (the four books of Moses.)

Refusniks: Israeli citizens who refuse to serve in the IDF or obey specific orders due to disagreement with the policies of their government such as the continuing occupation of Palestinian territory.

Chapter Twelve:

Knesset: the legislative branch of the Israeli government.

Sephardic: descendants of Jews who lived in Spain and Portugal, and later in North Africa, Asia Minor and other countries around the world.

Kadima: centrist Israeli political party established by right-wing moderates in November 2005 to support Ariel Sharon's unilateral disengagement plan from the coastal strip of Gaza.

Intifada: a term describing the popular Palestinian uprising against the Israeli occupation of the West Bank.

Hamas: the largest Palestinian Islamist party, currently controlling the Gaza Strip. Regarded as a terrorist organization by Israel and the US, Hamas was founded in 1987 to liberate Palestine from Israeli occupation and establish an Islamic state.

Courage to Refuse: a peace organization founded by Israeli soldiers from all branches of the IDF who refuse to serve in the occupied Territories beyond the 1967 borders of Israel.

Peace Now: a peace activist group, established in Israel to promote a two-state solution which adherents believe will resolve the Israeli-Palestinian conflict.

Epilogue:

Hezbollah: Shi'a Islamic military group and political party based in Lebanon.

Yisrael Beiteinu: extreme nationalist political party in Israel – popular among settlers in the Occupied Territories.

Likud: traditional right wing political party in Israel, currently led by Binyamin Netanyahu.

al-Qaeda: terrorist Islamic group committed to the destruction of Israel and the overthrow of western democracies.

Ayatollahs: Islamic spiritual leaders controlling the Iranian government.

Author's note

Much research went into the writing of this novel. I am indebted to the following:

Israel Shahak – Jewish Fundamentalism in Israel, Jewish History, Jewish Religion – the weight of three thousand years, Open Secrets – Israeli Nuclear and Foreign Policies.

Joe Sacco – Palestine.

Raja Shehadeh – When the Bulbul Stopped Singing & Strangers in the House.

Theo Richmond – Konin a Quest.

Gershom Gorenberg – The End of Days.

Eva Etzioni-Halevy – The Divided People.

Paul Findley – They Dare to Speak Out.

Dan Kurzman – The Bravest Battle – The 28 Days of the Warsaw Ghetto Uprising.

Greg Philo and Mike Berry – Bad News from Israel.

Baruch Kimmerling – Politicide.

Edward W Said and Christopher Hitchens – Blaming the Victims.

Shlomo Sand – The Invention of the Jewish People.

Martin Gilbert – Never Again – History of the Holocaust.

I would also like to thank Peter Cowlam for pro-ofreading the novel. Fiona Akers and Philippa Langley for their insights and encouragement. The staff of Grosvenor Publishers for their guidance and support throughout the publishing process.

About the Author

Geoff Akers was born in Peebles, Scotland in 1954, and studied at Aberdeen University where his interest in modern history and literature was fostered. He became particularly interested in poetry written during the First World War and wrote his honours dissertation on the work of Isaac Rosenberg.

He taught English and history for over fifteen years before giving up to become a full-time novelist. His first novel, **Beating for Light - the story of Isaac Rosenberg,** published in 2006, was critically well received, promoting interest in the life and times of the relatively obscure Jewish war poet.

Geoff is a keen traveller and photographer and has been to many countries in the Middle East, including Israel, Jordan and Egypt. He also loves walking and cycling in the hills of Scotland. Geoff is married and lives in Edinburgh with his wife, Fiona.

Lightning Source UK Ltd.
Milton Keynes UK
UKOW040327230313

208063UK00001B/12/P